MEET TRIGGER ARGEE . . .

Half a block from the shopping center, a row of spacers on planet-leave came rollicking cheerily toward her. . . . Trigger shifted toward the edge of the sidewalk to let them pass. As the line swayed up on her left, there was a shadowy settling of an aircar at the curb to her right.

With loud outcries of glad recognition and whoops of laughter, the line swung in about her, close. Bodies crowded against her; a hand was clapped over her mouth. Other hands held her arms. Her feet came off the ground and she had a momentary awareness of being rushed expertly forward.

There was a lurching twist as the aircar shot upward.

SHE'S ABOUT TO ENTER THE MYSTERY OF HER LIFE, IN

Also by James H. Schmitz

THE DEMON BREED
THE UNIVERSE AGAINST HER

ACE
SCIENCE
FICTION

Legacy

JAMES H. SCHMITZ

SF
ace books
A Division of Charter Communications Inc.
A GROSSET & DUNLAP COMPANY
360 Park Avenue South
New York, New York 10010

LEGACY

Copyright © 1962 by James H. Schmitz

Originally published as
A TALE OF TWO CLOCKS

An ACE Book

Cover art by Bob Adragna

First Ace printing: May 1979

Printed in U.S.A

This book is dedicated affectionately
to my father

1

It was the time of sunrise in Coyce, the White City, placidly beautiful capital of Maccadon, the University World of the Hub.

In the Colonial School's sprawling five-mile complex of buildings and tropical parks, the second student shift was headed for breakfast, while a larger part of the fourth shift moved at a more leisurely rate toward their bunks. The school's organized activities were not much affected by the hour, but the big exercise quadrangle was almost deserted for once. Behind the railing of the firing range a young woman stood by herself, gun in hand, waiting for the automatic range monitor to select a new string of targets for release.

She was around twenty-four, slim and trim in the school's comfortable hiking outfit. Tan shirt and knee-length shorts, knee stockings, soft-soled shoes. Her sun hat hung on the railing, and the dawn wind whipped strands of shoulder-length, modishly white-silver hair along her cheeks. She held a small, beautifully worked handgun loosely beside her—the twin-barrelled sporting Denton which gunwise citizens of the Hub rated as a weapon for the precisionist and expert only. In institutions like the Colonial School it wasn't often seen.

At the exact instant the monitor released its new flight of targets, she became aware of the aircar gliding down toward her from the administration buildings on the right. Startled, she glanced sideways long enough to identify the car's two occupants, shifted her attention back to the cluster of targets speeding toward her, studied the flight pattern for another unhurried half-second, finally raised the Denton. The little gun spat its noiseless, invisible needle of destruction eight times. Six small puffs of crimson smoke hung in the air. The two remaining targets swerved up in a mocking curve and shot back to their discharge huts.

The girl bit her lip in moderate annoyance, safetied and holstered the gun and waved her hand left-right at the range attendant to indicate she was finished. Then she turned to face the aircar as it settled slowly to the ground twenty feet away. Her gray eyes studied its occupants critically.

"Fine example you set the students!" she remarked. "Flying right into a hot gun range!"

Doctor Plemponi, principal of the Colonial School, smiled soothingly. "Eight years ago, your father bawled me out for the very same thing,

Trigger! Much more abusively, I must say. You know that was my first meeting with old Runser Argee, and I—"

"Plemp!" Mihul, Chief of Physical Conditioning, Women's Division, cautioned sharply from the seat behind him. "Watch what you're doing, you ass!"

Confused, Doctor Plemponi turned to look at her. The aircar dropped the last four feet to a jolting landing. Mihul groaned. Plemponi apologized. Trigger walked over to them.

"Does he do that often?" she asked interestedly.

"Every other time!" Mihul asserted. She was a tall, lean, muscular slab of a woman, around forty. She gave Trigger a wink behind Plemponi's back. "We keep the chiropractors on stand-by duty when we go riding with Plemp."

"Now then! Now then!" Doctor Plemponi said. "You distracted my attention for a moment, that's all. Now, Trigger, the reason we're here is that Mihul told me at our prebreakfast conference you weren't entirely happy at the good old Colonial School. So climb in, if you don't have much else to do, and we'll run up to the office and discuss it." He opened the door for her.

"Much else to do!" Trigger gave him a look. "All right, Doctor. We'll run up and discuss it."

She went back for her sun hat, climbed in, closed the door and sat down beside him, shoving the holstered Denton forward on her thigh.

Plemponi eyed the gun dubiously. "Brushing up in case there's another grabber raid?" he inquired. He reached out for the guide stick.

Trigger shook her head. "Just working off hostility, I guess." She waited till he had lifted the car off the ground in a reckless swoop. "That business yesterday—it really was a grabber raid?"

"We're almost sure it was," Mihul said behind her, "though I did hear some talk they might have been after those two top-secret plasmoids in your Project."

"That's not very likely," Trigger remarked. "The raiders were a half mile away from where they should have come down if the plasmoids were what they wanted. And from what I saw of them, they weren't nearly a big enough gang for a job of that kind."

"I thought so, too," Mihul said. "They were topflight professionals, in any case. I got a glimpse of some of their equipment. Knockout guns—foggers—and that was a fast car!"

"Very fast car," Trigger agreed. "It's what made me suspicious when I first saw them come in."

"They also," said Mihul, "had a high-speed interplanetary hopper waiting for them in the hills. Two more men in it. The cops caught them, too." She added, "They were grabbers, all right!"

"Anything to indicate whom they were after?" Trigger asked.

"No," Mihul said. "Too many possibilities. Twenty or more of the students in that area at the time had important enough connections to class as grabber bait. The cops won't talk except to admit they were tipped off about the raid. Which was obvious. The way they popped up out of nowhere and closed in on those boys was a beautiful sight to see!"

"I," Trigger admitted, "didn't see it. When that car homed in, I yelled a warning to the nearest bunch of students and dropped flat behind a rock. By the time I risked a look, the cops had them."

"You showed very good sense," Plemponi told her earnestly. "I hope they burn those thugs! Grabbing's a filthy business."

"That large object coming straight at you," Mihul observed calmly, "is another aircar. In this lane it has the right of way. You do not have the right of way. Got all that, Plemp?"

"Are you sure?" Doctor Plemponi asked her bewilderedly. "Confound it! I shall blow my siren."

He did. Trigger winced. "There!" Plemponi said triumphantly as the other driver veered off in fright.

Trigger told herself to relax. Aircars were so nearly accident-proof that even Plemponi couldn't do more than snarl up traffic in one. "Have there been other raids in the school area since I left?" she asked, as he shot up out of the quadrangle and turned toward the balcony of his office.

"That was just under four years ago, wasn't it?" Mihul said. "No, you were still with us when we had the last one . . . Six years back. Remember?"

Trigger did. Two students had been picked up on that occasion—sons of some Federation official. The grabbers had made a clean getaway, and it had been several months later before she heard the boys had been redeemed safely.

Plemponi descended to a teetery but gentle

landing on the office balcony. He gave Trigger a self-satisfied look. "See?" he said tersely. "Let's go in, ladies. Had breakfast yet, Trigger?"

Trigger had finished breakfast a half-hour earlier, but she accepted a cup of coffee. Mihul, all athlete, declined. She went over to Plemponi's desk and stood leaning against it, arms folded across her chest, calm blue eyes fixed thoughtfully on Trigger. With her lithe length of body, Mihul sometimes reminded Trigger of a ferret, but the tanned face was a pleasant one and there was humor around the mouth. Even in Trigger's pregraduate days, she and Mihul had been good friends.

Doctor Plemponi removed a crammed breakfast tray from a wall chef, took a chair across from Trigger, sat down with the tray on his knees, excused himself, and began to eat and talk simultaneously.

"Before we go into that very reasonable complaint you made to Mihul yesterday," he said, "I wish you'd let me point out a few things."

Trigger nodded. "Please do."

"You, Trigger," Plemponi told her, "are an honored guest here at the Colonial School. You're the daughter of our late friend and colleague Runser Argee. You were one of our star pupils—not just as a small-arms medallist either. And now you're the secretary and assistant of the famous Precolonial Commissioner Holati Tate—which makes you almost a participant in what may well turn out to be the greatest scientific event of the century . . . I'm referring, of course," Plemponi added, "to Tate's discovery of the Old Galactic plasmoids."

"Of course," agreed Trigger. "And what is all this leading up to, Plemp?"

He waved a piece of toast at her. "No. Don't interrupt! I still have to point out that because of the exceptional managerial abilities you revealed under Tate, you've been sent here on detached duty for the Precolonial Department to aid the Commissioner and Professor Mantelish in the University League's Plasmoid Project. That means you're a pretty important person, Trigger! Mantelish, for all his idiosyncrasies, is undoubtedly the greatest living biologist in the League. And the Plasmoid Project here at the school is without question the League's most important current undertaking."

"So I've been told," said Trigger. "That's why I want to find out what's gone haywire with it."

"In a moment," Plemponi said. "In a moment." He located his napkin, wiped his lips carefully. "Now I've mentioned all this simply to make it very, very clear that we'll do anything we can to keep you satisfied. We're delighted to have you with us. We are honored!" He beamed at her. "Right?"

Trigger smiled. "If you say so. And thanks very much for all the lovely compliments, Doctor. But now let's get down to business."

Plemponi glanced over at Mihul and looked evasive. "That being?" he asked.

"You know," Trigger said. "But I'll put it into specific questions if you like. Where's Commissioner Tate?"

"I don't know."

"Where is Mantelish?"

He shook his head. "I don't know that either." He began to look unhappy.

"Oh?" said Trigger. "Who does know then?"

"I'm not allowed to tell you," Doctor Plemponi said firmly.

Trigger raised an eyebrow. "Why not?"

"Federation security," Plemponi said, frowning. He added, "I wasn't supposed to tell you that either, but what could I do?"

"Federation security? Because of the plasmoids?"

"Yes . . . Well . . . I'd—I don't know."

Trigger sighed. "Is it just me you're not supposed to tell these things to?"

"No, no, no," Plemponi said hastily. "Nobody. I'm not supposed to admit to anyone that I know anything of the whereabouts of Holati Tate or Professor Mantelish."

"Fibber!" Trigger said quietly. "So you know!"

Plemponi looked appealingly at Mihul. She was grinning. "My lips are sealed, Trigger! I can't help it. Please believe me."

"Let me sum it up then," Trigger said, tapping the arm of her chair with a finger tip. "Eight weeks ago I get pulled off my job in the Manon System and sent here to arrange the organizational details of this Plasmoid Project. The only reason I took on the job, as a temporary assignment, was that

Commissioner Tate convinced me it was important to him to have me do it. I even let him talk me into doing it under the assumed name of Ruya Farn and"—she reached up and touched the side of her head—"and to dye my hair. For no sane reason that I could discover! He said the U-League had requested it."

Doctor Plemponi coughed. "Well, you know, Trigger, how sensitive the League is to personal notoriety."

The eyebrow went up again. "Notoriety?"

"Not in the wrong sense!" Plemponi said hastily. "But your name *has* become much more widely known than you may believe. The news viewers mentioned you regularly in their reports on Harvest Moon and the Commissioner. Didn't they, Mihul?"

Mihul nodded. "You made good copy, kid! We saw you in the solidopics any number of times."

"Well, maybe," Trigger said. "The cloak and dagger touches still don't make much sense to me. But let's forget them and go on.

"When we get here, I manage to see Mantelish just once to try to find out what his requirements will be. He's pretty vague about them. Commissioner Tate is in and out of the Project—usually out. He's also turned pretty vague. About everything. Three weeks ago today I'm told he's gone. Nobody here can, or will, tell me where he's gone or how he can be contacted. The same thing in the Maccadon Precol office. Same thing at the Evalee Home office. Same thing at the U-League—any office. Then I try to contact Mantelish. I'm informed he's with Tate! The two of them have left word I'm to carry on."

She spread her hands. "Carry on with what? I've done all I can do until I get further instructions from the people supposedly directing this supposedly very urgent and important project! Mantelish doesn't even seem to have a second in command . . ."

Plemponi nodded. "I was told he hadn't selected his Project assistants yet."

"Except," said Trigger, "for that little flock of Junior Scientists who keep themselves locked in with the plasmoids. They know less than nothing and would be too scared to tell me that if I asked them."

Plemponi looked confused for a moment. "The last sentence—" He checked himself. "Well, let's not quibble. Go on."

Trigger said, "That's it. Holati didn't need me on this job to begin with. There's nothing involved about the organizational aspects. Unless something begins to happen—and rather soon—there's no excuse for me to stay here."

"Couldn't you," Plemponi suggested, "regard this as a kind of well-earned little vacation?"

"I've tried to regard it as that. Holati impressed on me that one of us had to remain in the area of the Project at all times, so I haven't even been able to leave the school grounds. I've caught up with my reading, and Mihul has put me through two of her tune-up commando courses. But the point is that I'm not on vacation. I don't believe Precol would feel that any of my present activites come under the heading of detached duty work!"

There was a short silence. Plemponi stared down at his empty tray, said, "Excuse me," got up and walked over to the wall chef with the tray.

"Wrong slot," Trigger told him.

He looked back. "Eh?"

"You want to put it in the disposal, don't you?"

"Thanks," Plemponi said absently. "Always doing that. Confusing them . . ." He dropped the tray where it belonged, shoved his hands into the chef's cleaning recess and waved them around, then came back, still looking absent-minded, and stopped before Trigger's chair. He studied her face for a moment.

"Commissioner Tate gave me a message for you," he said suddenly.

Trigger's eyes narrowed slightly. "When?"

"The day after he left." Plemponi lifted a hand. "Now wait! You'll see how it was. He called in and said, and I quote, 'Plemp, you don't stand much of a chance at keeping secrets from Trigger, so I'll give you no unnecessary secrets to keep. If this business we're on won't let us get back to the Project in the next couple of weeks, she'll get mighty restless. When she starts to complain—but no earlier—just tell her there are reasons why I can't contact her at present, or let her know what I'm doing, and that I *will* contact her as soon as I possibly can.' End of quote."

"That was all?" asked Trigger.

"Yes."

"He didn't say a thing about how long this situation might continue?"

"No. I've given you the message word for word. My memory is excellent, Trigger."

"So it could be more weeks? Or months?"

"Yes. Possibly. I imagine . . ." Plemponi had begun to perspire.

"Plemp," said Trigger, "will you give Holati a message from me?"

"Gladly!" said Plemponi. "What—oh, oh!" He flushed.

"Right," said Trigger. "You can contact him. I thought so."

Doctor Plemponi looked reproachful. "That was unfair, Trigger! You're quick-witted."

Trigger shrugged. "I can't see any justification for all this mystery, that's all." She stood up. "Anyway, here's the message. Tell him that un-less somebody—rather promptly—gives me a good sane reason for hanging around here, I'll ask Precol to transfer me back to the Manon job."

Plemponi tut-tutted gloomily. "Trigger," he said, "I'll do my best about the message. But otherwise—"

She smiled nicely at him. "I know," she said, "your lips are sealed. Sorry if I've disturbed you, Plemp. But I'm just a Precol employee, after all. If I'm to waste their time, I'd like to know at least why it's necessary."

Plemponi watched her walk out of the room and off down the adjoining hall. In his face consterna-tion struggled with approval.

"Lovely little figure, hasn't she?" he said to Mihul. He made vague curving motions in the air with one hand, more or less opposing ones with the other. "That sort of an up-and-sideways lilt when she walks."

"Uh-huh," said Mihul. "Old goats."

"Eh?" said Doctor Plemponi.

"I overheard you discussing Trigger's lilt with Mantelish."

Plemponi sat down at his desk. "You shouldn't eavesdrop, Mihul," he said severely. "I'd better get that message promptly to Tate, I suppose. She meant what she said, don't you think?"

"Every bit of it," said Mihul.

"Tate warned me she might get very difficult about this time. She's too conscientious, I feel."

"She also," said Mihul, "has a boy friend in the Manon System. They've been palsy ever since they went through the school here together."

"Ought to get married then," Plemponi said. He shuddered. "My blood runs cold every time I think of how close those grabbers got to her yesterday!"

Mihul shrugged. "Relax! They never had a chance. The characters Tate has guarding her are the fastest-moving squad I ever saw go into action."

"That," Plemponi said reflectively, "doesn't sound much like our Maccadon police."

"I don't think they are. Imported talent of some kind, for my money. Anyway, if someone wants to pick up Trigger Argee here, he'd better come in with a battleship."

Plemponi glanced nervously across the balcony at the cloudless blue sky about the quadrangle.

"The impression I got from Holati Tate," he said, "is that somebody might."

2

THERE WAS A TUBE PORTAL at the end of the hall outside Doctor Plemponi's office. Mihul stepped into
the portal, punched the number of her personal
quarters, waited till the overhead light flashed
green a few seconds later, and stepped out into
another hall seventeen floors below Plemponi's
office and a little over a mile and a half away from
it.

Mihul crossed the hall, went into her apartment, locked the door behind her and punched a
shield button. In her bedroom, she opened a wall
safe and swung out a high-powered transmitter.
She switched the transmitter to active.

"Yes?" said a voice.

"Mihul here," said Mihul. "Quillan or the
Commissioner . . ."

"Quillan here," the transmitter said a few seconds later in a different voice, a deep male one.
"Go ahead, doll."

Mihul grunted. "I'm calling," she said, "because I feel strongly that you boys had better take some immediate action in the Argee matter."

"Oh?" said the voice. "What kind of action?"

"How the devil would I know? I'm just telling you I can't be responsible for her here much longer."

"Has something happened?" Quillan asked quickly.

"If you mean has somebody taken another swing at her, no. But she's all wound up to start swinging herself. She isn't going to do much waiting either."

Quillan said thoughtfully, "Hasn't she been that way for quite a while?"

"Not like she's been the last few days." Mihul hesitated. "Would it be against security if you told me whether something has happened to her?"

"Happened to her?" Quillan repeated cautiously.

"To her mind."

"What makes you think so?"

Mihul frowned at the transmitter.

"Trigger always had a temper," she said. "She was always obstinate. She was always an individualist and ready to fight for her own rights and anyone else's. But she used to show good sense. She's got one of the highest I.Q.s we ever processed through this place. The way she's acting now doesn't look too rational."

"How would she have acted earlier?" Quillan asked.

Mihul considered. "She would have been very

annoyed with Commissioner Tate," she said. "I don't blame her for that—I'd be, too, in the circumstances. When he got back, she'd have wanted a reasonable explanation for what has been going on. If she didn't get one that satisfied her, she'd have quit. But she *would* have waited till he got back. Why not, after all?"

"You don't think she's going to wait now?"

"I do not," Mihul said. "She's forwarded him a kind of ultimatum through Plemponi. Communicate-or-else, in effect. Frankly, I wouldn't care to guarantee she'll stay around to hear the answer."

"Hm . . . What do you expect she'll do?"

"Take off," Mihul said. "One way or the other."

"Ungh," Quillan said disgustedly. "You make it sound like the chick's got built-in space drives. You can stop her, can't you?"

"Certainly I can stop her," Mihul said. "If I can lock her in her room and sit on her to make sure she doesn't leave by the window. But 'unobtrusively?' You're the one who stressed she isn't to know she's being watched."

"True," Quillan said promptly. "I spoke like a loon, Mihul."

"True, Major Quillan, sir," said Mihul. "Now try again."

The transmitter was silent a few seconds. "Could you guarantee her for three days?" he asked.

"I could not," said Mihul. "I couldn't guarantee her another three hours."

"As bad as that?"

"Yes," said Mihul. "As bad as that. She was controlling herself with Plemponi. But I've been observing her in the physical workouts. I've fed it to her as heavy as I could, but there's a limit to what you can do that way. She's kept herself in very good shape."

"One of the best, I've been told," said Quillan.

"Condition, I meant," said Mihul. "Anyway, she's trained down fine right now. Any more of it would just maker her edgier. You know how it goes."

"Uh-huh," he said. "Fighter nerves."

"Same deal," Mihul agreed.

There was a short pause. "How about slapping a guard on all Colonial school exits?" he suggested.

"Can you send me an army?"

"No."

"Then forget it. She was a student here, remember? Last year a bunch of our students smuggled the stuffed restructured mastodon out and left it in the back garden of the mayor of Ceyce, just for laughs. Too many exits. And Trigger was a trickier monkey than most that way, when she felt like it. She'll fade out of here whenever she wants to."

"It's those damn tube portal systems!" said Quillan, with feeling. "Most gruesome invention that ever hit the tailing profession." He sighed. "You win, Mihul! The Commissioner isn't in at the moment. But whether he gets in or not, I'll have someone over today to pick her up. Matter of fact, I'll come along myself."

"Good for you, boy!" Mihul said relievedly. "Did you get anything out of yesterday's grabbers?"

"A little. 'Get her, don't harm her' were their instructions. Otherwise it was like with those other slobs. A hole in the head where the real info should be. But at least we know for sure now that someone is specifically after Argee. The price was kind of interesting."

"What was it?"

"Flat half million credits."

Mihul whistled. "Poor Trigger!"

"Well, nobody's very likely to earn the money."

"I hope not. She's a good kid. All right, Major. Signing off now."

"Hold on a minute," said Quillan. "You asked a while ago if the girl had gone ta-ta."

"So I did," Mihul said, surprised. "You didn't say. I figured it was against security."

"It probably is," Quillan admitted. "Everything seems to be, right now. I've given up trying to keep up with that. Anyway—I don't know that she has. Neither does the Commissioner. But he's worried. And Argee has a date she doesn't know about with the Psychology Service, four days from now."

"The eggheads?" Mihul was startled. "What do they want with her?"

"You know," Quillan remarked reflectively, "that's odd! They didn't think to tell me."

"Why are you letting me know?" Mihul asked.

"You'll find out, doll," he said.

The U-League guard leaning against the wall

opposite the portal snapped to attention as it opened. Trigger stepped out. He gave her a fine flourish of a salute.

"Good morning, Miss Farn."

"Morning," Trigger said. She flashed him a smile. "Did the mail get in?"

"Just twenty minutes ago."

She nodded, smiled again and walked past him to her office. She always got along fine with cops of almost any description, and these League boys were extraordinarily pleasant and polite. They were also, she'd noticed, a remarkably muscled group.

She locked the office door behind her—part of the Plasmoid Project's elaborate security precautions—went over to her mail file and found it empty. Which meant that whatever had come in was purely routine and already being handled by her skeleton office staff. Later in the day she might get a chance to scrawl Ruya Farn's signature on a few dozen letters and checks. Big job! Trigger sat down at her desk.

She brooded there a minute or two, tapping her teeth with her thumbnail. The Honorable Precolonial Commissioner Tate, whatever else might be said of him, undoubtedly was one of the brainiest little characters she'd ever come across. He probably saw some quite valid reason for keeping her here, isolated and uninformed. The question was what the reason could be.

Security . . . Trigger wrinkled her nose. Security didn't mean a thing. Everybody and everything associated with the Old Galactic plasmoids had been wrapped up in Federation security measures since the day the plasmoid discovery was announced. And she'd been in the middle of the operations concerning them right along. Why should Holati Tate have turned secretive on her now? When even blabby old Plemponi could contact him.

It was more than a little annoying . . .

Trigger shrugged, reached into a desk drawer and took out a small solidopic. She set it on the desk and regarded it moodily.

The face of an almost improbably handsome young man looked back at her. Startling dark-blue eyes; a strong chin, curly brown hair. There was a gleam of white teeth behind the quick, warm smile which always awoke a responsive glow in her.

She and Brule Inger had been the nearest thing to engaged for the last two and a half years, ever since Precol sent them out together to its project on Manon Planet. They'd been dating before that, while they were both still attending the Colonial School. But now she was here, perhaps stuck here indefinitely—unless she did something about it—and Brule was on Manon Planet. By the very fastest subspace ships the Manon System was a good nine days away. For the standard Grand Commerce express freighter or the ordinary liner it was a solid two-months' run. Manon was a *long* way away!

It was almost a month since she'd even heard from Brule. She could make up another personal tape to him today if she felt like it. He would get it in fourteen days or so via a Federation packet. But she'd already sent him three without reply. Brule wasn't at all good at long distance love-making, and she didn't blame him much. She was a little awkward herself when it came to feeding her personal feelings into a tape. And—because of security again—there was very little else she could feed into it. She couldn't even let Brule know just where she was.

She put the solido back in its drawer, reached for one of the bank of buttons on the right side of the desk and pushed it down. A desk panel slid up vertically in front of her, disclosing a news viewer switched to the index of current headlines.

Trigger glanced over the headlines, while a few items dissolved slowly here and there and were replaced by more recent developments. Under the "Science" heading a great deal seemed to be going on, as usual, in connection with plasmoid experiments around the Hub.

She dialed in the heading, skimmed through the first item that appeared. Essentially it was a summary of reports on Hubwide rumors that nobody could claim any worthwhile progress in determining what made the Old Galactic plasmoids tick. Which, so far as Trigger knew, was quite true. Other rumors, rather unpleasant ones, were that the five hundred or so scientific groups to whom individual plasmoids had been issued by the Federation's University League actually had gained important information, but were keeping it to themselves.

The summary plowed through a few of the learned opinions and counteropinions most recently obtained, then boiled them down to the statement that a plasmoid might be compared to an engine which appeared to lack nothing but an energy source. Or perhaps more correctly—assuming it might have an as yet unidentified energy source—a starter button. One group claimed to have virtually duplicated the plasmoid loaned to it by the Federation, producing a biochemical structure distinguishable from the Old Galactic model only by the fact that it had—quite predictably—fallen apart within hours. But plasmoids didn't fall apart. The specimens undergoing study had shown no signs of deterioration. A few still absorbed nourishment from time to time; some had been observed to move slightly. But none could be induced to operate. It was all very puzzling!

It *was* very puzzling, Trigger conceded. Back in the Manon System, when they had been discovered, the plasmoids were operating with high efficiency on the protein-collecting station which the mysterious Old Galactics appeared to have abandoned, or forgotten about, some hundreds of centuries ago. It was only when humans entered the base and switched off its mechanical operations that the plasmoids stopped working—and then, when the switches which appeared to have kept them going were expectantly closed again, they had stayed stopped.

Personally, Trigger couldn't have cared less if they never did move. It was nice that old Holati Tate had made an almost indecently vast fortune out of his first-discovery rights to the things, because she was really very fond of the Commissioner when he wasn't being irritating. But in some obscure way she found the plasmoids themselves and the idea of unlimited plastic life which they embodied rather appalling. However, she was in a minority there. Practically everybody else seemed to feel that plasmoids were the biggest improvement since the creation of Eve.

She switched the viewer presently to its local-news setting and dialed in the Manon System's reference number. Keeping tab on what was going on out there had become a private little ritual of late. Occasionally she even picked up references to Brule Inger, who functioned nowadays as Precol's official greeter and contact man in the system. He was very popular with the numerous important Hub citizens who made the long run out to the Manon—some bent on getting a firsthand view of the marvels of Old Galactic science, and a great many more bent on getting an early stake in the development of Manon Planet, which was rapidly approaching the point where its status would shift from Precol Project to Federation Territory, opening it to all qualified comers.

Today there was no news about Brule. Grand Commerce had opened its first business and recreation center on Manon, not ten miles from the Precol Headquarters dome where Trigger recently had been working. The subspace net which was being installed about the Old Galactic base was very nearly completed. The permanent Hub population on Manon Planet had just passed the forty-three thousand mark. There had been, Trigger recalled, a trifle nostalgically, barely eight hundred Precol employees, and not another human being, on that world in the days before Holati Tate announced his discovery.

She was just letting the viewer panel slide back into the desk when the office ComWeb gave forth with a musical ping. She switched it on.

"Hi, Rak!" she said cheerily. "Anything new?"

The bony-faced young man looking out at her wore the lusterless black uniform of a U-League Junior Scientist. His expression was worried.

He said, "I believe there is, Miss Farn." Rak was the group leader of the thirty-four Junior Scientists the League had installed in the Project. Like all the Juniors, he took his duties very seriously. "Unfortunately it's nothing I can discuss over a communicator. Would it be possible for you to come over and meet with us during the day?"

"That," Trigger stated, "was a ridiculous question, Rak! Want me over right now?"

He grinned. "Thanks, Miss Farn! In twenty minutes then? I'll get my advisory committee together and we can meet in the little conference room off the Exhibition Hall."

Trigger nodded. "I'll be wandering around the Hall. Just send a guard out to get me when you're ready."

3

SHE SWITCHED OFF THE ComWeb and stood up. Rak and his group were stuck with the Plasmoid Project a lot more solidly than she was. They'd been established here, confined to their own wing of the Project area, when she came in from Manon with the Commissioner. Until the present security rulings were relaxed—which might not be for another two years—they would remain on the project.

Trigger felt a little sorry for them, though the Junior Scientists didn't seem to mind the setup. Dedication stood out all over them. Since about half were young women, one could assume that at any rate they weren't condemned to a completely monastic existence.

A couple of workmen were guiding a dozen big cleaning robots around the Plasmoid Exhibition Hall, which wouldn't be open to students or vis-

itors for another few hours. Trigger strolled across
the floor of the huge area toward a couple of
exhibits that hadn't been there the last time she'd
come through. Life-sized replicas of two O. G.
Plasmoids—Numbers 1432 and 1433—she discovered. She regarded the waxy-looking, lump-
ish, partially translucent forms with some distaste. She'd been all over the Old Galactic Station
itself, and might have stood close enough to the
originals of these models to touch them. Not that
she would have.

She glanced at her watch, walked around a
scale model of Harvest Moon, the O.G. station,
which occupied the center of the Hall, and went
on among the exhibits. There were views taken on
Manon Planet in one alcove, mainly of Manon's
aerial plankton belt and of the giant plasmoids
called Harvesters which had moved about the
belt, methodically engulfing its clouds of living
matter. A whale-sized replica of a Harvester
dominated one end of the Hall, a giant dark-green
sausage in external appearance, though with
some extremely fancy internal arrangements.

"Miss Farn . . ."

She turned. A League cop, standing at the entrance of a hallway thirty feet away, pitched her
the old flourish and followed it up with a bow.
Excellent manners these guard boys had!

Trigger gave him a smile.

"Coming," she said.

Junior Scientist Rak and his advisory committee—two other young men and a young
woman—were waiting in the conference room for

her. They all stood up when she came in. This room marked the border of their territory; they would have violated several League rules by venturing out into the hall through which Trigger had entered.

And that would have been unthinkable.

Rak did the talking, as on the previous occasions when Trigger had met with this group. The advisory committee simply sat there and watched him. As far as Trigger could figure it, they were present at these sessions only to check Rak if it looked as if he were about to commit some ghastly indiscretion.

"We were wondering, Miss Farn," Rak said questioningly, "whether you have the authority to requisition additional University League guards for the Plasmoid Project?"

Trigger shook her head. "I've got no authority of any kind that I know of, as far as the League is concerned. No doubt Professor Mantelish could arrange it for you."

Rak nodded. "Is it possible for you to contact Professor Mantelish?"

"No," Trigger said. She smiled. "Is it possible for you to contact him?"

Rak glanced around his committee as if looking for approval, then said, "No, it isn't. As a matter of fact, Miss Farn, we've been isolated here in the most curious fashion for the past few weeks."

"So have I," said Miss Farn.

Rak looked startled. "Oh!" he said. "We were hoping you would be willing to give us a little information."

"I would," Trigger assured him, "if I had any to give. I don't, unfortunately." She considered. "Why do you feel additional League guards are required?"

"We heard," Rak remarked cautiously, "that there were raiders in the Colonial School area yesterday."

"Grabbers," Trigger said. "They wouldn't bother you. Your section of the project is supposed to be raidproof anyway."

Rak glanced at his companions again and apparently received some undetectable sign of consent. "Miss Farn, as you know, our group has been entrusted with the care of two League plasmoids here. Are you aware that six of the plasmoids which were distributed to responsible laboratories throughout the Hub have been lost to unknown raiders?"

She was startled. "No, I didn't know that. I heard there'd been some unsuccessful attempts to steal distributed plasmoids."

"These six attempts," Rak said primly, "were completely successful. One must assume that the victimized laboratories also had been regarded as raidproof."

Trigger admitted it was a reasonable assumption.

"There is another matter," Rak went on. "When we arrived here, we understood Doctor Gess Fayle was to bring Plasmoid Unit 112-113 to this project. It seems possible that Doctor Fayle's failure to appear indicates that League Headquarters does not consider the project a sufficienty safe place for 112-113."

"Why don't you ask Headquarters?" Trigger suggested.

They stirred nervously.

"That would be a violation of the Principle of the Chain of Command, Miss Farn!" Rak explained.

"Oh," she said. The Juniors were overdisciplined, all right. "Is that 112-113 such a particularly important item?"

"If Doctor Fayle is in personal charge of it," Rak said carefully, "I would say yes."

Recalling her meetings with Doctor Gess Fayle in the Manon System, Trigger silently agreed. He was one of the U-League's big shots, a political scientist who had got himself appointed as Mantelish's chief assistant when that eminent biologist was first sent to Manon to take over League operations there. Trigger had disliked Fayle on sight, and hadn't changed her mind on closer acquaintance.

"I remember that 112-113 unit now," she said suddenly. "Big, ugly thing—well, that describes a lot of them, doesn't it?"

Rak and the others looked quietly affronted. In a moment, Trigger realized, one of them was going to go into a lecture on functional esthetics unless she could head them off—and she'd already heard quite enough about functional esthetics in connection with the plasmoids.

"Now, 113," she hurried on, "is a very small

plasmoid"—she held her hands fifteen inches or so apart—"like that; and it's attached to the big one. Correct?"

Rak nodded, a little stiffly. "Essentially correct, Miss Farn."

"Well," Trigger said, "I can't blame you for worrying a bit. How about your Guard Captain? Isn't it all right to ask him about reinforcements?"

Rak pursed his lips. "Yes. And I did. This morning. Before I called you."

"What did he say?"

Rak grimaced unhappily. "He implied, Miss Farn, that his present guard complement could handle any emergency. How would he know?"

"That's his job," Trigger pointed out gently. The Juniors did look badly worried. "He didn't have any helpful ideas?"

"None," said Rak. "He said that if someone wanted to put up the money to hire a battle squad of Special Federation Police, he could always find some use for them. But that's hopeless, of course."

Trigger straightened up. She reached out and poked Rak's bony chest with a finger tip. "You know something?" she said. "It's not!"

The four faces lit up together.

"The fact is," Trigger went on, "that I'm handling the Project budget until someone shows up to take over. So I think I'll just buy you that Federation battle squad, Rak! I'll get on it right away." She stood up. The Juniors bounced automatically out of their chairs. "You go tell your guard Captain," she instructed them from the hall door, "there'll be a squad showing up in time for dinner tonight."

The Federation Police Office in Ceyce informed Trigger that a Class A Battle Squad—twenty trained men with full equipment—would report for two months' duty at the Colonial School during the afternoon. She made them out a check and gave it the Ruya Farn signature via telewriter. The figure on that check was going to cause some U-League auditor's eyebrows to fly off the top of his head one of these days; but if the League insisted on remaining aloof to the problems of its Plasmoid Project, a little financial anguish was the least it could expect in return.

Trigger felt quite cheerful for a while.

Then she had a call from Precol's Maccadon office. She was requested to stand by while a personal interstellar transmission was switched to her ComWeb.

It looked like her day! She hummed softly, waiting. She knew just one individual affluent enough to be able to afford personal interstellar conversations; and that was Commissioner Tate. Fast work, Plemp, she thought approvingly.

But it was Brule Inger's face that flashed into view on the ComWeb. Trigger's heart jumped. Her breath caught in her throat.

"Brule!" she yelled then. She shot up out of her chair. "Where are you calling from?"

Brule's eyes crinkled around the edges. He gave her the smile. The good old smile. "Unfortunate-

ly, darling, I'm still in the Manon System." He
blinked. "What happened to your hair?"

"Manon!" said Trigger. She started to settle
back, weak with disappointment. Then she shot
up again. "Brule! Lunatic! You're blowing a
month's salary a minute on this! I love you!
Switch off, fast!"

Brule threw back his head and laughed. "You
haven't changed much in two months, anyway!
Don't worry. It's for free. I'm calling from the
yacht of a friend."

"Some friend!" Trigger said, startled.

"It isn't costing her anything either. She had to
transmit to the Hub today anyway. Asked me if I'd
like to take over the last few minutes of contact
and see if I could locate you . . . Been missing me
properly, Trigger?"

Trigger smiled. "Very properly. Well, that was
lovely of her! Someone I know?"

"Hardly," said Brule. "Nelauk arrived a week or
so after you left. Nelauk Pluly. Her father's the
Pluly Lines. Let's talk about you. What's the
silver-haired idea?"

"Got talked into it," she told him. "It's all the
rage again right now." He surveyed her critically.
"I like you better as a redhead."

"So do I." Oops, Trigger thought. Security,
girl! "So I'll change back tonight," she went on
quickly. "Golly, Brule. It's nice to see that homely
old mug again!"

"Be a lot nicer when it won't have to be over a
transmitter."

"Right you are!"

"When are you coming back?"

She shook her head glumly. "Don't know."

He was silent a moment. "I've had to take a bit of chitchat now and then," he remarked, "about you and old Tate vanishing together."

Trigger felt herself coloring. "So don't take it," she said shortly. "Just pop them one!"

The smile returned. "Wouldn't be gentlemanly to pop a lady, would it?"

She smiled back. "So stay away from the ladies!" Somehow Brule and Holati Tate never had worked up a really warm regard for each other. It had caused a little trouble before.

"Okay to tell me where you are?" he asked.

"Afraid not, Brule."

"Precol Home Office apparently knows," he pointed out.

"Apparently," Trigger admitted.

They looked at each other a moment; then Brule grinned. "Well, keep your little secret!" he said. "All I really want to know is when you're getting back."

"Very soon, I hope, Brule," Trigger said unhappily. Then there was a sudden burst of sound from the ComWeb—gusts of laughing, chattering voices; a faint wash of music. Brule glanced aside.

"Party going on," he explained. "And here comes Nelauk! She wanted to say hello to you."

A dozen feet behind him, a figure strolled gracefully into view on the screen and came forward. A slender girl with high-piled violet hair and eyes that very nearly matched the hair's tint. She was dressed in something resembling a dozen blossoms—blossoms which, in Trigger's opinion, had been rather carelessly scattered. But presumably it was a very elegant party costume. She was quite young, certainly not yet twenty.

Brule laid a brotherly hand on a powdered shoulder. "Meet Trigger, Nelauk!"

Nelauk murmured it was indeed an honor, one she had long looked forward to. The violet eyes blinked sleepily at Trigger.

Trigger gave her a great big smile. "Thanks so much for arranging for the call. I've been wondering how Brule was doing."

Wrong thing to say, probably, she thought. She was right. Nelauk reached for it with no effort.

"Oh, he's doing wonderfully!" she assured Trigger without expression. "I'm keeping an eye on him. And this small favor—it was the very least I could do for Brule. For you, too, of course, Trigger dear."

Trigger held the smile firmly.

"Thanks so much, again!" she said.

Nelauk nodded, smiled back and drifted gracefully off the screen. Brule blew Trigger a kiss. "They'll be cutting contact now. See you very, very soon, Trigger, I hope."

His image vanished before she could answer.

She paced her office, muttering softly. She went over to the ComWeb once, reached out toward it and drew her hand back again.

Better think this over.

It might not be an emergency. Brule didn't exactly chase women. He let them chase him now and then. Long before she left Manon, Trigger had discovered without much surprise, that the wives, daughters and girl friends of visiting Hub tycoons were as susceptible to the Inger charm as any Precol clerks. The main difference was that they were a lot more direct about showing it.

It hadn't really worried her. In fact, she found Brule's slightly startled reports of maneuverings of various amorous Hub ladies very entertaining. But she had put in a little worrying about something else. Brule's susceptibility seemed to be more to the overwhelming mass display of wealth with which he was suddenly in almost constant contact. Many of the yachts he went flitting around among as Precol's representative were elaborate spacegoing palaces, and it appeared Brule Inger was soon regarded as a highly welcome guest on most of them.

Brule talked about that a little too much.

Trigger resumed her pacing.

Little Nelauk mightn't be twenty yet, but she'd flipped out a challenge just now with all the languid confidence of a veteran campaigner. Which, Trigger thought cattily, little Nelauk undoubtedly was.

And a girl, she added cattily, whose father represented the Pluly Lines did have some slight reason for confidence . . .

"Miaow!" she reproved herself. Nelauk, to be honest about it, was also a dish.

But if she happened to be serious about Brule, the dish Brule might be tempted by was said Pluly Lines.

Trigger went over to the window and looked

down at the exercise quadrangle forty floors below.

"If he's that much of a meathead!" she thought.

He could be that much of a meathead. He was
also Brule. She went back to her desk and sat
down. She looked at the ComWeb. A girl had a
right to consider her own interests.

And there was the completely gruesome possibility now that Holati Tate might call in at any
moment, give her an entirely reasonable, satisfactory, valid, convincing explanation for everything that had happened lately—and then show
her why it would be absolutely necessary for her
to stay here a while longer.

If it was a choice between inconveniencing
Holati Tate and losing that meathead Brule—

Trigger switched on the ComWeb.

4

THE HEAD OF THE PERSONNEL department of Precol's
Maccadon office said, "You don't want me,
Argee. That's not my jurisdiction. I'll connect you
with Undersecretary Rozan."

Trigger blinked. "Under—" she began. But he'd
already cut off.

She stared at the ComWeb, feeling a little shak-
en. All she'd done was to say she wanted to apply
for a transfer! Undersecretary Rozan was one of
Precol's Big Four. For a moment, Trigger had an
uncanny notion. Some strange madness was
spreading insidiously through the Hub. She
shook the thought off.

A businesslike blonde showed up in the screen.
She might be about thirty-five. She smiled a
small, cold smile.

"Rozan," she said. "You're Trigger Argee. I
know about you. What's the trouble?"

Trigger looked at her, wondering. "No trouble," she said. "Personnel just routed me through to you."

"They've been instructed to do so," said Rozan. "Go ahead."

"I'm on detached duty at the moment."

"I know."

"I'd like to apply for a transfer back to my previous job. The Manon System."

"That's your privilege," said Rozan. She half turned, swung a telewriter forward and snapped it into her ComWeb. She glanced out at Trigger's desk. "Your writer's connected, I see. We'll want thumbprint and signature."

She slid a form into her telewriter, shifted it twice as Trigger deposited thumbprint and signature and drew it out. "The application will be processed promptly, Argee. Good day."

Not a gabby type, that Rozan.

If not gabby, the Precol blonde was a woman of her word. Trigger had just started lunch when the office mail-tube receiver tinkled brightly at her. She reached in, took out a flat plastic carrier, snapped it open. The paper that unfolded itself in her hand was her retransfer application.

At the bottom of the form was stamped "Application Denied," followed by the signature of the Secretary of the Department of Precolonization, Home Office, Evalee.

Trigger's gaze shifted incredulously from the signature to the two words, and back. They'd taken the trouble to get that signature transmitted from Evalee just to make it clear that there were no

heads left to be gone over in the matter. Precol was
not transferring her back to Manon. That was final. Then she realized that there was a second
sheet attached to the application form.

On it in handwriting were a few more words:
"In accordance with the instructions of Commissioner Tate." And a signature, "Rozan." And
three final words: "Destroy this note."

Trigger crumpled up the application in one
hand. Her other hand darted to the ComWeb.

Then she checked herself. To fire an as-of-now
resignation back at Precol had been the immediate impulse. But something, some vague
warning chill, was saying it might be a very poor
impulse to follow.

She sat back to think it over.

It was very probable that Undersecretary Rozan
disliked Holati Tate intensely. A lot of the Home
Office big shots disliked Holati Tate. He'd
stamped on their toes more than once—very justi-
fiably; but he'd stamped. The Home Office
wouldn't go an inch out of its way to do something just because Commission Tate happened to
want it done.

So somebody else was backing up Commissioner Tate's instructions.

Trigger shook her head helplessly.

The only somebody else who *could* give instructions to the Precolonization Department was
the Council of the Federation!

And how could the Federation possibly care
what Trigger Argee was doing? She made a small,
incredulous noise in her throat.

Then she sat there a while, feeling frightened.

The fright didn't really wear off, but it settled down slowly inside her. Up on the surface she began to think again.

Assume it's so, she instructed herself. It made no sense, but everything else made even less sense. Just assume it's so. Set it up as a practical problem. Don't worry about the why . . .

The problem became very simple then. She wanted to go to Manon. The Federation—or something else, something quite unthinkable at the moment but comparable to the Federation in power and influence—wanted to keep her here.

She uncrumpled the application, detached Rozan's note, tore up the note and dropped its shreds into the wall disposal. That obligation was cancelled. She didn't have any other obligations. She'd liked Holati Tate. When all this was cleared up, she might find she still liked him. At the moment she didn't owe him a thing.

Now. Assume they hadn't just blocked the obvious route to Manon. They couldn't block all routes to everywhere; that was impossible. But they could very well be watching to see that she didn't simply get up and walk off. And they might be very well prepared to take quite direct action to stop her from doing it.

She would, Trigger decided, leave the method she'd use to get out of the Colonial School unobserved to the last. That shouldn't present any serious difficulties.

Once she was outside, what would she do?

Principally, she had to buy transportation. And

that—since she had no intention of spending a few months on the trip, and since a private citizen didn't have the ghost of a chance at squeezing aboard a Federation packet on the Manon run—was going to be expensive. In fact, it was likely to take the bulk of her savings. Under the circumstances, however, expense wasn't important. If Precol refused to give her back her job when she showed up on Manon, a number of the industrial outfits preparing to move in as soon as the plant got its final clearance would be very happy to have her. She'd already turned down a dozen offers at considerably more than her present salary.

So . . . she'd get off the school grounds, take a tube strip into downtown Ceyce, step into a ComWeb booth, and call Grand Commerce transportation for information on the earliest subspace runs to Manon.

She'd reserve a berth on the first fast boat out. In the name of—let's see—in the name of Birna Drellgannoth, who had been a friend of hers when they were around the age of ten. Since Manon was a Precol preserve, she wouldn't have to meet the problem of precise personal identification, such as one ran into when booking passage to some of the member worlds.

The ticket office would have her thumbprints then. That was unavoidable. But there were millions of thumbprints being deposited every hour of the day on Maccadon. If somebody started checking for her by that method, it should take them a good long while to sort out hers.

Next stop—the Ceyce branch of the Bank of Maccadon. And it was lucky she'd done all her banking in Ceyce since she was a teen-ager, because she would have to present herself in person to draw out her savings. She'd better lose no time getting to the bank either. It was one place where theoretical searchers could expect her to show up.

She could pay for her ship reservation at the bank. Then to a store for some clothes and a suitcase for the trip . . .

And, finally, into some big middle-class hotel where she would stay quietly until a few hours before the ship was due to take off.

That seemed to cover it. It probably wasn't foolproof. But trying to work out a foolproof plan would be a waste of time when she didn't know just what she was up against. This should give her a running start, a long one.

When should she leave?

Right now, she decided. Commissioner Tate presumably would be informed that she had applied for a transfer and that the transfer had been denied. He knew her too well not to become suspicious if it looked as if she were just sitting there and taking it.

She got her secretary on the ComWeb.

"I'm thinking of leaving the office," she said. "Anything for me to take care of first?"

It was a safe question. She'd signed the day's mail and checks before lunch.

"Not a thing, Miss Farn."

"Fine," said Ruya Farn. "If anyone wants me in

the next three or four hours, I'll be either down in the main library or out at the lake."

And that would give somebody two rather extensive areas to look for her, if and when they started to look—along with the fact that, for all anyone knew, she might be anywhere between those two points.

A few minutes later, Trigger sauntered, humming blithely, into her room and gave it a brief survey. There were some personal odds and ends she would have liked to take with her, but she could send for them from Manon.

The Denton, however, was coming along. The little gun had a very precisely calibrated fast-acting stunner attachment, and old Runser Argee had instructed Trigger in its use with his customary thoroughness before he formally presented her with the gun. She had never had occasion to turn the stunner on a human being, but she'd used it on game. If this cloak and dagger business became too realistic, she'd already decided she would use it as needed.

She slipped the Denton into the side pocket of a lightweight rain robe, draped the robe over her arm, slung her purse beside it, picked up the sun hat and left the room.

The Colonial School's kitchen area was on one of the underground levels. Unless they'd modified their guard system very considerably since Trigger had graduated, that was the route by which she would leave.

As far as she could tell they hadn't modified

anything. The whole kitchen level looked so unchanged that she had a moment of nostalgia.
Groups of students went chattering along the
hallways between the storerooms and the cooking
and processing plants. The big mess hall, Trigger
noticed in passing, smelled as good as it always
had. Bells sounded the end of a period and a
loudspeaker system began directing Class so and
so to Room such and such. Standing around were
a few uniformed guards—mainly for the purpose
of helping out newcomers who had lost their direction.

She came out on the equally familiar big and
brightly lit platform of the loading ramp. Some
sixty or seventy great cylindrical vans floated
alongside the platform, most of them disgorging
their contents, some still sealed.

Trigger walked unhurriedly down the ramp,
staying in the background, observing the move-
ments of two ramp guards and marking four vans
which were empty and looked ready to go.

The driver of the farthest of the four empties
stood in the back of his vehicle, a few feet above
the platform. When Trigger came level with him,
he was studying her. He was a big young man
with tousled black hair and a rough-and-ready
look. He was grinning very faintly. He knew the
ways of Colonial School students.

Trigger raised her left hand a few inches, three
fingers up. His grin widened. He shook his head
and raised both hands in a corresponding gesture.
Eight fingers.

Trigger frowned at him, stopped and looked

back along the row of vans. Then left hand up again—four fingers and thumb.

The driver made a circle with finger and thumb. A deal, for five Maccadon crowns. Which was about standard fare for unauthorized passage out of the school.

Trigger wandered on to the end of the platform, turned and came back, still unhurriedly but now close to the edge of the ramp. Down the line, another van slammed open in back and a stream of crates swooped out, riding a gravity beam from the roof toward a waiting storeroom carrier. The guard closest to Trigger turned to watch the process. Trigger took six quick steps and reached her driver.

He put down a hand to help her step up. She slipped the five-crown piece into his palm.

"Up front," he whispered hoarsely. "Next to the driver's seat and keep down. How far?"

"Nearest tube line."

He grinned again and nodded. "Can do."

Twenty minutes later Trigger was in a downtown ComWeb booth. There had been a minor modification in her plans and she'd stopped off in a store a few doors away and picked up a carefully nondescript street dress and a scarf. She changed into the dress now and bundled the school costume into a deposit box, which she dispatched to Central Deposit with a one-crown piece, getting a numbered slip in return. It had occurred to her that there was a chance otherwise of getting caught in a Colonial School roundup, if it was brought to Doctor Plemponi's attention that

there appeared to be considerably more students
out on the town at the moment than could be
properly overlooked.

Or even, Trigger thought, if somebody simply
happened to have missed Trigger Argee.

She slipped the rain robe over her shoulders,
dropped a coin into the ComWeb, and covered the
silver-blonde hair with the scarf. The screen lit
up. She asked for Grand Commerce Transportation.

Waiting, she realized suddenly that so far she
was rather enjoying herself. There had been a
little argument with the van driver who, it turned
out, had ideas of his own about modifying Trigger's plans—a complication she'd run into fre-
quently in her school days too. As usual, it didn't
develop into a very serious argument. Truckers
who dealt with the Colonial School knew, or
learned in one or two briefly horrid lessons, that
Mihul's commando-trained charges were prone
to ungirlish methods of discouragement when ar-
gued with too urgently.

The view screen switched on. The transportation clerk's glance flicked over Trigger's street
dress when she told him her destination. His expression remained bland. Yes, the Dawn City was
leaving Ceyce Port for the Manon System tomorrow evening. Yes, it was subspace express—one
of the newest and fastest, in fact. His eyes slipped
over the dress again. Also one of the most luxuri-
ous, he might add. There would be only two
three-hour stops in the Hub beyond Maccadon—
one each off Evalee and Garth. Then a straight

dive to Manon unless, of course, gravitic storm shifts forced the ship to surface temporarily. Average time for the Dawn City on the run was eleven days; the slowest trip so far had required sixteen.

"But unfortunately, madam, there are only a very few cabins left—and not very desirable ones, I'm afraid." He looked apologetic. "There hasn't been a vacancy on the Manon run for the past three months."

"I can stand it, I imagine," Trigger said. "How much for the cheapest?"

The clerk cleared his throat gently and told her.

She couldn't help blinking, though she was braced for it. But it was more than she had counted on. A great deal more. It would leave her, in fact, with exactly one hundred and twenty-six crowns out of her entire savings, plus the coins she had in her purse.

"Any extras?" she asked, a little hoarsely.

He shrugged. "There's Traveler's Rest," he said negligently. "Nine hundred for the three dive periods. But Rest is optional, of course. Some passengers prefer the experience of staying awake during a subspace dive." He smiled—rather sadistically, Trigger felt—and added, "Till they've lived through one of them, that is."

Trigger nodded. She'd lived through quite a few of them. She didn't like subspace particularly—nobody did—but except for an occasional touch of nausea or dizziness at the beginning of a dive, it didn't bother her much. Many people got hallucinations, went into states of panic or just got very sick. "Anything else?" she asked.

"Just the usual tips and things," said the clerk. He looked surprised. "Do you—does madam wish to make the reservation?"

"Madam does," Trigger told him coldly. "How long will it hold?"

It would be good up to an hour before take-off time, she learned. If not claimed then, it would be filled from the last-minute waiting list.

She left the booth thoughtfully. At least the Dawn City would be leaving in less than twenty-six hours. She wouldn't have to spend much of her remaining capital before she got off Maccadon.

She'd skip meals, she decided. Except breakfast next morning, which would be covered by her hotel room fee.

And it wasn't going to be any middle-class hotel.

There was no one obviously waiting for her at the Bank of Maccadon. In fact, since that venerable institution covered a city block, with entrances running up from the street level to the fifty-eighth floor, a small army would have been needed to make sure of spotting her.

She had to identify herself to get into the vaults, but there was a solution to that. Seven years ago when Runser Argee died suddenly and she had to get his property and records straightened out, a gray-haired little vault attendant with whom she dealt with had taken a fatherly interest in her.

When she saw he was still on the job, Trigger was certain the matter would go off all right.

It did. He didn't take a really close look at her until she shoved her signature and Federation identification in front of him. Then his head bobbed up briskly. His eyes lit up.

"Trigger!" He bounced out of his chair. His right hand shot out. "Good to see you again! I've been hearing about you."

They shook hands. She put a finger to her lips. "I'm here incog!" she cautioned in a low voice. "Can you handle this quietly?"

The faded blue eyes widened slightly, but he asked no questions. Trigger Argee's name was known rather widely, as a matter of fact, particularly on her home world. And as he remembered Trigger, she wasn't a girl who'd go look for a spotlight to stand in.

He nodded. "Sure can!" He glanced suspiciously at the nearest customers, then looked down at what Trigger had written. He frowned. "You drawing out everything? Not leaving Ceyce for good, are you?"

"No," Trigger said. "I'll be back. This is just a temporary emergency."

That was all the explaining she had to do. Four minutes later she had her money. Three minutes after that she had paid for the Dawn City reservation as Birna Drellgannoth and deposited her thumbprints with the ticket office. Counting what was left, she found it came to just under a hundred and thirty-eight.

Definitely no dinner tonight! She needed a suitcase and a change of clothing. And then she'd just better go sit in that hotel room.

The street level traffic was moderate around the bank, but it began to thicken as she approached a shopping center two blocks farther on. Striding along, neither hurrying nor idling, Trigger decided she had it made. The only real chance to catch up with her had been at the bank. And the old vault attendant wouldn't talk.

Half a block from the shopping center, a row of spacers on planet-leave came rollicking cheerily toward her, uniform jackets unbuttoned, three Ceyce girls in arm-linked formation among them, all happily high. Trigger shifted toward the edge of the sidewalk to let them pass. As the line swayed up on her left, there was a shadowy settling of an aircar at the curb to her right.

With loud outcries of glad recognition and whoops of laughter, the line swung in about her, close. Bodies crowded against her; a hand was clapped over her mouth. Other hands held her arms. Her feet came off the ground and she had a momentary awareness of being rushed expertly forward.

Then she was in the car, half on her side over the rear seat, two very strong hands clamping her wrists together behind her back. As she sucked in her breath for a yell, the door snapped shut behind her, cutting off the rollicking "ha-ha-ha's" and other noises outside.

There was a lurching twist as the aircar shot upward.

5

THE MAN WHO HELD TRIGGER'S wrists shifted his grip up her arms, and turned her a little so that she could sit upright on the seat, faced half away from him. She had got only a glimpse of him as he caught her, but he seemed to be wearing the same kind of commercial spacer's uniform as the group which had hustled her into the car. The other man in the car, the driver, sat up front with his back to them. He looked like any ordinary middle-aged civilian.

Trigger let her breath out slowly. There was no point in yelling now. She could feel her legs tremble a little, but she didn't seem to be actually frightened. At least, not yet.

"Spot anything so far?" the man who held her asked. It was a deep voice. It sounded matter-of-fact, quite unexcited.

"Three possibles anyway," the driver said with

equal casualness. He didn't turn his head. "Make it two . . . One very definite possible now, I'd say!"

"Better feed it to her then."

The driver didn't reply, but the car's renewed surge of power pushed Trigger down hard on the seat. She couldn't see much more than a shifting piece of the sky line through the front view plate. Their own car seemed to be rising at a tremendous rate. They were probably, she thought, already above the main traffic arteries over Ceyce.

"Now, Miss Argee," the man sitting beside her said, "I'd like to reassure you a little first."

"Go ahead and reassure me," Trigger said unsteadily.

"You're in no slightest danger from us," he said. "We're your friends."

"Nice friends!" remarked Trigger.

"I'll explain it all in a couple of minutes. There may be some fairly dangerous characters on our tail at the moment, and if they start to catch up—"

"Which they seem to be doing," the driver interrupted. "Hang on for a few fast turns when we hit the next cloud bank."

"We'll probably shake them there," the other man explained to Trigger. "In case we don't though, I'll need both hands free to handle the guns."

"So?" she asked.

"So I'd like to slip a set of cuffs on you for just a few minutes. I've been informed you're a fairly tricky lady, and we don't want you to do anything thoughtless. You won't have them on very long. All right?"

Trigger bit her lip. It wasn't all right, and she didn't feel at all reassured so far.

"Go ahead," she said.

He let go of her left arm, presumably to reach for the handcuffs. She twisted around on him and went into fast action.

She was fairly proficient at the practice of un-armed mayhem. The trouble was that the big ape she was trying the stuff on seemed at least as adept and with twice her muscle. She lost a precious instant finding out that the Denton was no longer in her robe pocket. After that she never got back the initiative. It didn't help either that the car suddenly seemed to be trying to fly in three directions at once.

All in all, about forty seconds passed before she was plumped back on the seat, her hands behind her again, linked at the wrists by the smooth plastic cords of the cuffs. The ape stood behind the driver, his hands resting on the back of the seat. He wasn't, Trigger observed bitterly, even breathing hard. The view plate was full of the cottony whiteness of a cloud heart. They seemed to be dropping again.

One more violent swerve and they came flashing out into wet gray cloud-shadow and on into brilliant sunlight.

A few seconds passed. Then the ape remarked, "Looks like you lost them, chum."

"Right," said the driver. "Almost at the river now. I'll turn north there and drop down."

"Right," said the ape. "Get us that far and we'll be out of trouble."

A few minutes passed in silence. Presently

Trigger sensed they were slowing and losing altitude. Then a line of trees flashed by in the view plate. "Nice flying!" the ape said. He punched the driver approvingly in the shoulder and turned back to Trigger.

They looked at each other for a few seconds. He was tall, dark-eyed, very deeply tanned, with thick sloping shoulders. He probably wasn't more than five or six years older than she was. He was studying her curiously, and his eyes were remarkably steady. Something stirred in her for a moment, a small chill of fear. Something passed through her thoughts, a vague odd impression, like a half aroused memory, of huge, cold, dangerous things far away. It was gone before she could grasp it more clearly. She frowned.

The ape smiled. It wasn't, Trigger saw, an entirely unpleasant face. "Sorry the party got rough," he said. "Will you give parole if I take those cuffs off and tell you what this is about?"

She studied him again. "Better tell me first," she said shortly.

"All right. We're taking you to Commissioner Tate. We'll be there in about an hour. He'll tell you himself why he wanted to see you."

Trigger's eyes narrowed for an instant. Secretly she felt very much relieved. Holati Tate, at any rate, wouldn't let anything really unpleasant happen to her—and she would find out at last what had been going on.

"You've got an odd way of taking people places," she observed.

He laughed. "The grabber party wasn't

scheduled. You'd indicated you wanted to speak
to the Commissioner. We were sent to the Colonial School to pick you up and escort you to him.
When we found out you'd disappeared, we had to
do some fast improvising. Not my business to tell
you the reasons for that."

Trigger said hesitantly, "Those people who
were chasing this car—"

"What about them?" he asked thoughtfully.

"Were they after me?"

"Well," he said, "they weren't after me. Better
let the Commissioner tell you about that, too.
Now—how about parole?"

She nodded. "Till you turn me over to the
Commissioner."

"Fair enough," he said. "You're his problem
then." He took a small flat piece of metal out of a
pocket and reached back of her with it. He didn't
seem to do more than touch the cuffs, but she felt
the slick coils loosen and drop away.

Trigger rubbed her wrists. "Where's my gun?"
she asked.

"I've got it. I'll give it to the Commissioner."

"How did you people find me so fast?"

"Police keep bank entrances under twenty-four
hour visual survey. We had someone watching
their screens. You were spotted going in." He sat
down companionably beside her. "I'd introduce
myself, but I don't know if that would fit in with
the Commissioner's plans."

Trigger shrugged. It still was quite possible, she
decided, that her own plans weren't completely
spoiled. Holati and his friends didn't necessarily

know about that vault account. If they did know she'd had one and had closed it out, they could make a pretty good guess at what she'd done with the money. But if she just kept quiet, there might be an opportunity to get back to Ceyce and the Dawn City by tomorrow evening.

"Cigarette?" the Commissioner's overmuscled henchman inquired amiably.

Trigger glanced at him from the side. Not amiably. "No, thanks."

"No hard feelings, are there?" He looked surprised.

"Yes," she said evenly. "There are."

"Maybe," the driver suggested from the front, "what Miss Argee could do with is a shot of Puya. Flask's in my coat pocket. Left side."

"There's an idea," remarked Trigger's companion. He looked at her. "It's very good Puya."

"So choke on it," Trigger told him gently. She settled back into the corner of the seat and closed her eyes. "You can wake me up when we get to the Commissioner."

"In some way," Holati Tate said, "this little item here seems to be at the core of the whole plasmoid problem. Know what it is?"

Trigger looked at the little item with some revulsion. Dark green, marbled with pink streakings, it lay on the table between them, rather like a plump leech a foot and a half long. It was motionless except that the end nearest her shifted in a short arc from side to side, as if the thing suffered from a very slow twitch.

"One of the plasmoids obviously," she said. "A

jumpy one." She blinked at it. "Looks like that 113. Is it?"

She glanced around. Commissioner Tate and Professor Mantelish, who sat in an armchair off to her right, were staring at her, eyebrows up, apparently surprised about something. "What's the matter?" she asked.

"We're just wondering," said Holati, "how you happen to remember 113, in particular, out of the thousands of plasmoids on Harvest Moon."

"Oh. One of the Junior Scientists on your Project mentioned the 112-113 unit. That brought it to mind. Is this 113?"

"No," said Holati Tate. "But it appears to be a duplicate of it." He was a mild-looking little man, well along in years, sparse and spruce in his Precol uniform. The small gray eyes in the sun-darkened, leathery face weren't really mild, if you considered them more closely, or if you knew the Commissioner.

"Have to fill you in on some of the background first, Trigger girl," he'd said, when she was brought to his little private office and inquired with some heat what the devil was up. The tall grabber hadn't come into the office with her. He asked the Commissioner from the door whether he should get Professor Mantelish to the conference room, and the Commissioner nodded. Then the door closed and the two of them were alone.

"I know it's looked odd," Commissioner Tate admitted, "but the circumstances have been very odd. Still are. And I didn't want to worry you any more than I had to."

Trigger, unmollified, pointed out that the

methods he'd used not to worry her hardly had been soothing.

"I know that, too," said the Commissioner. "But if I'd told you everything immediately, you would have had reason enough to be worried for the past two months, rather than just for a day or so. The situation has improved now, very considerably. In fact, in another few days you shouldn't have any more reason to worry at all." He smiled briefly. "At least, no more than the rest of us."

Trigger felt a bit dry-lipped suddenly. "I do at present?" she asked.

"You did till today. There's been some pretty heavy heat on you, Trigger girl. We're switching most of it off tonight. For good, I think."

"You mean some heat will be left?"

"In a way," he said. "But that should be cleared up too in the next three or four days. Anyway we can drop most of the mystery act tonight."

Trigger shook her head. "It isn't being dropped very fast!" she observed.

"I told you I couldn't tell it backwards," the Commissioner said patiently. "All right if we start filling in the background now?"

"I guess we'd better," she admitted.

"Fine," said Commissioner Tate. He got to his feet. "Then let's go join Mantelish."

"Why the professor?"

"He could help a lot with the explaining. If he's in the mood. Anyway he's got a kind of pet I'd like you to look at."

"A pet!" cried Trigger. She shook her head

again and stood up resignedly. "Lead on, Commissioner!"

They joined Mantelish and his plasmoid weird-
ie in what looked like the dining room of what
had looked like an old-fashioned hunting lodge
when the aircar came diving down on it between
two ice-sheeted mountain peaks. Trigger wasn't
sure in just what section of the main continent
they were; but there were only two or three
alternatives—it was high in the mountains, and
night came a lot faster here than it did around
Ceyce.

She greeted Mantelish and sat down at the table. Then the Commissioner locked the doors and
introduced her to the professor's pet.

"It's labelled 113-A," he said now. "Even the
professor isn't certain he could distinguish between the two. Right, Mantelish?"

"That is true," said Mantelish, "at present." He
was a very big, rather fat but healthy-looking old
man with a thick thatch of white hair and a ruddy
face. "Without a physical comparison—" He
shrugged.

"What's so important about the critter?" Trigger asked, eyeing the leech again. One good thing
about it, she thought—it wasn't equipped to eye
her back.

"It goes back to the time," the Commissioner
said, "when Mantelish and Fayle and Azol were
conducting the first League investigation of the
plasmoids on Harvest Moon. You recall the situation?"

"If you mean their attempts to get the things to show some signs of life, I do, naturally."

"One of them got lively enough for poor old Azol, didn't it?" Professor Mantelish rumbled from his armchair.

Trigger grimaced. Doctor Azol's fate might be one of the things that had given her a negative attitude towards plasmoids. With Mantelish and Doctor Gess Fayle, Azol had been the third of the three big U-League boys in charge of the initial investigation on Harvest Moon. As she remembered it, it was Azol who discovered that Plasmoids occasionally could be induced to absorb food. Almost any kind of food, it turned out, so long as it contained a sufficient quantity of protein. What had happened to Azol looked like a particularly unfortunate result of the discovery. It was assumed an untimely coronary had been the reason he had fallen helplessly into the feeding trough of one of the largest plasmoids. By the time he was found, all of him from the knees on up already had been absorbed.

"I meant your efforts to get them to work," she said.

Commissioner Tate looked at Mantelish. "You tell her about that part of it," he suggested.

Mantelish shook his head. "I'd get too technical," he said resignedly. "I always do. At least they say so. You tell her."

But Holati Tate's eyes had shifted suddenly to the table. "Hey, now!" he said in a low voice.

Trigger followed his gaze. After a moment she

made a soft, sucking sound of alarmed distaste.

"Ugh!" she remarked. "It's moving!"

"So it is," Holati said.

"Towards me!" said Trigger. "I think—"

"Don't get startled. Mantelish!"

Mantelish already was coming up slowly behind Trigger's chair. "Don't move!" he cautioned her.

"Why not?" said Trigger.

"Hush, my dear." Mantelish laid a large, heavy hand on each of her shoulders and bore down slightly. "It's sensitive! This is very interesting. Very."

Perhaps it was. She kept watching the plasmoid. It had thinned out somewhat and was gliding very slowly but very steadily across the table. Definitely in her direction.

"Ho-ho!" said Mantelish in a thunderous murmur. "Perhaps it likes you, Trigger! Ho-ho!" He seemed immensely pleased.

"Well," Trigger said helplessly, "I don't like it!" She wriggled slightly under Mantelish's hands. "And I'd sooner get out of this chair!"

"Don't be childish, Trigger," said the professor annoyedly. "You're behaving as if it were, in some manner, offensive."

"It is," she said.

"Hush, my dear," Mantelish said absently, putting on a little more pressure. Trigger hushed resignedly. They watched. In about a minute, the gliding thing reached the edge of the table. Trigger gathered herself to duck out from under Mantelish's hands and go flying out of the chair if it looked as if the plasmoid was about to drop into her lap.

But it stopped. For a few seconds it lay motionless. Then it gradually raised its front end and began waving it gently back and forth in the air. At her, Trigger suspected.

"Yipes!" she said, horrified.

The front end sank back. The plasmoid lay still again. After a minute it was still lying still.

"Show's over for the moment, I guess," said the Commissioner.

"I'm afraid so," said Professor Mantelish. His big hands went away from Trigger's aching shoulders. "You startled it, Trigger!" he boomed at her accusingly.

6

THE POINT OF IT, Holati Tate explained, was that this had been more activity than 113-A normally displayed over a period of a week. And 113-A was easily the most active plasmoid of them all nowadays.

"It is, of course, possible," Mantelish said, arousing from deep thought, "that it was attracted by your body odor."

"Thank you, Mantelish!" said Trigger.

"You're welcome, my dear." Mantelish had pulled his chair up to the table; he hitched himself forward in it. "We shall now," he announced, "try a little experiment. Pick it up, Trigger."

She stared at him. "Pick it up! No, Mantelish. We shall now try some other little experiment."

Mantelish furrowed his Jovian brows. Holati gave her a small smile across the table. "Just touch it with the tip of a finger," he suggested. "You can do that much for the professor, can't you?"

"Barely," Trigger told him grimly. But she reached out and put a cautious finger tip to the less lively end of 113-A. After a moment she said, "Hey!" She moved the finger lightly along the thing's surface. It had a velvety, smooth, warm feeling, rather like a kitten. "You know," she said surprised, "it feels sort of nice! It just looks disgusting."

"Disgusting!" Mantelish boomed, offended again.

The Commissioner held up a hand. "Just a moment," he said. He'd picked up some signal Trigger hadn't noticed, for he went over to the wall now and touched something there. A release button apparently. The door to the room opened. Trigger's grabber came in. The door closed behind him. He was carrying a tray with a squat brown flask and four rather small glasses on it.

He gave Trigger a grin. She gave him a tentative smile in return. The Commissioner had introduced him: Heslet Quillan—Major Heslet Quillan, of the Subspace Engineers. For a Subspace Engineer, Trigger had thought skeptically, he was a pretty good grabber. But there was a qualified truce in the room. It would last, at least, until Holati finished his explaining. There was no really good reason not to include Major Quillan in it.

"Ah, Puya!" Professor Mantelish exclaimed, advancing on the tray as Quillan set it on the table. Mantelish seemed to have forgotten about plasmoid experiments for the moment, and Trigger didn't intend to remind him. She drew her hand back quietly from 113-A. The professor unstoppered the flask. "You'll have some, Trigger, I'm sure? The only really good thing the benighted world of Rumli ever produced."

"My great-grandmother," Trigger remarked, "was a Rumlian." She watched him fill the four glass with a thin purple liquid. "I've never tried it; but yes, thanks."

Quillan put one of the glasses in front of her.

"And we shall drink," Mantelish suggested, with a suave flourish of his Puya, "to your great-grandmother!"

"We shall also," suggested Major Quillan, pulling a chair up to the table for himself, "Advise Trigger to take a very small sip on her first go at the stuff."

Nobody had invited him to sit down. But nobody was objecting either. Well, that fitted, Trigger thought.

She sipped. It was tart and hot. Very hot. She set the glass back on the table, inhaled with difficulty, exhaled quiveringly. Tears gathered in her eyes.

"Very good!" she husked.

"Very good," the Commissioner agreed. He put down his empty glass and smacked his lips lightly. "And now," he said briskly, "let's get on with this conference."

Trigger glanced around the room while Quillan refilled three glasses. The small live coal she had swallowed was melting away; a warm glow began

to spread through her. It did look like the dining
room of a hunting lodge. The woodwork was
dark, old-looking, worn with much polishing.
Horned heads of various formidable Maccadon
life-forms adorned the walls.

But it was open season now on a different kind
of game. Three men had walked briskly past them
when Quillan brought her in by the front door.
They hadn't even looked at her. There were
sounds now and then from some of the other
rooms, and that general feeling of a considerable
number of people around—of being at an operating headquarters of some sort, which hummed
with quiet activity.

One of the things, Holati Tate said, which had
not become public knowledge so far was that Professor Mantelish actually succeeded in getting
some of the plasmoids on the Old Galactic base
back into operation. One plasmoid in particular.

The reason the achievement hadn't been announced was that for nearly six weeks no one
except the three men directly involved in the experiments had known about them. And during
that time other things occurred which made sub-
sequent publicity seem very inadvisable.

Mantelish scowled. "We made up a report to
the League the day of the initial discovery," he
informed Trigger. "It was a complete and detailed
report!"

"True," Holati said, "but the report the
U-League got didn't happen to be the one Professor Mantelish helped make up. We'll go into that
later. The plasmoid the professor was experimenting with was the 112-113 unit."

He shifted his gaze to Mantelish. "Still want me to tell it?"

"Yes, yes!" Mantelish said impatiently. "You will oversimplify grossly, of course, but it should do for the moment. At a more leisurely time I shall be glad to give Trigger an accurate description of the processes."

Trigger smiled at him. "Thank you, Professor!" She took her second sip of the Puya. Not bad.

"Well, Mantelish was dosing this plasmoid with mild electrical stimulations," Holati went on. "He noticed suddenly that as he did it other plasmoids in that section of Harvest Moon were indicating signs of activity. So he called in Doctor Fayle and Doctor Azol."

The three scientists discovered quickly that stimulation of the 112 part of the unit was in fact producing random patterns of plasmoid motion throughout the entire base, while an electrical prod at 113 brought everything to an abrupt stop again. After a few hours of this, 112 suddenly extruded a section of its material, which detached itself and moved off slowly under its own power through half the station, trailed with great excitement by Mantelish and Azol. It stopped at a point where another plasmoid had been removed for laboratory investigations, climbed up and settled down in the place left vacant by its predecessor. It then reshaped itself into a copy of the predecessor, and remained where it was. Obviously a replacement.

There was dignified scientific jubilation among the three. This was precisely the kind of information the U-League—and everybody else—had been hoping to obtain. 112-113 tentatively could be assumed to be a kind of monitor of the station's activities. It could be induced to go into action and to activate the other plasmoids. With further observation and refinement of method, its action undoubtedly could be shifted from the random to the purposeful. Finally, and most importantly, it had shown itself capable of producing a different form of plasmoid life to fulfill a specific requirement.

In essence, the riddles presented by the Old Galactic Station appeared to be solved.

The three made up their secret report to the U-League. Included was a recommendation to authorize distribution of ten per cent of the less significant plasmoids to various experimental centers in the Hub—the big and important centers which had been bringing heavy political pressure to bear on the Federation to let them in on the investigation. That should keep them occupied, while the U-League concluded the really important work.

"Next day," said Holati, "Doctor Gess Fayle presented Mantelish with a transmitted message from U-League Headquarters. It contained instructions to have Fayle mount the 112-113 unit immediately in one of the League ships at Harvest Moon and bring it quietly to Maccadon."

Mantelish frowned. "The message was faked!" he boomed.

"Not only that," said Holati. "The actual report Doctor Fayle had transmitted the day before to the League was revised to the extent that it omitted any reference to 112-113." He glanced thoughtfully at Mantelish. "As a matter of fact, it was almost a month and a half before League Headquarters became aware of the importance of the unit."

The professor snorted. "Azol," he explained to Trigger, "had become a victim of his scientific zeal. And I—"

"Doctor Azol," said the Commissioner, "as you may remember, had his little mishap with the plasmoid just two days after Fayle departed."

"And I," Mantelish went on, "was involved in other urgent research. How was I to know what that villain Fayle had been up to? A vice president of the University League!"

"Well," Trigger said, "what had Doctor Fayle been up to?"

"We don't know yet," Holati told her. "Obviously he had something in mind with the faked order and the alteration of the report. But the only thing we can say definitely is that he disappeared on the League ship he had requisitioned, along with its personnel and the 112-113 plasmoid, and hasn't shown up again.

"And that plasmoid unit now appears to have been almost certainly the key unit of the entire Old Galactic Station—the unit that kept everything running along automatically there for thirty thousand years."

He glanced at Quillan. "Someone at the door. We'll hold it while you see what they want."

7

THE BURLY CHARACTER WHO had appeared at the door said diffidently that Professor Mantelish had wanted to be present while his lab equipment was stowed aboard. If the professor didn't mind, things were about that far along.

Mantelish excused himself and went off with the messenger. The door closed. Quillan came back to his chair.

"We're moving the outfit later tonight," the Commissioner explained. "Mantelish is coming along—plus around eight tons of his lab equipment. Plus his special U-League guards."

"Oh?" Trigger picked up the Puya glass. She looked into it. It was empty. "Moving where?" she asked.

"Manon," said the Commissioner. "Tell you about that later."

Every last muscle in Trigger's body seemed to

go limp simultaneously. She settled back slightly
in the chair, surprised by the force of the reaction.
She hadn't realized by now how keyed up she
was! She sighed a small sigh. Then she smiled at
Quillan.

"Major," she said, "how about a tiny little refill
on that Puya—about half?"

Quillan took care of the tiny little refill.

Commissioner Tate said, "By the way, Quillan
does have a degree in subspace engineering and
gets assigned to the Engineers now and then. But
his real job's Space Scout Intelligence."

Trigger nodded. "I'd almost guessed it!" She
gave Quillan another smile. She nearly gave
113-A a smile.

"And now," said the Commissioner, "we'll talk
more freely. We tell Mantelish just as little as we
can. To tell you the truth, Trigger, the professor is
a terrible handicap on an operation like this. I
understand he was a great friend of your father's."

"Yes," she said. "Going over for visits to Mantelish's garden with my father is one of the earliest
things I remember. I can imagine he's a problem!"
She shifted her gaze curiously from one to the
other of the two men. "What are you people doing? Looking for Gess Fayle and the key unit?"

Holati Tate said, "That's about it. We're one of a
few thousand Federation groups assigned to the
same general job. Each group works at its special-
ties, and the information gets correlated." He
paused. "The Federation Council—they're the
ones we're working for directly—the Council's
biggest concern is the very delicate political situa-

tion that's involved. They feel it could develop suddenly into a dangerous one. They may be right."

"In what way?" Trigger asked.

"Well, suppose that key unit is lost and stays lost. Suppose all the other plasmoids put together don't contain enough information to show how the Old Galactics produced the things and got them to operate."

"Somebody would get that worked out pretty soon, wouldn't they?"

"Not necessarily, or even probably, according to Mantelish and some other people who know what's happened. There seem to be too many basic factors missing. It might be necessary to develop a whole new class of sciences first. And that could take a few centuries."

"Well," Trigger admitted, "*I* could get along without the things indefinitely."

"Same here," the plasmoid nabob agreed ungratefully. "Weird beasties! But—let's see. At present there are twelve hundred and fifty-eight member worlds to the Federation, aren't there?"

"More or less."

"And the number of planetary confederacies, subplanetary governments, industrial, financial and commercial combines, assorted power groups, etc. and so on, is something I'd hate to have to calculate."

"What are you driving at?" she asked.

"They've all been told we're heading for a new golden age, courtesy of the plasmoid science. Practically everybody has believed it. Now there's considerable doubt."

"Oh," she said. "Of course—practically everybody is going to get very unhappy, eh?"

"That," said Commissioner Tate, "is only a little of it."

"Yes, the thing isn't just lost. Somebody's got it."

"Very likely."

Trigger nodded. "Fayle's ship might have got wrecked accidentally, of course. But the way he took off shows he planned to disappear—a crack-up on top of that would be too much of a coincidence. So any one of umpteen thousands of organizations in the Hub might be the one that has that plasmoid now!"

"Including," said Holati, "any one of the two hundred and fourteen restricted worlds. Their treaties of limitation wouldn't have let them get into the plasmoid pie until the others had been at it a decade or so. They would have been quite eager . . ."

There was a little pause. Then Trigger said, "Lordy! The thing could even set off another string of wars—"

"That's a point the Council is nervous about," he said.

"Well, it certainly is a mess. You would have thought the Federation might have had a Security Chief in on that first operation. Right there on Harvest Moon!"

"They did," he said. "It was Fayle."

"Oh! Pretty embarrassing." Trigger was silent a moment. "Holati, could those things ever become as valuable as people keep saying? It's all sounded a little exaggerated to me."

The Commissioner said he'd wondered about it too. "I'm not enough of a biologist to make an educated guess. What it seems to boil down to is that they might. Which would be enough to tempt a lot of people to gamble very high for a chance to get control of the plasmoid process—and we know definitely that some people are gambling for it."

"How do you know?"

"We've been working a couple of leads here. Pretty short leads so far, but you work with what you can get." He nodded at the table. "We picked up the first lead through 113-A."

Trigger glanced down. The plasmoid lay there some inches from the side of her hand. "You know," she said uncomfortably, "old Repulsive moved again while we were talking! Towards my hand." She drew the hand away.

"I was watching it," Major Quillan said reassuringly from the end of the table. "I would have warned you, but it stopped when it got as far as it is now. That was around five minutes ago."

Trigger reached back and gave old Repulsive a cautious pat. "Very lively character! He does feel pleasant to touch. Kitty-cat pleasant! How did you get a lead through him?"

"Mantelish brought it back to Maccadon with him, mainly because of its similarity to 113. He was curious because he couldn't even guess at what its function was. It was just lying there in a cubicle. So he did considerable experimenting with it while he waited for Gess Fayle to show up—and League Headquarters fidgeted around, hoping to get the kind of report from Mantelish and Fayle that Mantelish thought they'd already received. They were wondering where Fayle was, too. But they knew Fayle was Security, so they didn't like to get too nosy."

Trigger shook her head. "Wonderful! So what happened with 113-A?"

"Mantelish began to get results with it," the Commissioner said. "One experiment was rather startling. He'd been trying that electrical stimulation business. Nothing happened until he had finished. Then he touched the plasmoid, and it fed the whole charge back to him. Apparently it was a fairly hefty dose."

She laughed delightedly. "Good for Repulsive! Stood up for his rights, eh?"

"Mantelish gained some such impression anyway. He became more cautious with it after that. And then he learned something that should be important. He was visiting another lab where they had a couple of plasmoids which actually moved now and then. He had 113-A in his coat pocket. The two lab plasmoids stopped moving while he was there. They haven't moved since."

"Like the Harvest Moon plasmoids when they stimulated 113?"

"Right. He thought about that, and then located another moving plasmoid. He dropped in to look it over, with 113-A in his pocket again, and it stopped. He did the same thing in one more place and then quit. There aren't that many moving plasmoids around. Those three labs are still wondering what hit their specimens."

She studied 113-A curiously. "A mighty mite! What does Mantelish make of it?"

"He thinks the 112-113 unit forms a kind of self-regulating system. The big one induces plasmoid activity, the little one modifies it. This 113-A might be a spare regulator. But it seems to be more than a spare—which brings us to that first lead we got. A gang of raiders crashed Mantelish's lab one night."

"When was that?"

"Some months ago. Before you and I left Manon. The professor was out, and 113-A had gone along in his pocket as usual. But his two lab guards and one of the raiders were killed. The others got away. Gess Fayle's defection was a certainty by then, and everybody was very nervous. The Feds got there, fast, and dead-brained the raider. They learned just two things. One, he'd been mind-blocked and couldn't have spilled any significant information even if they had got him alive. The other item they drew from his brain was a clear impression of the target of the raid—the professor's pal here."

"Uh-huh," Trigger said, lost in thought. She poked Repulsive lightly. "That would be Fayle and his associates then. Or somebody who knew about them. Did they want to kill it or grab it?"

The Commissioner looked at her. "Grab it, was the dead-brain report. Why?"

"Just wondering. Would make a difference, wouldn't it? Did they try again?"

"There've been five more attempts," he said.

"And what's everybody concluded from that?"

"They want 113-A in a very bad way. So they need it."

"In connection with the key unit?" Trigger asked.

"Probably."

"That makes everything look very much better, doesn't it?"

"Quite a little," he said. "The unit may not work, or may not work satisfactorily, unless 113-A is in the area. Mantelish talks of something he calls proximity influence. Whatever that is, 113-A has demonstrated it has it."

"So," Trigger said, "they might have two thirds of what everybody wants, and you might have one third. Right here on the table. How many of the later raiders did you catch?"

"All of them," said the Commissioner. "Around forty. We got them dead, we got them alive. It didn't make much difference. They were hired hands. Very expensive hired hands, but still just that. Most of them didn't know a thing we could use. The ones that did know something were mind-blocked again."

"I thought," Trigger said reflectively, "you could unblock someone like that."

"You can, sometimes. If you're very good at it and if you have time enough. We couldn't afford to wait a year. They died before they could tell us anything."

There was a pause. Then Trigger asked, "How did you get involved in this, personally?"

"More or less by accident," the Commissioner said. "It was in connection with our second lead."

"That's me, huh?" she said unhappily.

"Yes."

"Why would anyone want to grab me? I don't know anything."

He shook his head. "We haven't found out yet. We're hoping we will, in a very few days."

"Is that one of the things you can't tell me about?"

"I can tell you most of what I know at the moment," said the Commissioner. "Remember the night we stopped off at Evalee on the way in from Manon?"

"Yes," she said. "That big hotel!"

8

"ABOUT AN HOUR AFTER YOU'D decided to hit the bunk," Holati said, "I portaled back to your rooms to pick up some Precol reports we'd been setting up."

Trigger nodded. "I remember the reports."

"A couple of characters were working on your doors when I got there. They went for their guns, unfortunately. But I called the nearest Scout Intelligence office and had them dead-brained."

"Why that?" she asked.

"It could have been an accident—a couple of ordinary thugs. But their equipment looked a little too good for ordinary thugs. I didn't know just what to be suspicious of, but I got suspicious anyway."

"That's you, all right," Trigger acknowledged. "What were they?"

"They had an Evalee record which told us more

than the brains did. They were high-priced boys. Their brains told us they'd allowed themselves to be mind-blocked on this particular job. High-priced boys won't do that unless they can set their standard price very much higher. It didn't look at all any more as if they'd come to your door by accident."

"No," she admitted.

"The Feds got in on it then. There'd been that business in Mantelish's lab. There were similarities in the pattern. You knew Mantelish. You'd been on Harvest Moon with him. They thought there could be a connection."

"But what connection?" she protested. "I know I don't know anything that could do anybody any good!"

He shrugged. "I can't figure it either, Trigger girl. But the upshot of it was that I was put in charge of this phase of the general investigation. If there is a connection, it'll come out eventually. In any case, we want to know who's been trying to have you picked up and why."

She studied his face with troubled eyes.

"That's quite definite, is it?" she asked. "There couldn't possibly still be a mistake?"

"No. It's definite."

"So that's what the grabber business in the Colonial School yesterday was about . . ."

He nodded. "It was their first try since the Evalee matter."

"Why do you think they waited so long?"

"Because they suspected you were being guarded. It's difficult to keep an adequate number of men around without arousing doubts in interested observers."

Trigger glanced at the plasmoid. "That sounds," she remarked, "as if you'd let other interested observers feel you'd left them a good opening to get at Repulsive."

He didn't quite smile. "I might have done that. Don't tell the Council."

Trigger pursed her lips. "I won't. So the grabbers who were after me figured I was booby-trapped. But then they came in anyway. That doesn't seem very bright. Or did you do something again to make them think the road was clear?"

"No," he said. "They were trying to clear the road for themselves. We thought they would finally. The deal was set up as a one-two."

"As a what?"

"One-two. You slug into what could be a trap like that with one gang. If it was a trap, they were sacrifices. You hope the opposition will now relax its precautions. Sometimes it does—and a day or so later you're back for the real raid. That works occasionally. Anyway it was the plan in this case."

"How do you know?"

"They'd started closing in for the grab in Ceyce when Quillan's group located you. So Quillan grabbed you first."

She flushed. "I wasn't as smart as I thought, was I?"

The Commissioner grunted. "Smart enough to give us a king-sized headache! But *they* didn't have any trouble finding you. We discovered to-night that some kind of tracer material had been worked into all your clothes. Even the flimsies. Somebody may have been planted in the school laundry, but that's not important now." He looked at her for a moment. "What made you decide to take off so suddenly?" he asked.

Trigger shrugged. "I was getting pretty angry with you," she admitted. "More or less with everybody. Then I applied for a transfer, and the application bounced—from Evalee! I figured I'd had enough and that I'd just quietly clear out. So I did—or thought I did."

"Can't blame you," said Holati.

Trigger said, "I still think it would have been smarter to keep me informed right from the start of what was going on."

He shook his head. "I wouldn't be telling you a thing even now," he said, "if it hadn't been defi-nitely established that you're already involved in the matter. This could develop into a pretty messy operation. I wouldn't have wanted you in on it, if it could have been avoided. And if you weren't going to be in on it, I couldn't go spilling Federa-tion secrets to you."

"I'm in on it, definitely, eh?"

He nodded. "For the duration."

"But you're still not telling me everything?"

"There're a few things I can't tell you," he said. "I'm following orders in that."

Trigger smiled faintly "That's a switch! I didn't know you knew how."

"I've followed plenty of orders in my time," the

Commissioner said, "when I thought they made sense. And I think these do."

Trigger was silent a moment. "You said a while ago that most of the heat was to go off me tonight. Can you talk about that?"

"Yes, that's all right." He considered. "I'll have to tell you something else again first—why we're going to Manon."

She settled back in her chair. "Go ahead."

"Somebody got the idea that one of the things Gess Fayle might have done is to arrange things so he wouldn't have to come back to the Hub for a while. If he could set up shop on some outworld far enough away, and tinker around with that plasmoid unit for a year or so until he knew all about it, he might do better for himself than by simply selling it to somebody."

"But that would be pretty risky, wouldn't it?" said Trigger. "With just the equipment he could pack on a League transport."

"Not very much risk," said the Commissioner, "if he had an agreement to have an Independent Fleet meet him."

"Oh." She nodded.

"And by what is, at all events, an interesting coincidence," the Commissioner went on, "we've had word that an outfit called Vishni's Fleet hasn't been heard from for some months. Their I-Fleet area is a long way out beyond Manon, but Fayle could have made it there, at League ship speeds, in about twenty days. Less, if Vishni sent a few pilots to meet him and guide him out of sub-space. If he's bought Vishni's, he's had his pick of a few hundred uncharted habitable planets and a few thousand very expert outworlders to see nothing happens to him planetside. And Vishni's boys are exactly the kind of crumbs you could buy for a deal like that.

"Now, what's been done is to hire a few of the other I-Fleets around there and set them and as many Space Scout squadrons as could be kicked loose from duty elsewhere to surveying the Vishni territory. Our outfit is in charge of that operation. And Manon, of course, is a lot better point from which to conduct it than the Hub. If something is discovered that looks interesting enough to investigate in detail, we'll only be a week's run away.

"So we've been ready to move for the past two weeks now, which was when the first reports started coming in from the Vishni area—negative reports so far, by the way. I've kept stalling from day to day, because there were also indications that your grabber friends might be getting set to swing at you finally. It seemed tidier to get that matter cleared up first. Now they've swung, and we'll go."

He rubbed his chin. "The nice thing about it all," he remarked, "is that we're going there with the two items the opposition has revealed it wants. We're letting them know those items will be available in the Manon System henceforward. They might get discouraged and just drop the whole project. If they do, that's fine. We'll go ahead with cleaning up the Vishni phase of the operation.

"But," he continued, "the indications are they can't drop their project any more than we can drop looking for that key unit. So we'll expect them to show up in Manon. When they do, they'll be working in unfamiliar territory and in a system where they have only something like fifty thousand people to hide out in, instead of a planetary civilization. I think they'll find things getting very hot for them very fast in Manon."

"Very good," said Trigger. "That I like! But what makes you think the opposition is just one group? There might be a bunch of them by now. Maybe even fighting among themselves."

"I'd bet on at least two groups myself," he said. "And if they're fighting, they've got our blessing. They're still all opposition as far as we're concerned."

She nodded. "How are you letting them know about the move?"

'The mountains around here are lousy with observers. Very cute tricks some of them use—one boy has been sitting in a hollow tree for weeks. We let them see what we want to. This evening they saw you coming in. Later tonight they'll see you climbing into the ship with the rest of the party and taking off. They've already picked up messages to tell them just where the ship's going." He paused. "But you've got a job to finish up here first, Trigger. That'll take about four days. So it won't really be you they see climbing into the ship."

"What!" She straightened up.

"We've got a facsimile for you," he explained.

"Girl agent. She goes along to draw the heat to Manon."

Trigger felt herself tightening up slowly all over.

"What's this job you're talking about?" she asked evenly.

"Can't tell you in too much detail. But around four days from now somebody is coming in to Maccadon to interview you."

"Interview me? What about?"

He hesitated a moment. "There's a theory," he said, "that you might have information you don't know you have. And that the people who sent grabbers after you want that information. If it's true, the interview will bring it out."

Her mouth went dry suddenly. She turned her head to Quillan. "Major," she said, "I think I'd like that cigarette now."

He came over and lit one for her. Trigger thanked him and puffed. And she'd almost spilled everything, she was thinking. The paid-up reservation. Every last thing.

"I'd like to get it straight," she said. "What you're talking about sounds like it's a mind-search job, Holati."

"It's in that class," he said. "But it won't be an ordinary mind-search. The people who are coming here are top experts at that kind of work."

She nodded. "I don't know much about it . . . Do they think somebody's got to me with a hypno-spray or something? That I've been conditioned? Something like that?"

"I don't know, Trigger," he said. "It may be

something in that line. But whatever it is, they'll be able to handle it."

Trigger moistened her lips, "I was thinking, you know," she said. "Supposing I'm mind-blocked."

He shook his head. "I can tell you that, anyway," he said. "We already know you're not."

Trigger was silent a moment. Then she said, "After that interview's over, I'm to ship out to Manon—is that it?"

"That's right."

"But it would depend on the outcome of that interview too, wouldn't it?" Trigger pointed out. "I mean you can't really be sure what those people might decide, can you?"

"Yes, I can," he said. "This thing's been all scheduled out, Trigger. And the next step of the schedule for you is Manon. Nothing else."

She didn't believe him in the least. He couldn't know. She nodded.

"Guess I might as well play along." She looked at him. "I don't think I really had much choice, did I?"

"Afraid not," he admitted. "It's one of those things that just have to be done. But you won't find it all bad. Your companion, by the way, for the next three days will be Mihul."

"Mihul!" Trigger exclaimed.

"Right there," said Mihul's voice. Trigger swung around in her chair. Mihul stood in a door which had appeared in the full wall of the room. She gave Trigger a smile. Trigger looked back at the Commissioner.

"I don't get it," she said.

"Oh, Mihul's in Scout Intelligence," he said, "wouldn't be here if she weren't."

"Been an agent for eighteen years," Mihul said, coming forward. "Hi, Trigger, surprised?"

"Yes," Trigger admitted. "Very."

"They brought me into this job," Mihul said, "because they figured you and I would get along together just fine."

9

It was really infernally bad luck! Mihul was going to be the least easy of wardens to get away from . . . particularly in time to catch a liner tomorrow night. Mihul knew her much too well.

"Like to come along and meet your facsimile now?" Mihul inquired. She grinned. "Most people find the first time quite an experience."

Trigger stood up resignedly. "All right," she said. They were being polite about it, but it was clear that it was still a cop and prisoner situation. And old friend Mihul! She rekembered something then. "I believe Major Quillan has my gun."

He looked at her thoughtfully, not smiling. "No," he said. "Gave it to Mihul."

"That's right," said Mihul. "Let's go, kid."

They went out through the door that had appeared in the wall. It closed again behind them.

The facsimile stood up from behind a table at

which she had been sitting as Trigger and Mihul came into the room. She gave Trigger a brief, impersonal glance, then looked at Mihul.

Mihul performed no introductions.

"Dress, robe and scarf," she said to the facsimile. "The shoes are close enough." She turned to Trigger. "She'll be wearing your street clothes when she leaves" she said. "Could we have the dress now?"

Trigger pulled the dress over her head, tossed it to Mihul and stood in her underwear, looking at her double slip out of her street clothes. They did seem to be a very close match in size and proportions. Watching the shifting play of slim muscles in the long legs and smooth back, Trigger decided the similarity was largely a natural one. The silver-blonde hair was the same, of course. The gray eyes seemed almost identical—and the rest of the face was a little too identical! They must have used a life-mask there.

It was a bit uncanny. Like seeing one's mirror image start moving about independently. If the girl had talked, it might have reduced the effect. But she remained silent.

She put on the dress Trigger had been wearing and smoothed it down. Mihul surveyed the result. She nodded. "Perfect." She took Trigger's robe and scarf from the back of a chair where someone had draped them and handed them over.

"You won't wear the scarf," she said. "Just shove it into a pocket of the coat."

The girl slung the cloak over her shoulder and stood holding the scarf. Mihul looked her over once more. "You'll do," she said. She smiled briefly. "All right."

The facsimile glanced at Trigger again, turned and moved attractively out of the room. Trigger frowned.

"Something wrong?" Mihul asked. She had gone over to a wall basin and was washing out a tumbler.

"Why does she walk like that?"

"The little swing in the rear? She's studied it." Mihul half filled the tumbler with water, fished a transparent splinter of something out of a pocket and cracked the splinter over the edge of the glass. "Among your friends it's referred to as the Argee Lilt. She's got you down pat, kid."

Trigger didn't comment. "Am I supposed to put on her clothes?"

"No. We've got another costume for you." Mihul came over, holding out the glass. "This is for you."

Trigger looked at the glass suspiciously. "What's in it?"

The blue eyes regarded her mildly. "You could call it a sedative."

"Don't need any. Thanks."

"Better take it anyway." Mihul patted her hip with her other hand. "Little hypo gun here. That's the alternative."

"What!"

"That's right. Same type of charge as in your fancy Denton. Stuff in the glass is easier to take and won't leave you groggy."

"What's the idea?"

"I've known you quite a while," said Mihul. "And I was watching you the last twenty minutes in that room through a screen. You'll take off again if you get the least chance. I don't blame you a bit. You're being pushed around. But now it's my job to see you don't take off; and until we get to where you're going, I want to be sure you'll stay quiet."

She still held out the glass, in a long, tanned, capable hand. She stood three inches taller than Trigger, weighted thirty-five pounds more. Not an ounce of that additional thirty-five pounds was fat. If she'd needed assistance, the hunting lodge was full of potential helpers. She didn't.

"I never claimed I liked this arrangement," Trigger said carefully. "I did say I'd go along with it. I will. Isn't that enough?"

"Sure," Mihul said promptly. "Give word of parole?"

There was a long pause.

"No!" Trigger said.

"I thought not. Drink or gun?"

"Drink," Trigger said coldly. She took the glass. "How long will it put me out?"

"Eight to nine hours." Mihul stood by watchfully while Trigger emptied the tumbler. After a moment the tumbler fell to the floor. She reached out and caught Trigger as she started down.

"All right," she said across her shoulder to the open doorway behind her. "Let's move!"

Trigger awoke and instantly went taut with tension. She lay quiet a few seconds, not even opening her eyes. There was cool sunlight on her eyelids, but she was indoors. There was a subdued murmur of sound somewhere; after a moment she knew it came from a news viewer turned low, in some adjoining room. But there didn't seem to be anybody immediately around her. Warily she opened her eyes.

She was on a couch in an airy, spacious room furnished in the palest of greens and ivory. One entire side of the room was either a window or a solido screen. In it was a distant mountain range with many snowy peaks, an almost cloudless blue sky. Sun at midmorning or midafternoon.

Sun and all had the look of Maccadon—they probably still were on the planet. That was where the interview was to take place. But she also could have been sent on a three-day space cruise, which would be a rather good way to make sure a prisoner stayed exactly where you wanted her. This could be a spaceliner suite with a packaged view of any one of some hundreds of worlds, and with packaged sunlight thrown in.

There was one door to the room. It stood open, and the news viewer talk came from there.

Trigger sat up quietly and looked down at the clothes she wore. All white. A short-sleeved half-blouse of some soft, rather heavy, very comfortable unfamiliar stuff. Bare midriff. White kid trousers which flared at the thighs and were drawn in to a close fit just above the knees and down the calves, vanishing into kid boots with thick, flexible soles.

Sporting outfit . . . That meant Maccadon!

She pulled a handful of hair foward and looked at it. They'd recolored it—this time to a warm mahogany brown. She swung her legs off the couch and stood up quietly. A dozen soft steps across the springy thick-napped turf of ivory carpet took her to the window.

The news viewer clicked and went silent.

"Not bad," Trigger said. She saw a long range of woodlands and open heath, rising gradually into the flanks of the mountains. On the far right was the still, silver glitter of two lakes. "Where are we?"

"Byla Uplands Game Preserve. That's the game bird area before you." Mihul appeared in the doorframe, in an outfit almost a duplicate of Trigger's, in pearl-gray tones. "Feel all right?"

"Feeling fine," Trigger said. Byla Uplands— the southern tip of the continent. She could make it back to Ceyce in two hours or less! She turned and grinned at Mihul. "I also feel hungry. How long was I out?"

Mihul glanced at her wrist watch. "Eight hours, ten minutes. You woke up on schedule. I had breakfast sent up thirty minutes ago. I've already eaten mine—took one sniff and plunged in. It's good!" Mihul's hair, Trigger saw, had been cropped short and a streak of gray added over the right side; and they'd changed the color of her eyes to hazel. She wondered what had been done to her along that line. "Want to come in?" Mihul said. "We can talk while you eat."

Trigger nodded. "After I've freshened up."

The bathroom mirror showed they'd left her eyes alone. But there was a very puzzling impression that she was staring at an image considerably plumper, shorter, younger than it should be—a teen-ager around seventeen or eighteen. Her eyes narrowed. If they'd done flesh-sculpting on her, it could cause complications.

She stripped hurriedly and checked. They hadn't tampered with her body. So it had to be the clothes; though it was difficult to see how even the most cunning cut could provide such a very convincing illusion of being more rounded out, heavier around the thighs, larger breasts— just missing being dumpy, in fact. She dressed again, looked again, and came out of the bathroom, still puzzled.

"Choice of three game birds for breakfast." Mihul announced. "Never heard of any of them. All good. Plus regular stuff." She patted her flat midriff. "Ate too much!" she admitted. "Now dig in and I'll brief you."

Trigger dug in. "I had a look at myself in the mirror," she remarked. "What's this now-you-see-it-now-you-don't business of fifteen or so pounds of baby fat?"

Mihul laughed. "You don't really have it."

"I know that too. How do they do it?"

"Subcolor job in the clothes. They're not really white. Anyone looking at you gets his vision distorted a little without realizing it. Takes a wider view of certain areas, for example. You can play it around in a lot of ways."

"I never heard of that one," Trigger said. "You'd think it would be sensational in fashions."

"It would be. Right now it's top secret for as long as Intelligence can keep it that way."

Trigger chewed a savory morsel of something. "Then why did you tell me?"

"You're one of the gang, however reluctant. And you're good at keeping the mouth shut. Your name, by the way, is now Comteen Lod, just turned eighteen. I am your dear mama. You call me Drura. We're from Slyth-Talgon on Evalee, here for a few days shooting."

Trigger nodded. "Do we do any shooting?"

Mihul pointed a finger at a side table. The Denton lay there, looking like a toy beside a standard slender-barrelled sporting pistol. "Bet your life, Comteen!" she said. "I've always been too stingy to try out a first-class preserve on my own money. And this one is *first* class." She paused. "Comteen and Drura Lod really exist. We're a very fair copy of what they look like, and they'll be kept out of sight till we're done here. Now—"

She leaned back comfortably, tilting the chair and clasping her hands around one knee. "Aside from the sport, we're here because you're a convalescent. You're recovering from a rather severe attack of Dykart Fever. Heard of it?"

Trigger reflected. "Something you pick up in some sections of the Evalee tropics, isn't it?"

Mihul nodded. "That's what you did, child! Skipped your shots on the last trip we took—and six months later you're still paying for it. You were in one of those typical Dykart fever comas when we brought you in last night."

"Very clever!" Trigger commented acidly.

"Very." Mihul pursed her lips. "The Dykart bug causes temporary derangements, you know—spells during which convalescents talk wildly, imagine things."

Trigger popped another fragment of meat between her teeth and chewed thoughtfully, looking over at Mihul. "Very good duck or whatever!" she said. "Like imagining they've been more or less kidnapped, you mean?"

"Things like that," Mihul agreed.

Trigger shook her head. "I wouldn't anyway. You types are bound to have all the legal angles covered."

"Sure," said Mihul. "Just thought I'd mention it. Have you used the Denton much on game?"

"Not too often." Trigger had been wondering whether they'd left the stunner compartment loaded. "But it's a very fair gun for it."

"I know. The other one's a Yool. Good game gun, too. You'll use that."

Trigger swallowed. She met the calm eyes watching her. "I've never handled a Yool. Why the switch?"

"They're easy to handle. The reason for the switch is that you can't just stun someone with a Yool. It's better if we both stay armed, though it isn't really necessary—so much money comes to play around here they can afford to keep the Uplands very thoroughly policed, and they do. But an ace in the hole never hurts." She considered.

"Changed your mind about that parole business yet?"

"I hadn't really thought about it," Trigger said.

"I'd let you carry your own gun then."

Trigger looked reflective, then shook her head. "I'd rather not."

"Suit yourself," Mihul said agreeably. "In that case though, there should be something else understood."

"What's that?"

"We'll have up to three-four days to spend here together before Whatzzit shows up."

"Whatzzit?"

"For future reference," Mihul said, "Whatzzit will be that which—or he or she who—wishes to have that interview with you and has arranged for it. That's in case you want to talk about it. I might as well tell you that I'll do very little taking about Whatzzit."

"I thought," Trigger suggested, "I was one of the gang."

"I've got special instructions on the matter," Mihul said. "Anyway, Whatzzit shows up. You have your interview. After that we do whatever Whatzzit says we're to do. As you know."

Trigger nodded.

"Meanwhile," said Mihul, "we're here. Very pleasant place to spend three-four days in my opinion, and I think, in yours."

"Very pleasant," Trigger agreed. "I've been suspecting it was you who suggested it would be a good place to wait in."

"No," Mihul said. "Though I might have, if

anyone had asked me. But Whatzzit's handling all
the arrangements, it seems. Now we could have
fun here—which, I suspect, would be the purpose
as far as you're concerned."

"Fun?" Trigger said.

"To put you into a good frame of mind for that
interview, might be the idea," Mihul said. "I don't
know. Three days here should relax almost anyone. Get in a little shooting. Loaf around the
pools. Go for rides. Things like that. The only
trouble is I'm afraid you're nourishing dark notions which are likely to take all the enjoyment
out of it. Not to mention the possibility of really
relaxing."

"Like what?" Trigger asked.

"Oh," Mihul said, "there're all sorts of possibilities, of course." She nodded her head at the
guns. "Like yanking the Denton out of my holster
and feeding me a dose of the stunner. Or picking
up that coffee pot there and tapping me on the
skull with it. It's about the right weight."

Trigger said thoughtfully, "I don't think either
of those would work."

"They might," Mihul said. "They just might!
You're fast. You've been taught to improvise. And
there's something eating you. You're edgy as a
cat."

"So?" Trigger said.

"So," Mihul said, "there are a number of alternatives. I'll lay them out for you. You take your
pick. For one, I could just keep you doped. Three
days in dope won't hurt you, and you'll certainly
be no problem then. Another way—I'll let you

stay awake, but we stay in our rooms. I can lock you in at night, and that window is escape-proof. I checked. It would be sort of boring, but we can have tapes and stuff brought up. I'd have the guns put away and I'd watch you like a hawk every minute of the day."

She looked at Trigger inquiringly. "Like either of those?"

"Not much," Trigger said.

"They're safe," Mihul said. "Quite safe. Maybe I should . . . Well, the heat's off, and it's just a matter now of holding you for Whatzzit. There're a couple of other choices. One of them has an angle you won't like much either. On the other hand, it would give you a sporting chance to take off if you're really wild about it. And it's entirely in line with my instructions. I warned them you're tricky."

Trigger stopped eating. "Let's hear that one."

Mihul tilted the chair back a little farther and studied her a moment. "Pretty much like I said before. Everything friendly and casual. Gun a bit, swim a bit. Go for a ride or soar. Lie around in the sun. But because of those notions of yours, there'd be one thing added. An un-incentive."

"An un-incentive?" Trigger repeated.

"Exactly," said Mihul. "*That* isn't at all in line with my instructions. But you're a pretty dignifed little character, and I think it should work."

"Just what does this un-incentive consist of?" Trigger inquired warily.

"If you make a break and get away," Mihul said, "that's one thing. Something's eating you, and I'm not sure I like the way this matter's been handled. In fact, I don't like it. So I'll try to stop you from leaving, but if it turns out I couldn't, I won't hold any grudges. Even if I wake up with lumps."

She paused. "On the other hand," she said, "there we are—together for three-four days. I don't want to spend them fighting off attempts to clobber me every thirty seconds. So any time you try and miss, Comteen, mama is going to pin you down fast, and hot up your seat with whatever is handiest."

Trigger stared at her.

She cleared her throat.

"While I'm carrying a gun?" she said shakily. "Don't be ridiculous, Mihul!"

"You're not going to gun me for keeps to get out of a licking," Mihul said. "And that's all the Yool can do. How else will you stop me?"

Trigger's fingernails drummed the table top briefly. She wet her lips. "I don't know," she admitted.

"Of course," said Mihul, "all this unpleasantness can be avoided very easily. There's always the fourth method."

"What's that?"

"Just give parole."

"No parole," Trigger said thinly.

"All right. Which of the other ways will it be?"

Trigger didn't hesitate. "The sporting chance," she said. "The others aren't choices."

"Fair enough," said Mihul. She stood up and went over to the wall. She selected a holster belt from the pair hanging there and fastened it around her. "I rather thought you'd pick it," she said. She gave Trigger a brief grin. "Just make sure it's a good opening!"

"I will," Trigger said.

Mihul moved to the side table, took up the Denton, looked at it, and slid it into her holster. She turned to gaze out the window. "Nice country!" she said. "If you're done with breakfast, how about going out right now for a first try at the birds?"

Trigger hefted the coffee pot gently. It was about the right weight at that. But the range was a little more than she liked, considering the unincentive.

Besides, it might crack the monster's skull.

She set the pot gently down again.

"Great idea!" she said. "And I'm all finished eating."

10

HALF AN HOUR LATER THERE still hadn't been any decent openings. Trigger was maintaining a somewhat brooding silence at the moment. Mihul, beside her, in the driver's seat of the tiny sports hopper, chatted pleasantly about this and that. But she didn't appear to expect any answers.

There weren't many half-hours left to be wasted.

Trigger stared thoughtfully out through the telescopic ground-view plate before her, while the hopper soared at a thousand feet toward the two-mile square of preserve area which had been assigned to them to hunt over that morning. Dimly reflected in the view plate, she could see the head of the gun-pup who went with that particular area lifted above the seat-back behind her. He was gazing straight ahead between the two humans, absorbed in canine reflections.

There was plenty of bird life down there. Some were ogirinal Terran forms, maintained unchanged in the U-League's genetic banks. Probably many more were inspired modifications produced on Grand Commerce game ranches. At any other time, Trigger would have found herself enjoying the outing almost as much as Mihul.

Not now. Other things kept running through her head. Money, for example. They hadn't returned her own cash to her and apparently didn't intend to—at least not until after the interview. But Mihul was carrying at least part of their spending money in a hip pocket wallet. The rest of it might be in a concealed room safe or deposited with the resort hotel's cashier.

She glanced over at Mihul again. Good friend Mihul never before had looked quite so large, lithe, alert and generally fit for a rough-and-tumble. That un-incentive idea was fiendishly ingenious! It was difficult to plan things through clearly and calmly while one's self-esteem kept quailing at vivid visualizations of the results of making a mistake.

The hopper settled down near the center of their territory, guided the last half mile by Mihul who had fancied the looks of some shrub-cluttered ravines ahead. Trigger opened the door on her side. The gun-pup leaped lightly across the seat and came out behind her. He turned to look over his huntresses and gave them a wag, a polite but perfunctory one. Then he stood waiting for orders.

Mihul considered him. "Guess he's in charge

here," she said. She waved a hand at the pup. "Go find 'em, old boy! We'll string along."

He loped off swiftly, a lean brown houndlike creature, a Grand Commerce development of some aristocratic Terran breed and probably a considerable improvement on the best of his progenitors. He curved around a thick clump of shrubs like a low-flying hawk. Two plump feather-shapes, emerald-green and crimson, whirred up out of the near side of the shrubbery, saw the humans before them and rose steeply, picking up speed.

A great many separate, clearly detailed things seemed to be going on within the next four or five seconds. Mihul swore, scooping the Denton out of its holster. Trigger already had the Yool out, but the gun was unfamiliar; she hesitated. Fascinated, she glanced from the speeding, soaring feather-balls to Mihul, watched the tall woman straighten for an overhead shot, left hand grasping right wrist to steady the lightweight Denton—and in that particular instant Trigger knew exactly what was going to happen next.

The Denton flicked forth one bolt. Mihul stretched a little more for the next shot. Trigger wheeled matter-of-factly, dropping the Yool, left elbow close in to her side. Her left fist rammed solidly into Mihul's bare brown midriff, just under the arch of the rib cage.

That punch, in those precise circumstances, would have paralyzed the average person. It didn't quite paralyze Mihul. She dropped forward, doubled up and struggling for breath, but already twisting around toward Trigger. Trigger stepped across her, picked up the Denton, shifted its setting, thumbed it to twelve-hour stunner max, and let Mihul have it between the shoulder blades.

Mihul jerked forward and went limp.

Trigger stood there, shaking violently, looking down at Mihul and fighting the irrational conviction that she had just committed cold-blooded murder.

The gun-pup trotted up with the one downed bird. He placed it reverently by Mihul's outflung hand. Then he sat back on his haunches and regarded Trigger with something of the detached compassion of a good undertaker.

Apparently this wasn't his first experience with a hunting casualty.

The story Trigger babbled into the hopper's communicator a minute later was that Drura Lod had succumbed to an attack of Dykart fever coma—and that an ambulance and a fast flit to a hospital in the nearest city were indicated.

The preserve hotel was startled but reassuring. That the mother should be afflicted with the same ailment as the daughter was news to them but plausible enough. Within eight minutes, a police ambulance was flying Mihul and Trigger at emergency speeds towards a small Uplands City behind the mountains.

Trigger never found out the city's name. Three minutes after she'd followed Mihul's floating stretcher into the hospital, she quietly left the building again by a street entrance. Mihul's wallet

had contained two hundred and thirteen crowns.
It was enough, barely.

She got a complete change of clothes in the first
Automatic Service store she came to and left the
store in them, carrying the sporting outfit in a bag.
The aircab she hired to take her to Ceyce had to be
paid for in advance, which left her eighty-two
crowns. As they went flying over a lake a while
later, the bag with the sporting clothes and acces-
sories was dumped out of the cab's rear window.
It was just possible that the Space Scouts had been
able to put that tracer material idea to immediate
use.

In Ceyce a short two hours after she'd felled
Mihul, Trigger called the interstellar spaceport
and learned that the Dawn City was open to passengers and their guests.

Birna Drellgannoth picked up her tickets and
went on board, mingling unostentatiously with a
group in a mood of festive leave-taking. She went
fading even more unostentatiously down a hallway when the group stopped cheerfully to pose
for a solidopic girl from one of the news agencies.
She located her cabin after a lengthy search, set
the door to don't-disturb, glanced around the
cabin and decided to inspect it in more detail
later.

She pulled off her slippers, climbed on the out-
sized divan which passed here for a bunk, and
stretched out.

She lay there a while, blinking at the ceiling
and worrying a little about Mihul. Even theoreti-
cally a stunner-max blast couldn't cause Mihul

the slightest permanent damage. It might, however, leave her in a fairly peevish mood after the grogginess wore off, since the impact wasn't supposed to be pleasant. But Mihul had stated she would hold no grudges over a successful escape attempt; and even if they caught up with her again before she got to Manon, this attempt certainly had to be rated a technical success.

They might catch up, of course, Trigger thought. The Federation must have an enormous variety of means at its disposal when it set out seriously to locate one of its missing citizens. But the Dawn City would be some hours on its way before Mihul even began to think coherently again. She'd spread the alarm then, but it should be a while before they started to suspect Trigger had left the planet. Maccadon was her home world, after all. If she'd just wanted to hole up, that was where she would have had the best chance to do it successfully.

Evalee, the first Hub stop, was only nine hours' flight away; Garth lay less than five hours beyond Evalee. After that there was only the long subspace run to Manon . . .

They'd have to work very fast to keep her from leaving the Hub this time!

Trigger glanced over at the Denton lying by the bedside ComWeb on a little table at the head of the divan-thing. She was aware of a feeling of great contentment, of growing relaxation. She closed her eyes.

By and large, she thought—all things considered—she hadn't come off badly among the cloak and dagger experts! She was on her way to Manon.

Some hours later she slept through the Dawn City's thunderous takeoff.

When she woke up next she was in semidarkness. But she knew where she was and a familiar feeling of low-weight told her the ship was in flight. She sat up.

At her motion, the area about her brightened, and the cabin grew visible again. It was rather large, oval-shaped. There were three closed doors in the walls, and the walls themselves were light amber, of oddly insubstantial appearance. A rosy tinge was flowing up from the floor level through them, and as the color surged higher and deepened, there came an accompanying stir of far-off, barely audible music. The don't-disturb sign still reflected dimly from the interior panels of the passage door. Trigger found its control switch on the bedstand and shut it off.

At once a soft chiming sounded from the miniature ComWeb on the bedstand. Its screen filled with a pulsing glow, and there was a voice.

"This is a recording, Miss Drellgannoth," the voice told her. "If Room Service may intrude with an audio message, please be so good as to touch the blue circle at the base of your ComWeb."

Trigger touched the blue circle. "Go ahead," she invited.

"Thank you, Miss Drellgannoth," said the voice. "For the duration of the voyage your personal ComWeb will be opened to callers, for either audio or visual intrusion, only by your verbal permission or by your touch on the blue circle."

It stopped. Another voice picked up. "This is your Personal Room Stewardess, Miss Drellgannoth. Forgive the intrusion, but the ship will dive in one hour. Do you wish to have a rest cubicle prepared?"

"No, thanks," Trigger said. "I'll stay awake."

"Thank you, Miss Drellgannoth. As a formality and in accordance with Federation regulations, allow me to remind you that Federation Law does not permit the bearing of personal weapons by passengers during a dive."

Her glance went to the Denton. "All right," she said. "I won't. It's because of dive hallucinations, I suppose?"

"Thank you very much, Miss Drellgannoth. Yes, it is because of the misapprehensions which may be caused by dive hallucinations. May I be of service to you at this time? Perhaps you would like me to demonstrate the various interesting uses of your personal ComWeb Cabinet?"

Trigger's eyes shifted to the far end of the cabin. A rather large, very elegant piece of furniture stood there. Its function hadn't been immediately obvious, but she had heard of ComWeb Service Cabinets.

She thanked the stewardess but declined the offer. The lady switched off, apparently a trifle distressed at not having discovered anything Birna Drellgannoth's personal stewardess might do for Birna right now.

Trigger went curiously over to the cabinet. It opened at her touch and she sat down before it, glancing over its panels. A remarkable number of uses were indicated, which might make it confusing to the average Hub citizen. But she had been trained in communications, and the service cabinet was as simple as any gadget in its class could get.

She punched in the ship's location diagram. The Dawn City was slightly more than an hour out of Ceyce Port, but it hadn't yet cleared the subspace nets which created interlocking and impenetrable fields of energy about the Maccadon System. A ship couldn't dive in such an area without risking immediate destruction; but the nets were painstakingly maintained insurance against a day when subspace warfare might again explode through the Hub.

Trigger glanced over the diagrammed route ahead. Evalee . . . Garth. A tiny green spark in the far remoteness of space beyond them represented Manon's sun.

Eleven days or so. With the money to afford a rest cubicle, the time could be cut to a subjective three or four hours.

But it would have been foolish anyway to sleep through the one trip on a Hub luxury liner she was ever likely to take in her life.

She set the cabinet to a review of the Dawn City's passenger facilities, and was informed that everything would remain at the disposal of waking passengers throughout all dives. She glanced over bars, fashion shows, dining and gaming rooms. The Cascade Plunge, from the looks of it, would have been something for Mihul . . . "Our

Large Staff of Traveler's Companions"—just what
she needed. The Solido Auditorium ". . . and the
Inferno—our Sensations Unlimited Hall." A dul-
cet voice informed her regretfully that Federation
Law did not permit the transmission of full SU
effects to individual cabins. It did, however, permit a few sample glimpses. Trigger took her
glimpses, sniffed austerely, switched back to the
fashions.

There had been a neat little black suit on display there. While she didn't intend to start roam-
ing about the ship until it dived and the majority
of her fellow travelers were immersed in their rest
cubicles, she probably still would be somewhat
conspicuous in her Automatic Sales dress on a
boat like the Dawn City. That little black suit
hadn't looked at all expensive—

"Twelve hundred forty-two Federation credits?" she repeated evenly a minute later. "I see!"

Came to roughly eight hundred fifty Maccadon
crowns, was what she saw.

"May we model it in your suite, madam?" the
store manager inquired.

"No, thanks," Trigger told her. "Just looking
them over a bit." She switched off, frowned absently at a panel labeled "Your Selection of Per-
sonalized Illusion Arrangements," shook her
head, snapped the cabinet shut and stood up. It
looked like she had a choice between being conspicuous and staying in her cabin and playing
around with things like the creation of illusion
scenes.

And she was really a little old for that kind of
entertainment.

She opened the door to the narrow passageway outside the cabin and glanced tentatively along it. It was very quiet here. One of the reasons this was the cheapest cabin they'd had available presumably was that it lay outside the main passenger areas. To the right the corridor opened on a larger hall which ran past a few hundred yards of storerooms before it came to a stairway. At the head of the stairway, one came out eventually on one of the passenger levels. To the left the corridor ended at the door of what seemed to be the only other cabin in this section.

Trigger looked back toward the other cabin.

"Oh," she said. "Well . . . hello."

The other cabin door stood open. A rather odd-looking little person sat in a low armchair immediately inside it. She had lifted a thin, green-sleeved arm in a greeting or beckoning gesture as Trigger turned.

She repeated the gesture now. "Come here, girl!" she called amiably in a quavery old-woman voice.

Well, it couldn't do any harm. Trigger put on her polite smile and walked down the hall toward the open door. A quite tiny old woman it was, with a head either shaved or naturally bald, dressed in a kind of dark-green pajamas. Long glassy earrings of the same color pulled down the lobes of her small ears. The oddness of the face was due mainly to the fact that she wore a great deal of make-up, and that the make-up was a matching green.

She twisted her head to the left as Trigger came up, and chirped something. Another woman appeared behind the door, almost a duplicate of the first, except that this one had gone all out for pink. Tiny things. They both beamed up at her.

Trigger beamed back. She stopped just outside the door.

"Greetings," said the pink one.

"Greetings," Trigger replied, wondering what world they came from. The style wasn't exactly like anything she'd seen before.

"We," the green lady informed her with a not unkindly touch of condescension, "are with the Askab of Elfkund."

"Oh!" said Trigger in the tone of one who is impressed. Elfkund hadn't rung any bells.

"And with whom are you, girl?" the pink one inquired.

"Well," Trigger said, "I'm not actually *with* anybody."

The smiles faded abruptly. They glanced at each other, then looked back at Trigger. Rather severely, it seemed.

"Did you mean," the green one asked carefully, "that you are not a retainer?"

Trigger nodded. "I'm from Maccadon," she explained. "The name is Birna Drellgannoth."

"Maccadon," the pink one repeated. "You are a commoner then, young Birna?"

"Of course she is!" The green one looked offended. "Maccadon!" She got out of her chair with remarkable spryness and moved to the door. "It's quite drafty," she said, looking pointedly past Trigger. The door closed on Trigger's face. A second later, she heard the lock snap shut. A moment after that, the don't-disturb sign appeared.

Well, she thought, wandering back to her cabin, it didn't look as if she were going to be bothered with excessively friendly neighbors on this trip.

She had a bath and then discovered a mechanical stylist in a recess beside the bathroom mirror. She swung the gadget out into the room, set it for a dye removal operation and sat down beneath it. A redhead again a minute or so later, she switched the machine to Orado styles and left it to make up its electronic mind as to what would be the most suitable creation under the circumstances.

The stylist hovered above her for over a minute, muttering and clucking as it conducted an apparently disapproving survey of the job. Then it went swiftly and silently to work. When it shut itself off, Trigger checked the results in the mirror.

She wasn't too pleased. An upswept arrangement which brought out the bone structure of her face rather well but didn't do much else for her. Possibly the stylist had included the Automatic Sales dress in its computations.

Well, it would have to do for her first tour of the ship.

11

THE BEDSIDE COMWEB WARNED her politely that it was now ten minutes to dive point. Waking passengers who experienced subspace distress in any form could obtain immediate assistance by a call on any ComWeb. If they preferred, they could have their cabins kept under the continuous visual supervision of their personal steward or stewardess.

The Dawn City's passenger areas still looked rather well populated when Trigger arrived. But some of the passengers were showing signs of regretting their decision to stay awake. Presently she became aware of a faint queasiness herself.

It wasn't bad—mainly a sensation as if the ship were trying continuously to turn over on its axis around her and not quite making it—and she knew from previous experience that after the first hour or so she would be completely free of that.

She walked into a low, dimly lit, very swank-looking gambling room, still well patronized by the hardier section of her fellow travelers, searching for a place where she could sit down unobtrusively for a while and let the subspace reaction work itself out.

A couch beside a closed door near the unlit end of the room seemed about right for the purpose.

Trigger sat down and glanced around. There were a variety of games in progress, all unfamiliar to her. The players were mostly men, but a remarkable number of beautiful women, beautifully gowned, stood around the tables as observers. Traveler's Companions, Trigger realized suddenly—the Dawn City's employees naturally would be inured to subspace effects. From the scraps of talk she could pick up, the stakes seemed uniformly high.

A swirl of vertigo suddenly built up in her again. This one was stronger than most; for a moment she couldn't be sure whether she was going to be sick or not. She stood up, stepped over to the door a few feet away, pulled it open and went through, drawing it shut behind her.

There had been a shielding black-light screen in the doorway. On the other side was bottled sunshine.

She found herself on a long balcony which overlooked a formal garden enclosure thirty feet below. There was no one else in sight. She leaned back against the wall beside the door, closed her eyes and breathed slowly and deeply for some seconds. The sickish sensation began to fade.

When she opened her eyes again, she saw the little yellow man.

He stood motionless at the far end of the garden, next to some flowering shrubbery out of which he might have just stepped. He seemed to be peering along the sand path which curved in toward the balcony and vanished beneath it, below the point where Trigger stood.

It was sheer fright which immobilized her at first. Because there was not anything really human about that small, squat, manshaped figure. A dwarfish yellow demon he seemed, evil and menacing. The garden, she realized suddenly, might be an illusion scene. Or else—

The thing moved in that instant. It became a blur of motion along the curving path and disappeared under the balcony. After a second or so she heard the sound of a door closing some distance away. The garden lay still again.

Trigger stayed where she was, her knees shaking a little. The fright appeared to have driven every trace of nausea out of her, and gradually her heartbeat began to return to normal. She took three cautious steps forward to the balcony railing, where the tip of a swaying green tree branch was in reach.

She put her hand out hesitantly, felt the smooth vegetable texture of a leaf, grasped it, pulled it away. She moved back to the door and examined the leaf. It was a quite real leaf. Thin sap formed a bead of amber moisture at the break in the stalk as she looked at it.

No illusion structure could be elaborated to that extent.

So she'd just had her first dive hallucination—
and it had been a dilly!

Trigger dropped the leaf, pushed shakily at the
balcony door, and stepped back through the
black-light screen into the reassuring murmur of
human voices in the gambling room.

An hour later, the ship's loudspeaker system
went on. It announced that the Dawn City would
surface in fifteen minutes because of gravitic dis-
turbances, and proceed the rest of the way to
Evalee in normal space, arriving approximately
five hours behind schedule. Rest cubicle passengers would not be disturbed, unless this was specifically requested by a qualified associate.

Trigger turned her attention back to her viewer,
feeling rather relieved. She hadn't experienced
any further hallucinations, or other indications of
subspace distress; but the one she'd had would do
her for a while. The little viewer library she was in
was otherwise deserted, and she'd been going
about her studies there just the least bit nervously.

Subject of the studies were the Hub's principal
games of chance. She'd identified a few of those
she'd been watching—and one of them did look as
if someone who went at it with an intelligent
understanding of the odds—

A part of Trigger kept tut-tutting and shaking
its head at such reckless notions. But another part
pointed out that they couldn't be much worse off
financially than they were right now. So what if
they arrived in Manon dead-broke instead of practically? Besides, there was the problem of remaining inconspicuous till they got there. On the
Dawn City no one whose wardrobe was limited to

one Automatic Sales dress was going to remain
inconspicuous very long.

Trigger-in-toto went on calculating the odds for
various possible play combinations. She developed her first betting system, presently discovered several holes in it, and began to develop
another.

The loudspeaker system went on again. She
was too absorbed to pay much attention to it at
first. Then she suddenly straightened up and listened, frowning.

The man speaking now was the liner's First
Security Officer. He was being very polite and
regretful. Under Section such and such, Number
so and so, of the Federation's Legal Code, a cabin
by cabin search of the passenger area of the Dawn
City had become necessary. The persons of passengers would not be searched. Passengers might,
if they wished, be present while their cabins were
inspected; but this was not required. Baggage
need not be opened, providing its spyproofing
was not activated. Any information revealed by
the search which did not pertain to a violation of
the Code Section and Number in question would
not be recorded and could not be introduced as
future legal evidence under any circumstances.
Complaints regarding the search could be addressed to any Planetary Moderator's office.

This wasn't good at all! Trigger stood up. The
absence of luggage in her cabin mightn't arouse
more than passing interest in the searchers. Her
gun was a different matter. Discreet inquiries regarding a female passenger who carried a dou-

ble-barreled sporting Denton might be one of
the check methods used by the Scout Intelligence
boys if they started thinking of liners which recently had left Maccadon in connection with
Trigger's disappearance. There weren't likely to
be more than two or three guns of that type on
board, and it was almost certain that she would be
the only woman who owned one.

She'd better go get the Denton immediately
. . . and then vanish again into the public sections of the ship! Some Security officer with a
good memory and a habit of noticing faces might
identify her otherwise from the news viewer pictures taken on Manon.

And he just might start wondering then why
she was traveling as Birna Drellgannoth—and
start to check.

She paused long enough to get the Legal Code
article referred to into the viewer.

Somebody on board appeared to have got himself murdered.

She reached the cabin too late. A couple of
young Security men already were going over it.
Trigger said hello pleasantly. It was too bad, but it
wasn't their fault. They just had a job to do.

They smiled back at her, apologized for the
intrusion and went on with their business. She sat
down and watched them. The Denton was there in
plain sight. Dropping it into her purse now would
be more likely to fix it in their memory than leaving it where it was.

The gadgets they were using were in conceal-
ing casings, and she couldn't guess what they

were looking for by the way they used them. It didn't seem that either of them was trying to haul up an identifying memory about her. They did look a little surprised when the second cabin closet was opened and found to be as empty as the first; but no comments were made about that. Two minutes after Trigger had come in, they were finished and bowed themselves out of the cabin again. They turned then toward the cabin occupied by the ancient retainers of the Askab of Elfkund.

Trigger left her door open. This she wanted to hear, if she could.

She heard. The Elfkund door also stayed open, while the racket beyond it grew shriller by the moment. Finally a ComWeb chimed. A feminine voice spoke sternly. The Quavering outcries subsided. It looked as if Security had been obliged to call on someone higher up in the Elfkund entourage to come to its aid. Trigger closed her door grinning.

On the screen of her secluded library, she presently watched a great port shuttle swing in from Evalee to meet the hovering Dawn City. It would bring another five hundred or so passengers on board and take off the few who had merely been making the short run from Maccadon to Evalee in style. Solidopic operators were quite likely to be on the shuttle, so she had decided to keep away from the entry area.

The transfer operation was carried out very expeditiously, probably to make up for some of the time lost on the surface. When the shuttle shoved

off, the loudspeaker announced that normal space
flight would be maintained till after the stopover
at Garth. Trigger wandered thoughtfully back to
her cabin. She closed the door behind her.

Then she saw the man sitting by the ComWeb
cabinet. Her breath sucked in. She crouched a
little, ready to wheel and bolt.

"Take it easy, Trigger!" Major Quillan said. He
was in civilian clothes, of rather dudish cut.

Trigger swallowed. There was, too obviously,
no place to bolt to. "How did you find me?"

He shrugged. "Longish story. You're not under
arrest."

"I'm not?"

"No," said Quillan. "When we get to Manon,
the Commissioner will have a suggestion to make
to you."

"Suggestion?" Trigger said warily.

"I believe you're to take back your old Precol job
in Manon, but as cover for your participation in
our little project. If you agree to it."

"What if I don't?"

He shrugged again. "It seems you'll be writing
your own ticket from here on out."

Trigger stared at him, wondering. "Why?"

Quillan grinned. "New instructions have been
handed down," he said. "If you're still curious,
ask Whatzzit."

"Oh," Trigger said. "Then why are you here?"

"I," said Quillan, "am to make damn sure you
get to Manon. I brought a few people with me."

"Mihul, too?" Trigger asked, a shade diffidently.

"No. She's on Maccadon."

"Is she—how's she doing?"

"Doing all right," Quillan said. "She sends her regards and says a little less heft on the next solar plexus you torpedo should be good enough."

Trigger flushed. "She isn't sore, is she?"

"Not the way you mean." he considered. "Not many people have jumped Mihul successfully. In her cockeyed way, she seemed pretty proud of her student."

Trigger felt the flush deepen. "I got her off her guard," she said.

"Obviously," said Quillan. "In any ordinary argument she could pull your legs off and tie you up with them. Still, that wasn't bad. Have you talked to anybody since you came on board?"

"Just the room stewardess. And a couple of old ladies in the next cabin."

"Yeah," he said. "Couple of old ladies. What did you talk about?"

Trigger recounted the conversation. He reflected, nodded and stood up.

"I put a couple of suitcases in that closet over there," he said. "Your personal stuff is in them, de-tracered. Another thing—somebody checked over your finances and came to the conclusion you're broke."

"Not exactly broke," said Trigger.

Quillan reached into a pocket, pulled out an envelope and laid it on the cabinet. "Here's a little extra spending money then," he said. "The balance of your Precol pay to date. I had it picked up on Evalee this morning. Seven hundred twenty-eight FC."

"Thanks," Trigger said. "I can use some of that."

They stood looking at each other.

"Any questions?" he asked.

"Sure," Trigger said. "But you wouldn't answer them."

"Try me, doll," said Quillan. "But let's shift operations to the fanciest cocktail lounge on this thing before you start. I feel like relaxing a little. For just one girl, you've given us a fairly rough time these last forty-eight hours!"

"I'm sorry," Trigger said.

"I'll bet," said Quillan.

Trigger glanced at the closet. If he'd brought everything along, there was a dress in one of those suitcases that would have been a little too daring for Maccadon. It should, therefore, be just about right for a cocktail lounge on the Dawn City; and she hadn't had a chance to wear it yet. "Give me ten minutes to change."

"Fine." Quillan started toward the door. "By the way, I'm your neighbor now."

"The cabin at the end of the hall?" she asked startled.

"That's right." He smiled at her. "I'll be back in ten minutes."

Well, that was going to be cosy! Trigger found the dress, shook it out and slipped into it, enormously puzzled but also enormously relieved. That Whatzzitt!

Freshening up her make-up, she wondered how he had induced the Elfkund ladies to leave. Perhaps he'd managed to have a better cabin offered to them. It must be convenient to have that kind of a pull.

12

"WELL, WE DIDN'T JUST leave it up to them," Quillan said. "Ship's Engineering spotted a radiation leak in their cabin. Slight but definite. They got bundled out in a squawking hurry." He added, "They did get a better cabin though."

"Might have been less trouble to get me to move," Trigger remarked.

"Might have been. I didn't know what mood you'd be in."

Trigger decided to let that ride. This cocktail lounge was a very curious place. By the looks of it, there were thirty or forty people in their immediate vicinity; but if one looked again in a couple of minutes, there might be an entirely different thirty or forty people around. Sitting in easy chairs or at tables, standing about in small groups, talking, drinking, laughing, they drifted past slowly; overhead, below, sometimes tilted at

odd angles—fading from sight and presently returning.

In actual fact she and Quillan were in a little
room by themselves, and with more than ordinary
privacy via an audio block and a reconstruct
scrambler which Quillan had switched on at their
entry. "I'll leave us out of the viewer circuit,"
he remarked, "until you've finished your questions."

"Viewer circuit?" she repeated.

Quillan waved a hand around. "That," he said.
"There are more commercial and industrial spies,
political agents, top-class confidence men and
whatnot on board this ship than you'd probably
believe. A good percentage of them are pretty fair
lip readers, and the things you want to talk about
are connected with the Federation's hottest current secret. So while it's a downright crime not to
put you on immediate display in a place like this,
we won't take the chance."

Trigger let that ride too. A group had materialized at an oblong table eight feet away
while Quillan was speaking. Everybody at the
table seemed fairly high, and two of the couples
were embarrassingly amorous; but she couldn't
quite picture any of them as somebody's spies or
agents. She listened to the muted chatter. Some
Hub dialect she didn't know.

"None of those people can see or hear us then?"
she asked.

"Not until we want them to. Viewer gives you
as much privacy as you like. Most of the crowd
here just doesn't see much point to privacy. Like
those two."

Trigger followed his glance. At a tilted angle above them, a matched pair of black-haired, black-gowned young sirens sat at a small table, sipping their drinks, looking languidly around.

"Twins," Trigger said.

"No," said Quillan. "That's Blent and Company."

"Oh?"

"Blent's a lady of leisure and somewhat excessively narcissistic tendencies," he explained. He gave the matched pair another brief study. "Perhaps one can't really blame her. One of them's her facsimile. Blent—whichever it is—is never without her face."

"Oh," Trigger said. She'd been studying the gowns. "That," she said, a trifle enviously, "is why I'm not at all eager to go on display here."

"Eh?" said Quillan.

Trigger turned to regard herself in the wall mirror on the right, which, she had noticed, remained carefully unobscured by drifting viewers and viewees. A thoughtful touch on the lounge management's part.

"Until we walked in here," she explained, "I thought this was a pretty sharp little outfit I'm wearing."

"Hmmm," Quillan said judiciously. He made a detailed appraisal of the mirror image of the slim, green, backless, half-thigh-length sheath which had looked so breath-taking and seductive in a Ceyce display window. Trigger's eyes narrowed a little. The major had appraised the dress in detail before.

"It's about as sharp a little outfit as you could

get for around a hundred and fifty credits," he remarked. "Most of the items the girls are sporting here are personality conceptions. That starts at around ten to twenty times as high. I wasn't talking about displaying the dress. Now what were those questions?"

Trigger took a small sip of her drink, considering. She hadn't made up her mind about Major Quillan, but until she could evaluate him more definitely, it might be best to go by appearances. The appearances so far indicated small sips in his company.

"How did you people find me so quickly?" she asked.

"Next time you want to sneak off a civilized planet," Quillan advised her, "pick something like a small freighter. Or hire a small-boat to get you out of the system and flag down a freighter for you. Plenty of tramp captains will make a space stop to pick up a paying passenger. Liners we can check."

"Sorry," Trigger said meekly. "I'm still new at this buiness."

"And thank God for that!" said Quillan. "If you have the time and the money, it's also a good idea, of course, to zig a few times before you zag towards where you're really heading. Actually, I suppose, the credit for picking you up so fast should go to those collating computers."

"Oh?"

"Yes." Major Quillan looked broodingly at his drink for a moment. "There they sit," he remarked suddenly, "with their stupid plastic faces hanging out! Rows of them. You feed them something you don't understand. They don't understand it either. Nobody can tell me they can. But they kick it around and giggle a bit, and out comes some ungodly suggestion."

"So they helped you find me?" she said cautiously. It was clear that the major had strong feelings about computers.

"Oh, sure," he said. "It usually turns out it was a good idea to do what those CCs say. Anything unusual that shows up in the area you're working on gets chunked into the things as a matter of course. We were on the liners. Dawn City reports back a couple of murders. 'Dawn City to the head of the list!' cry the computers. Nobody asks why. They just plow into the ticket purchase records. And right there are the little Argee thumbprints!"

He looked at Trigger. "My own bet," he said, somewhat accusingly, "was that you were one of those that had just taken off. We didn't know about that ticket reservation."

"What I don't see," Trigger said, changing the subject, "is why two murders should seem so very unusual. There must be quite a few of them, after all."

"True," said Quillan. "But not murders that look like catassin killings."

"Oh!" she said startled. "Is that what these were?"

"That's what Ship Security thinks."

Trigger frowned. "But what could be the connection—"

Quillan reached across the table and patted her

hand. "You've got it!" he said with approval. "Exactly! No connection. Some day I'm going to walk down those rows and give them each a blast where it will do the most good. It will be worth being broken for."

Trigger said, "I thought that catassin planet was being guarded."

"It is. It would be very hard to sneak one out nowadays. But somebody's breeding them in the Hub. Just a few. Keeps the price up."

Trigger grimaced uncomfortably. She'd seen recordings of those swift, clever, constitutionally murderous creatures in action. "You say it looked like catassin killings. They haven't found it?"

"No. But they think they got rid of it. Emptied the air from most of the ship after they surfaced and combed over the rest of it with life detectors. They've got a detector system set up now that would spot a catassin if it moved twenty feet in any direction."

"Life detectors go haywire out of normal space, don't they?" she said. "That's why they surfaced then."

Quillan nodded. "You're a well-informed doll. They're pretty certain it's been sucked into space or disposed of by its owner, but they'll go on looking till we dive beyond Garth."

"Who got killed?"

"A Rest Warden and a Security officer. In the rest cubicle area. It might have been sent after somebody there. Apparently it ran into the two men and killed them on the spot. The officer got off one shot and that set off the automatic alarms. So pussy cat couldn't finish the job that time."

"It's all sort of gruesome, isn't it?" Trigger said.

"Catassins are," Quillan agreed. "That's a fact."

Trigger took another sip. She set down her glass. "There's something else," she said reluctantly.

"Yes?"

"When you said you'd come on board to see I got to Manon, I was thinking none of the people who'd been after me on Maccadon could know I was on the Dawn City. They might though. Quite easily."

"Oh?" said Quillan.

"Yes. You see I made two calls to the ticket office. One from a street ComWeb and one from the bank. If they already had spotted me by that tracer material, they could have had an audio pick-up on me, I suppose."

"I think we'd better suppose it," said Quillan. "You had a tail when you came out of the bank anyway." His glance went past her. "We'll get back to that later. Right now, take a look at that entrance, will you?"

Trigger turned in the direction he'd indicated.

"They do look like they're somebody important," she said. "Do you know them?"

"Some of them. That gentleman who looks like he almost has to be the Dawn City's First Captain really is the Dawn City's First Captain. The lady he's escorting into the lounge is Lyad Ermetyne. The Ermetyne. You've heard of the Ermetynes?"

"The Ermetyne Wars? Tranest?" Trigger said doubtfully.

"They're the ones. Lyad is the current head of the clan."

The history of Hub systems other than one's own became so involved so rapidly that its detailed study was engaged in only by specialists. Trigger wasn't one. "Tranest is one of the restricted planets now, isn't it?" she ventured.

"It is. Restriction is supposed to be a handicap. But Tranest is also one of the wealthiest individual worlds in the Hub."

Trigger watched the woman with some interest as the party moved along a dim corridor, followed by the viewer circuit's invisible pick-up. Lyad Ermetyne didn't look more than a few years older than she was herself. Rather small, slender, with delicately pretty features. She wore something ankle-length and long-sleeved in lusterless gray with an odd, smoky quality to it.

"Isn't she the empress of Tranest or something of the sort?" Trigger asked.

Quillan shook his head. "They've had no emperors there, technically, since they had to sign their treaty with the Federation. She just owns the planet, that's all."

"What would she be doing, going to Manon?"

"I'd like to know," Quillan said. "The Ermetyne's a lady of many interests. Now—see the plump elderly man just behind her?"

"The ugly one with the big head who sort of keeps blinking?"

"That one. He's Belchik Pluly and—"

"Pluly?" Trigger interrupted. "The Pluly Lines?"

"Yes. Why?"

"Oh—nothing really. I heard—a friend of

mine—Pluly's got a yacht out in the Manon System. And a daughter."

Quillan nodded. "Nelauk."

"How did you know?"

"I've met her. Quite a girl, that Nelauk. Only child of Pluly's old age, and he dotes on her. Anyway, he's been on the verge of being blacklisted by Grand Commerce off and on through the past three decades. But nobody's ever been able to pin anything more culpable on him than that he keeps skimming extremely close to the limits of a large number of laws."

"He's very rich, I imagine?" Trigger said thoughtfully.

"Very. He'd be much richer even if it weren't for his hobby."

"What's that?"

"Harems. The Pluly harems rate among the most intriguing and best educated in the Hub."

Trigger looked at Pluly again. "Ugh!" she said faintly.

Quillan laughed. "The Pluly salaries are correspondingly high. Viewer's dropping the group now, so there's just one more I'd like you to notice. The tall girl with black hair, in orange."

Trigger nodded. "Yes. I see her. She's beautiful."

"So she is. She's also Space Scout Intelligence. Gaya. Comes from Farnhart where they use the single name system. A noted horsewoman, very wealthy, socially established. Which is why we like to use her in situations like this."

Trigger was silent a moment. Then she said,

"What kind of situation is it? I mean, what's she doing with Lyad Ermetyne and the others?"

"She probably attached herself to the group as soon as she discovered Lyad had come on board. Which," Quillan said, "is exactly what I would have told Gaya to do if I'd spotted Lyad first."

Trigger was silent a little longer this time. "Were you thinking this Lyad could be . . ."

"One of our suspects? Well," said Quillan judiciously, "let's say Lyad has all the basic qualifications. Since she's come on board, we'd better consider her. When something's going on that looks more than usually tricky, Lyad is always worth considering. And there's one point that looks even more interesting to me now than it did at first."

"What's that?"

"Those two little old ladies I eased out of their rightful cabin."

Trigger looked at him. "What about them?"

"This about them. The Askab of Elfkund is, you might way, one of the branch managers of the Ermetyne interests in the Hub. He is also a hard-working heel in his own right. But he's not the right size to be one of the people we're thinking about. Lyad is. He might have been doing a job for her."

"Job?" she asked. She laughed. "Not with those odd little grannies?"

"We know the odd little grannies. They're the Askab's poisoners and pretty slick at it. They were sizing you up while you were having that little chat, doll. Probably not for a coffin this time. You were just getting the equivalent of a pretty thorough medical check-up. Presumably, though, for some sinister ultimate purpose."

"How do you know?" Trigger asked, very uncomfortably.

"One of those little suitcases in their cabin was a diagnostic recorder. It would have been standing fairly close to the door while you were there. If they didn't take your recordings out before I got there, they're still inside. They're being watched and they know it. It seemed like a good idea to keep the Askab feeling fairly nervous until we found out whether those sweethearts of his had been parked next door to you on purpose."

"Apparently they were," Trigger admitted. "Nice bunch of people!"

"Oh, they're not all bad. Lyad has her points. And old Belchik, for example, isn't really a heel. He just had no ethics. Or morals. And revolting habits. Anyway, all this brings up the matter of what we should do with you now."

Trigger set her glass down on the table.

"Refill?" Quillan inquired. He reached for the iced crystal pitcher between them.

"No," she said. "I just want to make a statement."

"State away." He refilled his own glass.

"For some reason," said Trigger, "I've been acting lately—the last two days—in a remarkably stupid manner."

Quillan choked. He set his glass down hastily, reached over and patted her hand. "Doll," he said, touched, "it's come to you! At last."

She scowled at him. "I don't usually act that way."

"That," said Quillan, "was what had me so baffled. According to the Commissioner and others, you're as bright in the head as a diamond, usually. And frankly—"

"I know it," Trigger said dangerously. "Don't rub it in!"

"I apologize," said Quillan. He patted her other hand.

"At any rate," Trigger said, drawing her hands back, "now that I've realized it, I'm going to make up for it. From here on out, I'll cooperate."

"To the hilt?"

She nodded. "To the hilt! Whatever that is."

"You can't imagine," said Quillan, "how much that relieves me." He filled her glass, giving her a relieved look. "I had definite instructions, of course, not to do anything like grabbing you by the back of the neck, flinging you into a rest cubicle and sitting on it, guns drawn, until we'd berthed in Precol Port. But I was tempted, I can tell you."

He paused and thought. "You know," he began again, "that really would be the best."

"No!" Trigger said indignantly. "When I said cooperate, I meant actively. Mihul said I'm considered one of the gang in this project. From now on I'll behave like one. And I'll also expect to be treated like one."

"Hm," said Quillan. "Well, there is something you can do, all right."

"What's that?"

"Go on display here, now."

"What for?" she asked.

"As bait, you sweet ninny! If the boss grabber is on this ship, we should draw a new nibble from him." He appraised the green dress in the mirror again. His expression grew absent. It might be best, Trigger suspected, a trifle uneasily, to keep Major Quillan's thoughts turned away from things like nibbling.

"All right," she said briskly. "Let's do that. But you'll have to brief me."

13

SHE HAD FELT SOMEWHAT self-conscious for the first
two or three minutes. But it helped when she
caught a glimpse of their own table drifting by
among the others and realized that the smiling
red-headed viewer image over there looked completely at her ease.

It helped, too, that Major Quillan turned suddenly into the light-but-ardent-conversation type
of companion. In the short preceding briefing he
had pointed out that a bit of flirting, etc., was a
necessary, or at least nearly necessary, part of the
act. Trigger was going along with the flirting; he
could be right about that. She intended to stay on
the alert for the etc.

They got nibbles very promptly. But not quite
the right kind.

The concealed table ComWeb murmured, "A

caller requests to be connected with Major Quillan. Is it permitted?"

"Oho!" Quillan said poisonously. "I suspected we should have stayed off circuit! Who's the caller?"

"The name given is Keth Deboll."

Quillan laughed. "Give the little wolf Major Quillan's regards and tell him it was a good try. I'll look him up tomorrow."

He gave Trigger a gentle wink. "Let 'em pant," he said. "At a distance!"

She smiled uncertainly. If he had a mustache, she thought, he'd be twirling it.

There were two more calls in the next few minutes, of similar nature. Quillan rebuffed them cheerfully. It was rather flattering in a way. She wondered how so many people in the cocktail lounge happened to know Quillan by name.

When the ComWeb reported the fourth caller, it sounded awed.

"The name given is the Lady Lyad Ermetyne!" it said.

Quillan beamed. "Lyad? Bless her heart! A pleasure. Put her through."

A screen shaped itself on the wall mirror to the right. Lyad Ermetyne's face appeared in it.

"Heslet Quillan!" She smiled. "So you aren't permanently lost to your friends, after all!" It was a light, liquid voice. It suited her appearance perfectly.

"Only to the frivolous ones," Quillan said. His thick black brows went up. His face took on a dedicated look. "I'm headed for Manon on duty."

She nodded. "Still with the Subspace Engineers?"

"And with the rank of major by now," Quillan said.

"Congratulations! But I'd already observed that your fabulous good fortune hasn't deserted you in the least." Lyad's glance switched to Trigger; she smiled again. It was a pleasant, easy smile that showed white teeth. "Would you shield your ComWeb, Quillan?"

"Shield it?" Quillan looked surprised. "Why, certainly!" He reached under the edge of the table. The drifting viewer images vanished. "Go ahead."

Lyad's eyes turned back to Trigger. They were off-color eyes, like amber or a light wine, fringed with long black lashes. Very steady, very knowing eyes. Trigger felt herself tensing.

"Forgive me the discourtesy of inquiring directly," the light voice said. "But you are Trigger Argee, aren't you?"

Quillan's hand slapped the table. He looked at Trigger and laughed. "Better give up, Trigger! I told you you were much more widely known than you believed."

"Well, Brule," Trigger muttered moodily to the solidopic propped upright against the pillow before her, "you'd bug those pretty blue eyes out if you knew who's invited me to dinner!"

Brule smiled back winningly. She lay on her cabin's bed, chin on her crossed arms, eyes a dozen inches from the pretty blue ones. She studied Brule's features soberly.

"Major Heslet Quillan," she announced suddenly in cold, even tones, "is a completely impossible character!"

It was no more than the truth. She didn't mind so much that Quillan wouldn't tell her what he thought of Lyad Ermetyne's standing on the suspect list now—there hadn't really been much opportunity for open conversation so far. But he and that unpleasant Belchik Pluly had engaged in some jovial back-slapping and rib-punching when he and Trigger went over to join Lyad's party at her request; and Quillan cried out merrily that he and Belchik had long had one great interest in common—ha-ha-ha! Then those two great buddies vanished together for a full hour to take in some very special, not publicly programmed Sensations Unlimited in the Dawn City's Inferno.

Lyad had smiled after them as they left. "Aren't men disgusting?" she said tolerantly.

That reflected on her, didn't it? She was supposed to be very good friends with somebody like that! Of course Quillan must have some bit of Intelligence business in mind with Pluly, but there should be other ways of going about it. And later, when she'd been just a little stiff with him, Quillan had had the nerve to tell her not to be a prude, doll!

Trigger shoved the solidopic under the pillow. Then she rolled on her side and blinked at the wall.

Naturally, Major Quillan's personal habits were none of her business. It was just that in less than an hour he was to pick her up and take her to the Ermetyne suite for that dinner. She was wondering how she should behave towards him.

Reasonably pleasant but cool, she decided. But again, not too cool, since she'd obligated herself to help him find out what the Tranest tycoonness was after. Any obvious lack of friendliness between them might make the job more difficult.

Trigger sighed. Things were getting complicated again.

While Quillan was indulging his baser nature among the questionable attractions of the Inferno, she'd shot three hundred of her Precol credits on a formal black gown . . . on what, yesterday, she would have considered a rather unbelievable gown. Even at an Ermetyne dinner she couldn't actually look dowdy in it. And then, accompanied by Gaya, who had turned out to be a very pleasant but not very communicative companion, she'd headed for a gambling room to make back the price of the gown.

It hadn't worked out. The game she'd particularly studied up on turned out to have a five hundred minimum play. Which finished that scheme. The system she'd planned to use looked very sound, but she needed more than one chance to try it in. She and Gaya sat down at another table, with a different game, where you could get in for fifty credits. In eight minutes Trigger lost a hundred and twenty and quit.

Gaya won seventy-five.

It had been an interesting day, but with some unsatisfactory aspects to it.

She hauled the solidopic out from under the pillow again.

"And you," she told Brule warningly, "seem to be playing around with some very bad company, my friend! Just luck I'm coming back to see you don't get into serious trouble!"

She'd showered and was studying the black gown's effect before the mirror when the ComWeb chimed.

"Permission for audio intrusion granted," Trigger said casually without looking around. She was getting used to this sort of thing.

"Thank you, Miss Drellgannoth," said the ComWeb. "A package from the Beldon Shop has been deposited in your mail transmitter." It signed off.

Beldon Shop? Trigger frowned, laid the gown across a chair and went over to the transmitter receptacle. She opened it. A flat small green package, marked "The Styles of Beldon," slid out. A delicate scent came trailing along with it. A small white envelope clung to the package's top.

Inside the envelope was a card. It read:

"A peace offering. Would you wear it to dinner in token of forgiveness? Very humbly, Q."

Trigger found herself smiling and wiped off the smile. Then she let it come back. No point in staying grim with the character! She pulled the package tab and it opened up. There were three smaller packages inside.

She opened the first of these and for a moment gazed doubtfully at four objects like green leaf buds, each the size of her thumb. She laid them down and opened the second package. This one contained a pair of very fancy high heels, green and pale gold.

Out of the third flowed something which was, at all events, extraordinarily beautiful material of some kind. Velvety green . . . shimmeringly alive. Its touch was a caress. Its perfume was like soft whispers. Lifting one end with great care between thumb and finger, Trigger let it unfold itself to the floor.

Tilting her head to the side, she studied the shimmering featherweight cat's cradle of jewel-green ribbons that hung there.

Wear it?

What *was* it?

She reflected, found her dressing gown in one of the suitcases, slipped it on, sat down before the ComWeb with the mysterious ribbon arrangement, and dialed Gaya's number.

The Intelligence girl was in her cabin and obviously had been napping. But she was wide awake now. "Shielded here!"she said quickly as soon as her image cleared. "Go ahead!"

"It's nothing important," Trigger said hastily. Gaya relaxed. "It's just—" she held up the ribbons. "Major Quillan sent me this."

Gaya uttered a small squeal. "Oh! Beautiful! A Beldon!"

"That's what it says."

Gaya smiled. "He must like you!"

"Oh?" said Trigger. She hesitated. Gaya's face grew questioning. She asked, "Is something the matter?"

"Probably not," said Trigger. She considered. "If you laugh," she warned, "I'll hate you." She indicated the ribbons again. "What is that Beldon really?"

Gaya blinked. "You haven't been around our decadent circles long enough," she said soberly. Then she did laugh. "Don't hate me, Trigger! Anyway, it's very high fashion. It's also"—her glance went quickly over Trigger—"in excellent taste, in this case. It's a Beldon gown."

A gown!

Some of the beautiful ribbons were wider than others. None of them looked as wide as they should have been. Not for a gown.

Dubiously, Trigger wriggled and fitted herself into the high fashion item. Even before she went over to the mirror in it, she knew it wouldn't do. Not possibly! Styles on many Hub worlds were rather bold of course, but she was sure this effect wasn't what the Beldon's designers had intended.

She stepped in front of the mirror. Her eyes widened. "Brother!" she breathed.

That Beldon did go with a woman like stripes went with a tiger! After one look, you couldn't quite understand why nature hadn't arranged for it first. But just as obviously there wasn't nearly enough Beldon around at the moment.

Trigger checked the time and began to feel harried. Probably she'd wind up wearing the black gown anyway, but at least she wanted to get this

matter worked out before she decided. She dialed
for a drink, took two swallows and reflected that
she might have put the thing on backwards. Or
upside down.

Five minutes later, she sat at the dresser, tapping her fingers on its glassy surface, gazing at the
small pile of green ribbons before her and whis-
tling softly. There was a thoroughly bared look on
her face. Suddenly she stood up and went back to
the ComWeb.

"Ribbons?" said the lady who was the Beldon
Shop's manager. 'That would be 741. A delightful
little creation!"

"Delightful," said Trigger. "May I see it on the
model?"

"Immediately, madam."

A few moments later, a long-limbed model
strolled into the view screen, displaying an ex-
quisite arrangement of burnt sienna ribbons plus
four largish leaf-like designs. Trigger glanced
quickly back to the table where she had put down
the strange green buds. They had quietly opened
out meanwhile.

She thanked the manager, switched off the
ComWeb, got into the Beldon again and attached
her leaf designs where the model had carried
them. They adhered softly, molding themselves
to her, neatly completing the costume.

She stepped into the high heels and looked in
the mirror again. She breathed "Brother!" again.
Maccadon wouldn't have approved. She wasn't
sure she approved either.

But one thing was certain—there wasn't the

remotest suggestion of dowdiness about a Beldon. Objectively, impersonally considered, the effect was terrific.

Feeling tawny and feline, Trigger slowly lifted one shoulder and lowered it again. She turned and strolled toward the full-length mirror across the cabin, admiring the shifts of the Beldon effect in the flow of motion.

Terrific!

With another drink, she could do it.

She dialed another drink and settled down with it beneath the mechanical stylist for a readjustment in the hairdo department. This time the stylist purred as it surveyed and hummed while it worked. And when the hairdo was done and Trigger moved to get up, its flexible little tool pads pulled her back gently into the seat and tilted up her chin. For a moment she was startled. Then she saw that the stylist had produced a shining make-up kit and was opening it. This time she was getting the works . . .

Twenty minutes later, Quillan's voice informed her via the ComWeb that he could be outside her cabin any time she was ready. Trigger told him cheerily to come right over, picked up her purse and swaggered toward the door, smiling a cool, feline smile.

"Prude, eh?" she muttered.

She opened the door.

"Ya-arghk!" cried Quillan, shaken.

14

THEY WERE OUT ON A TERRACE near the top of an illusion mountainside, in a beautiful evening. Dinner
had been old-style and delicious, served by its
creators, two slim, brown-skinned, red-lipped
girls who looked much too young to have ac-
quired such skills. They were natives of Tranest,
Lyad said proudly, and two of the finest food
technicians in the Hub. They were, at all events,
the two finest food technicians Trigger had run
into as yet.

The brandy which followed the dinner seemed
to represent no let-down to the connoisseurs
around Trigger. She went at it cautiously, though
she had swallowed a couple of wake-up capsules
just before they walked into the Ermetyne suite.
The capsules took effect in the middle of the first
course; and what she woke up to was a disconcert-

ing awareness of being the center of much careful attention. The boys were all giving her-plus-Beldon the eye, intensively; even Lyad's giant-sized butler or majordomo or whatever she'd called him, named Virod, ogled coldly out of the background. Trigger gave them the eye back, one after the other, in turn; and that stopped it. Lyad, beautifully wearing something which would have passed muster at the U-League's Annual Presidential Dinner in Ceyce, looked amused.

It wasn't till the end of the second course that Trigger began to feel at ease again. After that she forgot, more or less, about the Beldon. The talk remained light during dinner. When they switched off the illusion background for a look at the goings-on during the Garth stopover, she took the occasion to study her companions in more detail.

There were three men at the table; Lyad and herself. Quillan sat opposite her. Belchik Pluly's unseemly person, in a black silk robe which left his plump arms bare from the elbows down, was on Quillan's right.

The third man fascinated her. It was as if some strange cold creature had walked up out of a polar sea to come on board their ship.

It wasn't so much his appearance, though the green tip of a Vethi sponge lying coiled lightly about his neck probably had something to do with the impression. Trigger knew about Vethi sponges and their addicts, though she hadn't seen either before. It wasn't soo serious an addiction, except perhaps in the fact that it was rarely given up again. The sponges soothed jangled nerves, stabilized unstable emotions.

Balmordan didn't look like a man who needed one. He was big, not as tall as Quillan but probably heavier, with strong features, a boldly jutting nose. Bleak, pale eyes. He was about fifty and wore a richly ornamented blue shirt and trousers. The shirt hung loose, perhaps to conceal the flattened contours of his odd companion's body. Lyad had introduced him as a Devagas scientist and in a manner which indicated he was a man of considerable importance. That meant he was almost certainly a member of the Devagas hierarchy, which in itself would have made him very interesting.

Trigger had run into some of the odd-ball missionaries the Devagas kept sending about the Hub; and she'd sometimes speculated curiously regarding the leaders of that chronically angry, unpredictable nation which, on its twenty-eight restricted worlds, formed more than six percent of the population of the Hub. The Devagas seemed to like nobody; and certainly nobody liked them.

Balmordan didn't fit her picture of a Devagas leader too badly. His manner and talk were easygoing and agreeable. But his particular brand of ogle, when she first became aware of it, had been disquieting. Rather like a biologist planning the details of an interesting vivisection.

Of course he *was* a biologist.

But Trigger kept wondering why Lyad had invited him to dinner. She was positive, for one thing, that Belchik Pluly wasn't at all happy about Balmordan's presence.

Dinner was over before the Garth take-off, and they switched themselves back to the mountainside and took other chairs. A red-haired, green-eyed, tanned, sinuous young woman called Flam appeared from time to time to renew brandy glasses and pass iced fruits around. She gave Trigger coolly speculative looks now and then.

Then Virod showed up again with a flat tray of what turned out to be a very special brand of tobacco. Trigger declined. The men made connoisseur-type sounds of high appreciation, and everybody, including Lyad, lit up small pipes of a very special brand of coral and puffed away happily. Quillan looked up at Virod.

"Hi, big boy!" he said pleasantly. "How's everything been with you?"

Virod, in a wide-sleeved scarlet jacket and creased black trousers, bowed his shaved bullet head very slightly. "Everything's been fine, Major Quillan," he said. "Thank you." He turned and went out of the place. Trigger glanced after him. Virod awed her a little—he was really huge. Moving about among them, he had seemed like a softly padding elephant. And there was an elephant's steady deftness in the way he held out the tiny tobacco trays.

The Ermetyne winked at Quillan. "Quillan wrestled Virod to a pindown once," she said to Trigger. "A fifty-seven minute round, wasn't it?"

"Thereabouts," Quillan said. He added, "Trigger doesn't know yet that I was a sports bum in my youth."

"Really?" Trigger said.

He nodded. "Come from a long line of sports bums, as a matter of fact. But I broke tradition— went into business for myself finally. Nowadays I'm old and soft. Eh, Belchy?" The two great pals, sitting side by side, dug elbows at each other and ha-ha-ha'd. Trigger winced.

"Still in the same line of business, on the side?" Lyad inquired.

Quillan looked steadily at her and grinned. "More or less," he said.

"We might," Lyad said thoughtfully, "come back to that later. As for that match with Virod," she went on to Trigger, "it was really a terrific event! Virod was a Tranest arena professional be- fore I took him into my personal employ, and he's very, very rarely been beaten in any such contest." She laughed. "And before such a large group of people too! I'm afraid he's never quite forgiven you for that, Quillan."

"I'll keep out of his way," Quillan said easily.

"Did you people know," Lyad said, "that the trouble on the way between Maccadon and Evalee was caused by a catassin killing?" There was a touch of mischief in the question, Trigger thought.

There were assorted startled responses. The Ermetyne went briefly over some of the details Quillan had told; essentially it was the same story. "And do you know, Belchik, what the creature was trying to do? It was trying to get into the rest cubicle vaults. Just think, it might have been sent after you!"

It was rather cruel. Pluly's head jerked, and he blinked rapidly at Lyad, saying nothing. He was a badly scared little man at that moment. Trigger felt a little sorry for him, but not too sorry. Belchy's ogle had been of the straightforward, loose-lipped, drooling variety.

"You're safe when you're in one of those things, Belchik!" Quillan said reassuringly. "Wouldn't you feel a little safer there yourself, Lyad? If you say they're not even sure they've killed the creature . . ."

"I probably shall have a cubicle set up here," Lyad said. "But not as protection against a catassin. It would never get past Pilli, for one thing." She looked at Trigger. "Oh, I forgot. You haven't met Pilli. Virod!" she called.

Virod appeared at the far end of the terrace.

"Yes, First Lady?"

"Bring in Pilli," she told him.

Virod bowed. "Pilli is in the room, First Lady." He glanced about, went over to a massive easy chair a few feet way, and swung it aside. Something like a huge ball of golden fur behind it moved and sat up.

It was an animal of some sort. Its head seemed turned toward the group, but whatever features it had remained hidden under the fur. Then an arm like the arm of a bear reached out and Trigger saw a great furred hand that in shape seemed completely human clutch the chair's edge.

"He was resting," Lyad said. "Not sleeping.

Pilli doesn't sleep. He's a perfect guardian. Come here, Pilli—meet Trigger Argee."

Pilli swung up on his feet. It was an impressively effortless motion. There was a thick wide torso on short thick legs under the golden fur. The structure was gorilla-like. Pilli might weigh around four hundred pounds.

He started silently forward and Trigger felt a tingle of alarm. But he stopped six feet away. She looked at him. "Do I say something to Pilli?"

Lyad looked pleased. "No. He's a biostructure. A very intelligent one, but speech isn't included in his pattern."

Trigger kept looking at the golden-furred nightmare. "How can he see to guard you through all that hair?"

"He doesn't see," Lyad said. "At least not as we do. Pilli's part of one of our Tranest experiments—the original stock came from the Maccadon life banks, a small golden-haired Earth monkey. The present level of the experiment is on the fancy side—it has four hearts, for example, and what amounts to a second brain at the lower half of its spine. But it doesn't come equipped with visual organs. Pilli is one of twenty-three of the type. They have compensatory perception of a kind that is still quite mysterious. We hope to breed them past the speech barrier so they can tell us what they do instead of seeing . . . All right, Pilli. Run along!" She said to Balmordan, "I believe he doesn't like that Vethi thing of yours very much."

Balmordan nodded. "I had the same impression."

Perhaps, Trigger thought, that was why Pilli had been lurking so close to them. She watched the biostructure move off down the terrace, grotesque and huge. She had got its scent as it went past her, a fresh, rather pleasant whiff, like the smell of ripe apples. An almost amiable sort of nightmare figure, Pilli was; the apple smell went with that, seemed to fit it. But nightmare was there too. She found herself feeling rather sorry for Pilli.

"In a way," Lyad said, "Pilli brings us to that matter of business I mentioned this afternoon."

The group's eyes shifted over to her. She smiled.

"We have good scientists on Tranest," she said, "as Pilli, I think, demonstrates." She nodded at Balmordan. "There are good scientists in the Devagas Union. And everyone here is aware that the Treaties of Restriction imposed on both our governments have made it impossible for our citizens to engage seriously in plasmoid research."

Trigger nodded briefly as the light-amber eyes paused on her for a moment. Quillan had cautioned her not to show surprise at anything the Ermetyne might say or do. If Trigger didn't know what to say herself, she was merely to look inscrutable. "I'll scrut," he explained. "The others won't. I'll take over then and you just follow my lead. Get it?"

"Balmordan," Lyad said, "I understand you are

going to Manon to attend the seminars and demonstrations on the plasmoid station?"

"That is true, First Lady," said Balmordan.

"Now I," Lyad told the company, "shall be more honest. The information released in those seminars is of no value whatever. He"—she nodded at the Devagas scientist—"and I are going to Manon with the same goal in mind. That is to obtain plasmoids for our government laboratories."

Balmordan smiled amiably.

Trigger asked. "How do you intend to obtain them?"

"By offering very large sums of money, or equivalent inducements, to people who are in a position to get them for me," said Lyad.

Quillan tut-tutted disapprovingly. "The First Lady's mind," he told Trigger, "turns readily to illegal methods."

"When necessary," Lyad said undisturbed, "as it is here."

"How about you, sir?" Quillan asked Balmordan. "Are we to understand that you also would be interested in the purchase of a middling plasmoid or two?"

"I would be, naturally," Balmordan said. "But not at the risk of causing trouble for my government."

"Of course not," Quillan said. He thought a moment. "You, Belchy?" he asked.

Pluly looked alarmed. "No! No! No!" he said hastily. He blinked wildly. "I'll stick to the shipping business. It's safer."

Quillan patted him fondly on the shoulder. "That's one law-abiding citizen in this group!" He winked at Trigger. "Trigger's wondering," he told Lyad, "why she and I are being told these things."

"Well, obviously," Lyad said, "Trigger and you are in an excellent position—or will be, very soon—to act as middlemen in the matter."

"Wha . . ." Trigger began, astounded. Then, as all eyes swiveled over to her, she checked herself. "Did you really think," she asked Lyad, "that we'd agree to such a thing?"

"Certainly not," said Lyad. "I don't expect anyone to agree to anything tonight—though it's a safe assumption I'm not the only one here who has made sure this conversation is not being recorded, and will not be available for reconstruction. Well, Quillan?" She smiled.

"How right you are, First Lady!" Quillan said. He tapped a breast pocket. "Scrambler and distorter present and in action."

"And you, Balmordan?"

"I must admit," Balmordan said pleasantly, "that I thought it wise to take certain precautions."

"Very wise!" said Lyad. Her glance shifted, with some amusement in it, to Pluly. "Belchik?"

"You're a nerve-wracking woman, Lyad," Belchik said unhappily. "Yes. I'm scrambling, of course." He shuddered. "I can't afford to take chances. Not when you're around."

"Of course not, and even so," said Lyad, "there are still reasons why an unconsidered word might be embarrassing in this company. So, no, Trigger, I'm not expecting anybody to agree to anything tonight. I'm merely mentioning that I'm interested in the purchase of plasmoids. Incidentally, I'd be very much more interested even in seeing you, and Quillan, enter my employ directly. Yes, Belchik?"

Pluly had begun giggling wildly.

"I was—ha-ha—having the same idea!" he gasped. "About one of—ha-ha—of 'em anyway! I—"

He jerked and came to an abrupt stop, transfixed by Trigger's stare. Then he reached for his glass, blinking at top speed. "Excuse me," he muttered.

"Hardly, Belchik!" said Lyad. She gave Trigger a small wink. "But I can assure you, Trigger Argee, that you'd find my pay and working conditions very attractive indeed."

It seemed a good moment to look inscrutable. Trigger did.

"Serious about that, Lyad?" asked Quillan.

The Ermetyne said, "Certainly I'm serious. Both of you could be of great value to me at present." She looked at him a moment. "Did you ever happen to tell Trigger about the manner in which you re-established the family fortune?"

"Not in any great detail," Quillan said.

"A very good hijacker and smuggler went to waste when you signed up with the Engineers," Lyad said. "But perhaps not entirely to waste."

"Perhaps not," acknowledged Quillan. He

grinned. "But I'm a modest man. One fortune's enough for me."

"There was a time, you know," Lyad said, "when I was rather afraid it would be necessary to have you killed."

Quillan laughed. "There was a time," he admitted, "when I suspected you might be thinking along those lines, First Lady! Didn't lose too much, did you?"

"I lost enough!" Lyad said. She wrinkled her nose at him. "But that's all over and done with. And now—no more business tonight. I promise." She turned her head a little. "Flam!" she called.

"Yes, First Lady?" said the voice of the red-headed girl.

"Bring us Miss Argee's property, please."

Flam brought in a small package of flat disks taped together. Lyad took them.

"Sometimes," she told Quillan, "the Askab becomes a little independent. He's been spoken to. Here—you keep them for Trigger."

She tossed the package lightly over to them. Quillan put out a hand and caught it.

"Thanks," he said. He put the package in a pocket. "I'll call off my beagles."

"Suit yourself as to that," said the Ermetyne. "It won't hurt the Askab to stay frightened a little longer."

She checked herself. The room's ComWeb was signaling. Virod went over to it. A voice came through.

". . . The Garth-Manon subspace run begins in

one hour. Rest cubicles have been prepared . . ."

"That means me," Belchik Pluly said. He climbed hastily to his feet. "Can't stand dives! Get hallucinations. Nasty ones." He staggered a little then, and Trigger realized for the first time that Belchy had got pretty thoroughly drunk.

"Better give our guest a hand, Virod," Lyad called over her shoulder. "Happy dreams, Belchik! Are you going by Rest, Trigger? No? You're not, of course, Quillan. Balmordan?"

The Devagas scientist also shook his head.

"Then by all means," Lyad said, "let's stay together a little while longer."

15

"She," said Trigger, "is a remarkable woman."

"Yeah," said Quillan. "Remarkable."

"May I ask you, finally, a few pertinent questions?" Trigger inquired humbly.

"Not here, sweet stuff," said Quillan.

"You're a bossy sort of slob, Heslet Quillan," she said equably.

Quillan didn't answer. They had come down the stairway to the storerooms level and were walking along the big lit hallway toward their cabins. Trigger felt pleasantly relaxed. But she did have a great many pertinent questions to ask Quillan now, and she wanted to get started on them.

"Oh!" she said suddenly. Just as suddenly, Quillan's hand was on her shoulder, moving her along.

"Hush now," he said. "And keep walking."

"But you saw it, didn't you?" Trigger asked, trying to look back to the small open door into the storerooms they'd just passed.

Quillan sighed. "Certainly," he said. "Guy in space armor."

"But what's he doing there?"

"Checking something, I suppose." His hand left her shoulder; and, for just a moment, his finger rested lightly across her lips. Trigger glanced up at him. He was walking on beside her, not looking at her.

All right, she thought—she could take a hint. But she felt tense and uncomfortable now. Something was going on again, apparently.

They turned into the side passage and came up to her cabin. Trigger started to turn to face him, and Quillan picked her up and went on without a noticeable break in his stride. Close to her ear, his voice whispered, "Explain in a moment! Dangerous here."

As the door to the end cabin closed behind them, he put her back on her feet. He looked at his watch.

"We can talk here," he said. "But there may not be much time for conversation." He gestured toward a table against the wall. "Take a look at the setup."

Trigger looked. The table was littered with instruments, like an electronic work bench. A visual screen showed a view of both her own cabin and a section of the passage outside it, up to the point where it entered the big hall.

"What is it?" she asked uncertainly.

"Essentially," said Quillan, "we've set up a catassin trap."

"Catassin!" Trigger squeaked.

"That's right. Don't get too nervous though. I've caught them before. Used to be a sort of specialty of mine. And there's one thing about them—they'll blab their pointed little heads off if you can get one alive and promise it its catnip . . ." He'd shucked off his jacket and taken out of it a very large handgun with a bell-shaped mouth. He laid the gun down next to the view screen. "In case," he said, unreassuringly. "Now just a moment."

He sat down in front of the view screen and did something to it.

"All right," he said then. "We're here and set. Probability period starts in three minutes, continues for sixty. Signal on any blip. Otherwise no gabbing. And remember they're *fast*. Don't get sappy."

There was no answer. Quillan did something else to the screen and stood up again. He looked broodingly at Trigger. "It's those damn computers again!" he said. "*I* don't see any sense in it."

"In what?" she asked shakily.

"Everything that's happening around here is being fed back to them at the moment," he said. "When they heard about our invite to Lyad's dinner party, and who was to be present, they came up with a honey. In the time period I mentioned a catassin is supposed to show up at your cabin. They give it a pretty high probability."

Trigger didn't say anything. If she had, she probably would have squeaked again.

"Now don't worry," he said, squeezing her shoulder reassuringly between a large thumb and four slightly less large fingers. "Nice muscle!" he said absently. "The cabin's trapped and I've taken other precautions." He massaged the muscle gently. "Probably the only thing that will happen is that we'll sit around here for an hour or so, and then we'll have a hearty laugh together at those foolish computers!" He smiled.

"I thought," Trigger said without squeaking, "that everybody was pretty sure it was dead."

Quillan frowned. "Well, that's something else again! There are at least two ways I know of to sneak it past that search. Jump it out and in with a subtub is one—they could have done that from their own cabin as soon as they had its pattern. So I don't really think it's dead. It's just—"

"Quillan," a tiny voice said from the viewer.

He turned, took two steps, and sat down fast before the viewer. "Go ahead!"

"Fast motion in B section. Going your way."

Fast motion. A thought flicked up. "Quillan—" Trigger began.

He raised a shushing hand. "Get a silhouette?" he asked. His hands went to a set of control switches and stayed there.

"No. Pickup shows a haze like in the reconstruct." An instant's pause. "Leaving B section."

"Motion in C section," said another voice.

Quillan said, "All right. It's coming. No more verbal reports unless it changes direction. If you want to stay alive, don't move unless you're in armor."

There was silence. Quillan sat unmoving, eyes fixed on the screen. Trigger stood just behind him. Her legs had begun to tremble. She'd better tell him.

"Quillan—"

For an instant, in the screen, there was something like heat shimmer at the far end of the passage. Then she saw her cabin door pop open.

The interior of the cabin showed in a brief flare of blue light. In it was a shape. It vanished instantly again.

She heard Quillan make a shocked, incredulous sound. His left hand slashed at a switch on the panel.

Twenty feet from them, just behind the closed door to the passage, was a splatting noise like a tremendous slap. Then another noise, strangely like a brief cloudburst. Then silence again.

She realized Quillan was on his feet beside her, the oversized gun in his hand. It was pointed at the door. His eyes switched suddenly from the door to the screen and back again. She felt him relaxing slowly. Then she discovered she was clutching a handful of his shirt along with a considerable chunk of tough skin. She went on clutching it.

"Fly swatter got it!" he said. "Whew!" He looked down and patted the clutching hand. "No catassin! The trap in the cabin just wasn't fast enough. Had a gravity mine outside our door, just in case. *That* was barely fast enough!" For once, Quillan looked almost awed.

"L-l-l-like—" Trigger began. She tried again. "Like a little yellow man—"

"You saw it? In the cabin? Yes. Never saw anything just like it before!"

Trigger pressed her lips together to make them stay steady.

"I have," she said. "That's what I was trying to tell you."

Quillan stared at her for an instant. "You'll tell me about it in a couple of minutes. I've got some quick work to do first." He checked himself. A wide grin spread suddenly over his face. "Know something, doll?"

"What?"

"The damn computers!" Major Quillan said happily. "They goofed!"

The gravity mine would have reduced almost any life-form which moved into its field to a rather thin smear, but there wasn't even that left of the yellow demon-shape. Something, presumably something it was carrying, had turned it into a small blaze of incandescent energy as the mine flattened it out. Which explained the sound like a cloudburst. That had been the passage's automatic fire extinguishers going into brief but correspondingly violent action.

Quillan's group stayed out of sight for the time being. He'd barely got the mine put away, along with a handful of warped metal slugs, which was what the mine had left of their attacker's mechanical equipment, and Trigger's cabin door locked again, when three visitors came zooming down the storerooms hall in a small car. A ship's engineer and two assistants had arrived to check on what had started the extinguishers.

"They may," Quillan said hopefully, "just go away again." He and Trigger were watching the engineers through the viewer which had been extended to cover their end of the passage.

They didn't just go away again. They checked the extinguishers, looked at the floor, still wet but rapidly absorbing the last drops of the brief deluge. They exchanged puzzled comment. They checked everything once more. Finally the leader made use of the door announcer and asked if he might intrude.

Quillan switched off the viewer. "Come in," he said resignedly.

The door opened. The three glanced at Quillan, and then at Trigger-plus-Beldon. Their eyes widened only slightly. Duty on the Dawn City produced hardened men.

Neither Quillan nor Trigger could offer the slightest explanation as to what had started the extinguishers. The engineers apologized and withdrew. The door closed again.

Quillan switched on the viewer. Their voices came back into the cabin as they climbed into their car.

"So that's how it happened," one of the assistants was saying reflectively.

"Right," said the ship's engineer. "Like to burst into flames myself."

"Ha-ha-ha!" They drove off.

Trigger flushed. She looked at Quillan.

"Perhaps I ought to get into something else," she said. "Now that the party's over."

"Perhaps," Quillan admitted. "I'll have Gaya bring something down. We want to stay out of your cabin for an hour or so till everything's been checked. There'll be a few conferences to go through now."

Gaya arrived next, with clothes. Trigger retired to the cabin's bathroom with them and came out a few minutes later, dressed again. Meanwhile the Dawn City's First Security Officer also had arrived and was setting up a portable restructure stage in the center of the cabin. He looked rather grim, but he also looked like a very much relieved man.

"I suggest we run your sequence off first, Major," he said. "Then we can put them on together, and compare them."

Trigger sat down on a couch beside Gaya to watch. She'd been told that the momentary view of the little demon-shape in the cabin had been deleted from Security's copy of their own sequence and wasn't to be mentioned.

Otherwise there really was not too much to see. What the attacking creature had used to blur the restructure wasn't clear, except that it wasn't a standard scrambler. Amplifed to the limits of clarity and stepped down in time to the limit of immobility, all that emerged was a shifting haze of energy, which very faintly hinted at a dwarfish human shape in outline. A rather unusually small and heavy catassin, the Security chief pointed out, would present such an outline. That some-

thing quite material was finally undergoing dev-
astating structural disorganization on the gravity mine was unpleasantly obvious, but it produced no further information. The sequence
ended with the short blaze of heat which had set
off the extinguishers.

Then they ran the restructure of the preceding
double killing. Trigger watched, gulping a little,
till it came to the point where the haze shape
actually was about to touch its victims. Then she
studied the carpet carefully until Gaya nudged
her to indicate the business was over. Catassins
almost invariably used their natural equipment in
the kill; it was a swift process, of course, but
shockingly brutal, and Trigger didn't care to remember what the results looked like in a human
being. Both men had been killed in that manner;
and the purpose obviously was to conceal the fact
that the killer was not a catassin, but something
even more efficient along those lines.

It didn't occur to the Security chief to question
Trigger. A temporal restructure of a recent event
was a far more reliable witness than any set of
human senses and memory mechanisms. He left
presently, reassured that the catassin incident
was concluded. It startled Trigger to realize that
Security did not seem to be considering seriously
the possibility of discovering the human agent
behind the murders.

Quillan shrugged. "Whoever did it is covered
three ways in every direction. The chief knows it.
He can't psych four thousand people on general
suspicions, and he'd hit mind-blocks in every

twentieth passenger presently on board if he did. Anyway he knows we're on it, and that we have a great deal better chance of nailing the responsible characters eventually."

"More information for the computers, eh?" Trigger said.

"Uh-huh."

"You got this little chunk the hard way, I feel," she observed.

"True," Quillan admitted. "But we have to get it any way we can till we get enough to move on. Then we move." He looked at her, with an air of regarding a new idea. "You know," he said, "you don't do badly for an amateur!"

"She doesn't do badly," Gaya's voice said behind Trigger, "for anybody. How do you people feel about a drink? I thought I could use one myself after looking at the chief's restructure."

Trigger felt herself coloring. Praise from the cloak and dagger experts! For some reason it pleased her immensely. She turned her head to smile at Gaya, standing there with three glasses on a tray.

"Thanks!" she said. She took one of the glasses. Gaya held the tray out to Quillan and took the third glass herself.

It was some five minutes later when Trigger remarked, "You know, I'm getting sleepy."

Quillan looked around the viewer equipment he and Gaya were dismantling. "Why not hit the couch over there and take a nap?" he suggested. "It'll be about an hour before the boys can get down here for the real conference."

"Good idea." Trigger yawned, finished her drink, put the glass on a table, and wandered over to the couch. She stretched out on it. A drowsy somnolence enveloped her almost instantly. She closed her eyes.

Ten minutes later, Gaya, standing over her, announced, "Well, she's out."

"Fine," said Quillan, packaging the rest of the equipment. "Tell them to haul in the rest cubicle. I'll be done here in a minute. Then you and the lady warden can take over."

Gaya looked down at Trigger. There was a trace of regret in her face. "I think," she said, "she's going to be fairly displeased with you when she wakes up and finds she's on Manon."

"Wouldn't doubt it," said Quillan. "But from what I've seen of that chick, she's going to get fairly displeased with me from time to time on this operation anyway."

Gaya looked at his back.

"Major Quillan," she said, "would you like a tip from a keen-eyed operator?"

"Go ahead, ole keen-eyed op!" Quillan said in kindly tones.

"Not that you don't have it coming, boy," said Gaya. "But watch yourself! This one is dangerous. This one could sink you for keeps."

"You're going out of your mind, doll," said Quillan.

16

THE PRECOL HEADQUARTERS DOME on Manon Planet
was still in the spot where Trigger had left it,
looking unchanged; but everything else in the
area seemed to have been moved, improved, ex-
panded or taken away entirely, and unfamiliar
features had appeared. In the screens of Commissioner Tate's Precol offices, Trigger could see
both the new metropolitan-sized spaceport on
which the Dawn City had set down that morning,
and the towering glassy structures of the giant
shopping and recreation center, which had been
opened here recently by Grand Commerce in its
bid for a cut of prospective outworld salaries. The
salaries weren't entirely prospective either.

Ten miles away on the other side of Headquarters dome, new squares of living domes were
sprouting up daily. At this morning's count they
housed fifty-two thousand people. The Hub's

major industries and assorted branches of Federation government had established a solid foothold on Manon.

Trigger turned her head as Holati Tate came into the office. He closed the door carefully behind him.

"How's the little critter doing?" he asked.

"Still absorbing the goop," Trigger said. She held Mantelish's small mystery plasmoid cupped lightly between thumbs and fingers, its bottom side down in a shallow bowl half full of something which Mantelish considered to be nutritive for plasmoids, or at least for this one. Its sides pulsed lightly and regularly against her palms. "The level of the stuff keeps going down," she added.

"Good," said Holati. He pulled a chair up to the table and sat down opposite her. He looked broodingly at plasmoid 113-A.

"You really think this thing *likes* me—personally?" Trigger inquired.

Her boss said, "It's eating, isn't it? And moving. There were a couple of days before you got here when it looked pretty dead to me."

"Hard to believe," Trigger observed, "that a sort of leech-looking thing could distinguish between people."

"This one can. Do you get any sensations while holding it?"

"Sensations?" She considered. "Nothing particular. It's just like I said the other time—little Repulsive is rather nice to feel."

"For you," he said. "I didn't tell you everything."

"You rarely do," Trigger remarked.

"I'll tell you now," said Holati. "The day after we left, when it started acting very agitated and then very droopy, Mantelish said it might be missing the female touch it had got from you. He was being facetious, I think. But I couldn't see any reason not to try it, so I called in your facsimile and had her sit down at the table where the thing was lying."

"Yes?"

"Well, first it came flying up to her, crying 'Mama!' Not actually, of course. Then it touched her hand and recoiled in horror."

Trigger raised an eyebrow.

"It looked like it," he insisted. "We all commented on it. So then she reached out and touched it. Then she recoiled in horror."

"Why?"

"She said it had given her a very nasty electric jolt. Apparently like the one it gave Mantelish."

Trigger glanced down dubiously at Repulsive. "Gee, thanks for letting me hold it, Holati! It seems to have stopped eating now, by the way. Or whatever it does. Doesn't look much fatter if any, does it?"

The Commissioner looked. "No," he said. "And if you weighed it, you'd probably find it still weighs an exact three and a half pounds. Mantelish feels the thing turns any food intake directly into energy."

"Then it should be able to produce a very nice jolt at the moment," Trigger commented. "Now, what do I do with Repulsive?"

Holati took a towel from beneath the table and spread it out. "Absorbent material," he said. "Lay it on that and just let it dry. That's what we used to do."

Trigger shook her head. "Next thing, I'll be changing its diapers!"

"It isn't that bad," the Commissioner said. "Anyway, you will adopt baby, won't you?"

"I suppose I have to." She placed the plasmoid on the towel, wiped her hands and stepped back from it. "What happens if it falls on the floor?"

"Nothing," Holati said. "It just moves on in the direction it was going. Pretty hard to hurt those things."

"In that case," Trigger said, "let's check out its container now."

The Commissioner took Repulsive's container out of a desk safe and handed it to her. Its outer appearance was that of a neat modern woman's handbag with a shoulder strap. It had an antigrav setting which would reduce its overall weight, with the plasmoid inside, down to nine ounces if Trigger wanted it that way. It also had a combination lock, unmarked, virtually invisible, the settings of which Trigger already had memorized. Without knowing the settings, a determined man using a high-powered needle blaster might have opened the handbag in around nine hours. A very special job.

Trigger ran through the settings, opened the container and peered inside. "Rather cramped," she observed.

"Not for one of them. We needed room for the gadgetry."

"Yes," she said. "Subspace rotation." She shook her head. "Is that another Space Scout invention?"

"No," said Holati. "They stole it from Subspace Engineers. Engineers don't know we have it yet. Far as I know, nobody else has got it from them. Go ahead—give it a try."

"I was going to." Trigger snapped the container shut, slipped the strap over her shoulder and stood straight, left hand closed over the lower rim of the purselike object. She shifted the ball of her thumb and the tip of her middle finger to the correct spots and began to apply pressure. Then she started. Handbag and strap had vanished.

"Feels odd!" She smiled. "And to bring it back, I just have to be here—the same place—and say those words."

He nodded. "Want to try that now?"

Trigger waved her left hand gently through the air beside her. "What happens," she asked, "if the thing surfaces exactly where my hand happens to be?"

"It won't surface if there's anything bulkier than a few dust motes in the way. That's one improvement the Sub Engineers haven't heard about yet."

"Well . . ." She glanced around, picked up a plastic ruler from the desk behind her, and moved back a cautious step. She waved the ruler's tip gingerly about in the area where the handbag had been.

"Come, Fido!" she said.

Nothing happened. She drew the ruler back.

"Come, Fido!"

Handbag and strap materialized in mid-air and thumped to the floor.

"Convinced?" Holati asked. He picked up the handbag and gave it back to her.

"It seems to work. How long will that little plasmoid last if it's left in subspace like that?"

He shrugged. "Indefinitely, probably. They're tough. We know that twenty-four hours at a stretch won't bother it in the least, so we've set that as the limit it's to stay rotated except in emergencies."

"And you—and one other person I'm not to know about, but who isn't anywhere near here—can also bring it back?"

"Yes. If we know the place from which it's been rotated. So the agreement is that—again except in absolute emergencies—it will be rotated only from one of the six points specified and known to all three of us."

Trigger nodded. She opened the container and went over to the table where the plasmoid still lay on its towel. It was dry by now. She picked it up.

"You're a lot of trouble, Repulsive!" she told it. "But these people think you must be worth it." She slipped it into the container, and it seemed to snuggle down comfortably inside. Trigger closed the handbag, lightened it to half its normal weight, slipped the strap back over her left shoulder. "And now," she inquired, "what am I to do with the stuff I usually keep in a purse?"

"You'll be in Precol uniform while you're here. We've had a special uniform made for you. Extra pockets."

Trigger sighed.

"Oh, they're quite inconspicuous and convenient," he assured her. "We checked with the girls on that."

"I'll bet!" she said. "Did they okay the porgee pouch too?"

"Sure. Porgee doping is a big thing all over the Hub at the moment. Among the ladies anyway. Shows you're the delicate sort, or something like that. I forget what they said. Want to start carrying it?"

"Hand it over," Trigger said resignedly. "I did see quite a few pouches on the ship. Might as well get people used to thinking I've turned into a porgee sniffer."

Holati went back to the desk safe and took out a flat pouch, the length of his hand but narrower. He gave it to her. It appeared to be worked of gold thread; one side was studded with tiny pearls, the opposite surface was plain. Trigger laid the plain side against the cloth of her skirt, just below the right hip, and let go. It adhered there. She stretched her right leg out to the side and considered the porgee pouch.

"Doesn't look too bad," she conceded. "That's real porgee in the top section?"

"The real article. Close to nine hundred and fifty credits worth."

"Suppose somebody wants to borrow a sniff? Wouldn't be good to have them fumbling around the pouch very much!"

"They can't," said the Commissioner. "That's why we made it porgee. When you buy a supply, it has to be adjusted to your individual chemistry, exactly. That's mainly what makes it expensive. Try using someone else's, and it'll flip you across the room."

"Better get this adjusted to my chemistry then. I might have to take a demonstration sniff now and then to make it look right."

"We've already done that," he said.

"Good," said Trigger. "Now let's see!" She straightened up, left hand closed lightly around the bottom of the purse, right hand loose at her side. Her eyes searched the office briefly. "Some object around here you don't particularly value?" she asked. "Something largish?"

"Several," the Commissioner said. He glanced around. "That overgrown flower pot in the corner is one. Why?"

"Just practicing," said Trigger. She turned to face the flower pot. "That will do. Now—here I come along, thinking of nothing." She started walking toward the flower pot. "Then, suddenly, in front of me, there stands a plasmoid snatcher."

She stopped in mid-stride. Handbag and strap vanished, as her right hand slapped the porgee pouch. The Denton popped into her palm. The flower pot screeched and flew apart.

"Golly!" she said, startled. "Come, Fido!" Handbag and strap reappeared and she reached out and caught the strap. She looked around at Commissioner Tate.

"Sorry about your pot, Holati. I was just going to shake it up a little. I forgot you people had been handling my gun. I keep it switched to stunner myself when I'm carrying it," she added pointedly.

"Perfectly all right about the pot," the Commissioner said. "I should have warned you. Otherwise, I'd say all you'd need is a moment to see them coming."

Trigger spun the Denton to its stunner setting and laid it back inside the slit which had appeared along the side of the porgee pouch. She ran thumb and finger tip along the length of the slit, and the pouch was sealed again.

"That's the part that's worrying me," she admitted.

When Trigger presented herself at Commissioner Tate's personal quarters early that evening, she found him alone.

"Sit down," he said. "I've been trying to get hold of Mantelish for the past hour. He's over on the other side of the planet again."

Trigger sat down and lifted an eyebrow. "Should he be?"

"I don't think so," said Holati. "But I've been overruled on that. He's still the best man the Federation has working on the various plasmoid problems, so I'm not to interfere with his investigations any more than I can show is absolutely necessary. It's probably all right. Those U-League guards of his aren't a bad group."

"If they compare with the boys the League had watching the Plasmoid Project, they should be just about tops," Trigger said.

"The Space Scouts thank you for those kind words," the Commissioner told her. "Those weren't League guards. When it came to deciding who was to keep an eye on you, I overruled everybody."

She smiled. "I might have guessed it. What's there for the professor to be investigating on the other side of Manon?"

"He's hunting for some theoretical creatures he calls wild plasmoids."

"*Wild* plasmoids?"

"Uh-huh. His idea is that some of the plasmoids the Old Galactics were using on Manon might have got away from them, or just been left lying around, so to speak, and could have survived till now. He thinks they might even be reproducing themselves. He's looking for them with a special detector he built."

Trigger held up a finger on which was a slim gold ring with a small green stone in it. "Like this one?" she asked.

"He's got a large version of that type of detector with him too. But he thinks that if any wild plasmoids are around, they're likely to be along the lines of 113-A. So he's also constructed a detector which reacts to 113-A."

"I see." Trigger was silent a moment. "Does Mantelish have any idea why Repulsive is the only plasmoid known to which our ring detectors don't react?"

"Apparently he does," Holati said. "But when he starts in on those subjects, I find him difficult to follow." He looked soberly at Trigger. "There are times," he confessed, "when I suspect Professor Mantelish is somewhat daft. But probably he's just so brilliant that he keeps fading beyond my mental range."

Trigger laughed. "My father used to come home from a session with Mantelish muttering the same sort of thing." She glanced at the ring again. "By the way, have any plasmoids actually been stolen around here for us to detect?"

He nodded. "Quite a few have been snitched from Harvest Moon and various storage points by now. I wouldn't be surprised if some of them turn up here in the dome eventually. Not that it's a serious loss. What the thieves have been getting away with is small stuff—plasmoid nuts and bolts, so to speak. Still, each of those would still fetch around a hundred thousand credits, if you offered them to the right people. Incidentally, if asking you to this conference has interfered with any personal plans, just say so. We can put it off till tomorrow. Especially since it's beginning to look as if Mantelish won't make it here either."

"Either?" Trigger said.

"Quillan's already had to cancel. He got involved with something during the afternoon."

"Oh," she said coolly. She looked at her watch. "I do have a dinner date with Brule Inger in an hour and a half. But you said this meeting wasn't to take more than an hour anyway, didn't you?"

He nodded.

"Then I'm free. My quarters are arranged, and I'm ready to go back on my old job in the morning."

"Fine," said the Commissioner. "There are things I wanted to discuss with you privately anyway. If we can't get through to Mantelish in another ten minutes, we'll go ahead with that. I would have liked to have Quillan here to fill us in with data about some of the top-level crooks in the Hub. They're a specailty of his. I don't know too much about them myself."

He paused. "That Lyad Ermetyne now," he said, "looks as if she either already is part of the main problem or is working very hard to get there. She's had a Tranest warship stationed here for the past two weeks. A thing called the Aurora."

Trigger was startled. "But warships aren't allowed in Manon System!"

"It isn't in the system. It's stationed a half light-year away, where it has a legal right to be. Nothing to worry about as such. It's just a heavy armed frigate, which is the limit Tranest is allowed to build. Since it's Lyad's private boat, I imagine it's been souped up with everything they could throw in. Anyway, the fact that she sent it here ahead of her indicates she isn't just dropping in for a casual visit."

"She made that pretty clear herself!" Trigger said. "Why do you think she's being so open about it?"

He shrugged. "Might have a number of reasons. One could be that she'd get the beady eye anyway as soon as she showed up here. When Lyad goes anywhere, it's usually on business. After Quillan reported on your dinner party, I got all the information I could on her. The First Lady stacks up as a tough cookie! Also smart. Most of those Ermetynes wind up being dead-brained by some loving relative, and apparently they have to know how to whip up a sharp brew of poison before they're let into kindergarten. Lyad's been top dog among them since she was eighteen—"

His head turned. A bell had begun pinging in the next room. He stood up.

"Probably Mantelish's outfit on the transmitter," he said. "I told them to call as soon as they located him." He stopped at the door. "Care for a drink, Trigger girl? You know where the stuff is."

"Not just now, thanks."

The Commissioner came back in a couple of minutes. "Darn fool got lost in a swamp! They found him finally, but he's too tired to come over now."

He sat down and scratched his chin thoughtfully. "Do you remember the time you passed out on the Harvest Moon?" he asked.

Trigger looked at him, puzzled. "The time I what?"

"Passed out. Fainted. Went out cold."

"I? You're out of your mind, Holati! I never fainted in my life."

"Reason I asked," he said, "is that I've been told a spell in a rest cubicle—same thing as a rest cubicle anyway, only it's used for therapy—sometimes resolves amnesias."

"Amnesias! What are you talking about?"

The Commissioner said. "I'm talking about you. This is bound to be a jolt, Trigger girl. Might have been easier after a drink. But I'll just give it to you straight. About a week after Mantelish and his U-League crew first arrived here, you did pass out on one occasion while we were on the Harvest Moon with them. And afterwards you didn't remember doing it."

"I didn't?" Trigger said weakly.

"No. I thought it might have cleared up, and you just had some reason for not wanting to mention it." He got to his feet. "Like that drink now—before I go on with the details?"

She nodded.

17

HOLATI TATE BROUGHT HER the drink and went on with the details.

Trigger and he and a dozen or so of the first group of U-League investigators had been in what was now designated as Section 52 of Harvest Moon. The Commissioner was by himself, checking over some equipment which had been installed in one of the compartments. After a while Doctor Azol joined him and told him Mantelish and the others had gone on to another section. Holati and Azol finished the check-up together and were about to leave the area to catch up with the group, when Holati saw Trigger lying on the floor in an adjoining compartment.

"You seemed to be in some kind of coma," he said. "We picked you up and put you into a chair by one of the survey screens, and were trying to get out a call on Azol's suit communicator to the ambulance boat when you suddenly opened your eyes. You looked at me and said, 'Oh, there you are! I was just going to go looking for you.' "

"It was obvious that you didn't realize anything unusual had happened. Azol started to say something, but I stepped on his foot, and he caught on. In fact, he caught on so fast that I became a little suspicious of him."

"Poor Azol!" Trigger said.

"Poor nothing!" the Commissioner said cryptically. "I'll tell you about that some other time. I cautioned Doctor Azol to say nothing to anybody until the incident had been clarified, in view of the stringent security precautions being practiced . . . supposedly being practiced," he amended. Then he'd returned to Manon Planet with Trigger immediately, where she was checked over by Precol's medical staff. Physically there wasn't a thing wrong with her.

"And that," said Trigger, feeling a little frightened, "is something else I don't remember!"

"Well, you wouldn't," the Commissioner said. "You were fed a hypno-spray first. You went out for three hours. When you woke up, you thought you'd been having a good nap. Since the medics were sure you hadn't picked up some odd plasmoid infection, I wanted to know just what else had happened on Harvest Moon. One of those scientific big shots might also have used a hypno-spray on you, with the idea of turning you into a conditioned assistant for future shenanigans."

Trigger grinned faintly. "You do have a suspicious mind!" The grin faded. "Was that what they were going to find out in that mind-search interview on Maccadon I skipped out on?"

"It's one of the things they might have looked for," he agreed.

Trigger gazed at him very thoughtfully for a moment. "Well, I loused that deal up!" she remarked. "But why is everybody—" She shook her head. "Excuse me. Go on."

The Commissioner went on. "Old Doc Leeharvis was handling the hypnosis herself. She hit what she thought might be a mind-block when she tried to get you to remember what happened. We know now it wasn't a mind-block. But she wouldn't monkey with you any farther, and told me to get in an expert. So I called the Psychology Service's headquarters on Orado."

Trigger looked startled, then laughed. "The eggheads? You went right to the top there, didn't you?"

"Tried to," said Holati Tate. "It's a good idea when you want real service. They told me to stay calm and to say nothing to you. An expert would be shipped out promptly."

"Was he?"

"Yes."

Trigger's eyes narrowed a little. "Same old hypno-spray treatment?"

"Right," said Commissioner Tate. "He came, sprayed, investigated. Then he told me to stay calm, and went off looking puzzled."

"Puzzled?" she said.

"If I hadn't known before that experts come in

all grades," the Commissioner said, "I'd know it now. That first one they sent was just sharp enough to realize there might be something involved in the case he wasn't getting. But that was all."

Trigger was silent a moment. "So there've been more of those investigations I don't know about!" she observed, her voice taking on an edge.

"Uh-huh," the Commissioner said cautiously.

"How many?"

"Seven."

Trigger flushed, straightened up, eyes blazing, and pronounced a very unladylike word.

"Excuse me," she added a moment later. "I got carried away."

"Perfectly all right," said the Commissioner.

"I've been getting just a bit fed up anyway," Trigger went on, voice and color still high, "with people knocking me for a loop one way or another whenever they happen to feel like it!"

"Don't blame you a bit," he said.

"And please don't think I don't appreciate your calling in all those experts. I do. It's just their sneaky, underhanded, secretive methods I don't go for!"

"Exactly how I feel about it," said the Commissioner.

Trigger stared at him suspiciously. "You're a pretty sneaky type yourself!" she said. "Well, excuse the blowup, Holati. They probably had some reason for it. Have they found out anything at all with all the spraying and investigating?"

"Oh, yes. They seem to have made considerable

progress. The last report I had from them—about a month ago—shows that the original amnesia has been completely resolved."

Trigger looked surprised. "If it's been resolved," she said reasonably, "why don't I remember what happened?"

"You aren't supposed to become conscious of it before the final interview—I don't know the reason for that. But the memory is available now. On tap, so to speak. They'll give you a cue, and then you'll remember it."

"Just like that, eh?" She paused. "So the Psychology Service is Whatzzit."

"Whatzzit?" said the Commissioner.

She explained about Whatzzit. He grinned.

"Yes," he said. "They're the ones who've been giving the instructions, as far as you're concerned."

Trigger was silent a moment. "I've heard," she said, "the eggheads have terrific pull when they want to use it. You don't hear much about them otherwise. Let me think just a little."

"Go ahead," said Holati.

A minute ticked away.

"What it boils down to so far," Trigger said then, "is still pretty much what you told me on Maccadon. The Psychology Service thinks I know something that might help clean up the plasmoid problem. Or at least help explain it."

He nodded.

"And the people who've been trying to grab me very probably are doing it for exactly the same reason."

He nodded again. "That's almost certain."

"Do you think the eggheads might already have figured out what the connection is?"

The Commissioner shook his head. "If they had, we'd be doing something about it. The Federation Council is very nervous!"

"Well . . ." Trigger said. She pursed her lips. "That Lyad . . ." she said.

"What about her?"

"She tried to hire me," said Trigger. "Major Quillan reported it, I suppose?"

"Sure."

"And it wouldn't be just to steal some stupid plasmoid. Especially since you say a number of small ones are already available. Then there're the ones that raiders picked up in the Hub. She probably has a collection by now."

He nodded. "Probably."

"She seems to know quite a bit about what's been going on . . ."

"Very likely she does."

"Let's grab her!" said Trigger. "We can do it quietly. And she's too big to be mind-blocked. We'd get part of the answer. Perhaps all of it!"

Something flared briefly in the Commissioner's small gray eyes. He reached over and patted her knee.

"You're a girl after my own heart, Trigger girl," he said. "I'm for it. But half the Council would have fainted dead away if they'd heard you make that suggestion!"

"They're as touchy as that?" she asked, disappointed.

"Yes—and you can't quite blame them. Fumbles could be pretty bad. When it comes to someone around Lyad's level, our own group is restricted to defensive counteraction. If we get evidence against her, it'll be up to the diplomats to decide what's to be done about it. Tactfully. We wouldn't be further involved."

Trigger nodded, watching him. "Go on."

"Well, defensive counteraction can cover a lot of things, of course. If we actually run into the First Lady while we're engaged in it, we'll hold her—as long as we can. And from all accounts, now that she's showed up to take personal charge of things around here, we can expect some very fast, very direct action from Lyad."

"How fast?"

"My own guess," said the Commissioner, "would be around a week. If she hasn't moved by then, we might help things along a little."

"Make a few of those openings for her, eh? Well, that doesn't sound too bad." Trigger reflected. "Then there's Point Number Two," she said.

"What's that?"

She grimaced. "I'm not real keen on it," she confessed, "but I think we'd better do something about that interview with Whatzzit I ducked out of. If they still want to talk to me—"

"They do. Very much so."

"What's that business about their saying it was okay now for me to go on to Manon?"

Commissioner Tate tugged gently at his left ear

lobe. "Frankly," he said, "that's something that shook me a little."

"Shook you? Why?"

"It's that matter of experts coming in grades. The upper ranks in the Psychology Service are extremely busy people, I understand. After your first interview we were shifted upward promptly. A couple of middling high-bracket investigators took over for a while. But after the fourth interview I was told I'd have to bring you to the Hub to let somebody really competent handle the next stage of whatever they've been doing. They said they couldn't spare anybody of that caliber for a trip to Manon."

"Was that the real reason we went to Maccadon?" Trigger asked, startled.

"Sure. But we still hadn't got anywhere near the Service's top level then. As I get it, their topnotchers don't spend much time on individual cases. They keep busy with things on the scale of our more bothersome planetary cultures—and there are supposed to be only a hundred or so of them in that category. So I was more than a little surprised when the Service informed me finally one of those people was coming to Maccadon to conduct your ninth interview."

"One of the real eggheads!" Trigger smiled nervously. "And then I just took off! They can't have too good an opinion of me at the moment, you know."

"Apparently that didn't upset them in the least," the Commissioner said. "They told me to stay calm and make sure you got to Manon all right. Then they said they had a ship operating in this area, and they'd route it over to Manon after you arrived here."

"A ship?" Trigger asked.

"I've seen a few of their ships—they looked like oversized flying mountains. Camouflage jobs. What they actually are is spacegoing superlaboratories, from what I've heard. This one has a couple of those topnotchers on board, and one of them will take you on. It's due here in a day or so."

Trigger had paled somewhat. "You know," she said, "I feel a little shaken myself now."

"I'm not surprised," said the Commissioner.

She shook her head. "Well if they're topnotchers, they must know what they're doing." She gave him a smile. "Looks like I'm something extremely unusual! Like a bothersome planetary culture . . . Weak joke," she added.

The Commissioner ignored the weak joke. "There's another thing," he said thoughtfully.

"What's that?"

"When I mentioned your reluctance about being interviewed, they told me not to worry about it—that you wouldn't try to duck out again. That's why I was surprised when you brought up the matter of the interview yourself just now."

"Now that is odd," Trigger admitted after a pause. "How would they know?"

"Right," he said. He sighed. "Guess we're both a little out of our depth there. I've come close to getting impatient with them a few times—had the feeling they were stalling me off and holding back information. But presumably they do know what they're doing." He glanced at his watch. "That hour's about up now, by the way."

"Well, if there's something else that should be discussed I can break my dinner date," Trigger said, somewhat reluctantly. "I had a chance to talk with Brule at the spaceport for a while, when we came in this morning."

"I wasn't suggesting that," said Holati. "There still are things to be discussed, but a few hours one way or the other won't make any difference. We'll get together again around lunch tomorrow. Then you'll be filled in pretty well on all the main points of this business."

Trigger nodded. "Fine."

"What I had in mind right now was that the Service people suggested having you look over their last report on you after your arrival. You'd have just enough time for that before going to keep your date. Care to do it?"

"I certainly would!" Trigger said.

The transmitter signaled for attention while she was studying the report. Holati Tate went off to answer it. The report was rather lengthy, and Trigger was still going over it when he got back. He sat down again and waited.

When she looked up finally, he asked, "Can you make much sense of it?"

"Not very much," Trigger admitted. "It just states what seems to have happened. Not how or why. Apparently they did get me to develop a total recall of that knocked-out period in the last interview—I even reported hearing you and Doctor Azol moving around and talking in the next compartment."

He nodded. "I remember enough of my conversation with Azol to be able to verify that part of it."

"Then, some time before I actually fell down," said Trigger, "I was apparently already in that mysterious coma. Getting deeper into it. It started when I walked away from Mantelish's group, without having any particular reason for doing it. I just walked. Then I was in another compartment by myself and still walking, and the stuff kept getting deeper, until I lost physical control of myself and fell down. Then I lay there a while until you came down that aisle and saw me. And after you'd picked me up and put me in that chair—just like that, everything clears up! Except that I don't remember what happened and think I've just left Mantelish to go looking for you. I don't even wonder how I happen to be sitting there in a chair!"

The Commissioner smiled briefly. "That's right. You didn't."

Her slim fingers tapped the pages of the report, the green stone in the ring he'd given her to wear reflecting little flashes of light. "They seem quite positive that nobody else came near me during that period. And that nobody had used a hypnospray on me or shot a hypodermic pellet into me—anything like that—before the seizure or whatever it was came on. How do you suppose they could be so sure of that?"

"I wouldn't know," Holati said. "But I think we might as well assume they're right."

"I suppose so. What it seems to boil down to is they're saying I was undergoing something like a very much slowed-down, very profound emotional shock—source still undetermined, but profound enough to knock me completely out for a while. Only they also say that—for a whole list of reasons—it couldn't possibly have been an emotional shock after all! And when the effect left, it went instantaneously. That would be just the reverse to the pattern of an emotional shock, wouldn't it?"

"Yes," he said. "That occurred to me too, but it didn't explain anything to me. Possibly it's explained something to the Psychology Service."

"Well," Trigger said, "it's certainly all very odd. Very disagreeable, too!" She laid the report down on the arm of her chair and looked at the Commissioner. "Guess I'd better run now," she said. "But there was something you said before that made me wonder. There was really very little of Doctor Azol left after that plasmoid got through with him."

He nodded. "True."

"It wasn't Azol, was it?"

"No."

"Man, oh, man!" Trigger jumped up, bent over his chair and gave him a quick peck on an ear tip. "If I ask one more question, we'll be sitting here the next two hours. I'll run instead! See you around lunchtime, Commissioner!"

"Right, Trigger," he said, getting up.

He closed the door behind her and went back to the transmitter. He looked rather unhappy.

"Yes?" said a voice in the transmitter.

"She just left," Commissioner Tate said. "Get on the beam and stay there!"

18

"WELL," TRIGGER SAID, regarding Brule critically, "I just meant to say that you're getting the least little bit plump here and there, under all that tan. I'll admit it doesn't show yet when you're dressed."

Brule smiled tolerantly. In silver swimming trunks and sandals, he was obviously a very handsome hunk of young man, and he knew it. So did Trigger. So did a quartet of predatory young females eyeing them speculatively from a table only twenty feet away.

"I've come swimming here quite a bit since they opened the Center," he said. He flexed his right arm and regarded his biceps complacently. "That's just streamlined muscle you're looking at, sweetheart!"

Trigger reached over and poked the biceps with a finger tip. "Muscle?" she said, smiling at him. "It dents. See?"

He clasped his other hand over hers and squeezed it lightly.

"Oh, golly, Brule!" she said happily. "I'm so glad I'm back!"

He gave her the smile. "You're not the only glad one!"

She looked around, humming softly. They were having dinner in one of the Grand Commerce Center's restaurants. This one happened to be beneath the surface of the artificial swimming lake installed in the Center—a giant grotto surrounded by green-gold chasms of water on every side. Underwater swimmers and bottom walkers moved past beyond the wide windows. A streak of silvery swiftness against a dark red canyon wall before her was trying to keep away from a trio of pursuing spear fishermen. Even the lake fish were Hub imports, advertised as such by the Center.

Her eyes widened suddenly. "Hey!" she said.

"What?"

"That group of people up there!"

Brule looked. "What about them?"

"No suits, you idiot!"

He grinned. "Oh, a lot of them do that. Okay by Federation law, you know. And seeing Manon's so close to becoming open Federation territory, we haven't tried to enforce minor Precol regulations much lately."

"Well—" Trigger began. He was still smiling. "Have you been doing it?" she inquired suspiciously.

"Swimming in the raw? Certainly. Depends on

the company. If you weren't such a little prude, I'd
have suggested it tonight. Want to try it later?"

Trigger colored. Prude again, she thought.
"Nope," she said. "There are limits."

He patted her cheek. "On you it would look
cute."

She shook her head, aware of a small fluster of
guilt. There had been considerably less actual
coverage in the Beldon costume than there was in
the minute two-piece counterpart to Brule's silver
trunks she wore at the moment. She'd have to tell
Brule about the Beldon stunt, since it was more
than likely he'd hear about it from others—
Nelauk Pluly, for one.

But not now. Things were getting just a little
delicate along that line at the moment.

"Leave us change the subject, pig," she said
cheerfully. "Tell me what else you've been doing
besides acquiring a gorgeous tan."

A couple of hours later, things began to get
delicate again. Same subject. Trigger had been
somewhat startled at the spaceport when Brule
told her he had shifted his living quarters to a
Center apartment, and that a large number of Precol's executives were taking similar liberties.
Holati's stand-in, Acting Commissioner Chelly,
apparently hadn't been too successful at keeping
up personnel discipline.

She hadn't said anything. It was true that
Manon was still a precolonial planet only as a
technicality. They didn't know quite as much
about it as they had to know before it could be

officially released for unrestricted settling, but by
now there was considerable excuse for loosening
up on many of the early precautionary measures.
For one thing, there were just so many Hub people
around nowadays that it would have been a practical impossibility to enforce all Precol rules.

What bothered her mainly about the business of
Brule's Center apartment was that it might make
the end of the evening less pleasant than she
wanted it to be. Brule had become the least bit
swacked. Not at all offensively, but he tended to
get pretty ambitious then. And during the past
few hours she'd noticed that something had
changed in his attitude toward her. He'd always
been confident of himself when it came to wom-
en, so it wasn't that. It was perhaps, Trigger
thought, like an unspoken ultimatum along those
lines. And she'd felt herself freezing up a little in
response to the thought.

The apartment was very beautiful. Nelauk, she
guessed. Or somebody else like that. Brule's taste
was good, but he simply wouldn't have thought of
a lot of the details here. Neither, Trigger conceded, would she. Some of the details looked
pretty expensive.

He came back into the living room in a dressing
gown, carrying a couple of drinks. It was going to
get awkward, all right.

"Like it?" he asked, waving a hand around.

"It's beautiful," Trigger said honestly. She
smiled. She sipped at the drink and placed it on
the arm of her chair. "Somebody like an interior
decorator help you with it?"

Brule laughed and sat down opposite her with his drink. The laugh had sounded the least bit annoyed. "You're right," he said. "How did you guess?"

"You never went in for art exactly," she said. "This room is a work of art."

He nodded. He didn't look annoyed any more. He looked smug. "It is, isn't it?" he said. "It didn't even cost so very much. You just have to know how, that's all."

"Know how about what?" Trigger asked.

"Know how to live," Brule said. "Know what it's all about. Then it's easy."

He was looking at her. The smile was there. The warm, rich voice was there. All the old charm was there. It was Brule. And it wasn't. Trigger realized she was twisting her hands together. She looked down at them. The little jewel in the ring Holati Tate had given her to wear blinked back with crimson gleamings.

Crimson!

She drew a long, slow breath.

"Brule," she said.

"Yes?" said Brule. At the edge of her vision she saw the smile turn eager.

Trigger said, "Give me the plasmoid." She raised her eyes and looked at him. He'd stopped smiling.

Brule looked back at her a long time. At least it seemed a long time to Trigger. The smile suddenly returned.

"What's that supposed to mean?" he asked, almost plaintively. "If it's a joke, I don't get it."

"I just said," Trigger repeated carefully, "give me the plasmoid. The one you stole."

Brule took a swallow of his drink and put the glass down on the floor. "Aren't you feeling well?" he asked solicitously.

"Give me the plasmoid."

"Honestly, Trigger." He shook his head. He laughed. "What are you talking about?"

"A plasmoid. The one you took. The one you've got here."

Brule stood up. He studied her face, blinking, puzzled. Then he laughed, richly. "Trigger, I've fed you one drink too many! I never thought you'd let me do it. Be sensible now—if I had a plasmoid here, how could you tell?"

"I can tell. Brule, I don't know how you took it or why you took it. I don't really care." And that was a lie, Trigger thought dismally. She cared. "Just give it to me, and I'll put it back. We can talk about it afterwards."

"Afterwards," Brule said. The laugh came again, but it sounded a little hollow. He moved a step toward her, stopped again, hands on his hips. "Trigger," he said soberly, "if I've ever done anything you mightn't approve of, it was done for both of us. You realize that, don't you?"

"I think I do," Trigger said warily. "Yes. Give it to me, Brule."

Brule leaped forward. She slid sideways out of the chair to the floor as he leaped. She was crying inside, she realized vaguely. Brule was going to kill her now, if he could.

She caught his left foot with both hands as he came down, and twisted viciously.

Brule shouted something. His red, furious face swept by above. He thumped to the floor beside her, one leg flung across her thighs, gripping.

In colonial school Brule had received the same basic training in unarmed combat that Trigger had. He was close to eighty pounds heavier than Trigger, and it was still mostly muscle. But it was nearly four years now since he had bothered himself with drills.

And he hadn't been put through Mihul's advanced students' courses lately.

He stayed conscious a little less than nine seconds.

The plasmoids were in a small electronic safe built into a music cabinet. The stamp to the safe was in Brule's billfold.

There were three of them, about the size of mice, starfish-shaped lumps of translucent, hard, colorless jelly. They didn't move.

Trigger laid them in a row on the polished surface of a small table, and blinked at them for a moment from a streaming left eye. The right eye was swelling shut. Brule had got in one wild wallop somewhere along the line. She picked up a small jar, emptied some spicy-smelling, crumbly contents out on the table, dropped the plasmoids inside, closed the jar and left the apartment with it. Brule was just beginning to stir and groan.

Commissioner Tate hadn't retired yet. He let

her in without a word. Trigger put the jar down on a table.

"Three of your nuts and bolts in there," she said.

He nodded. "I know."

"I thought you did," said Trigger. "Thanks for the quick cure. But right at the moment I don't like you very much, Holati. We can talk about that in the morning."

"All right," said the Commissioner. He hesitated. "Anything that should be taken care of before then?"

"It's been taken care of," Trigger said. "One of our employees has been moderately injured. I dialed the medics to go pick him up. They have. Good night."

"You might let me do something for that eye," he said.

Trigger shook her head. "I've got stuff in my quarters."

She locked herself into her quarters, got out a jar of quick-heal and anointed the eye and a few other minor bruises. She put the jar away, made a mechanical check of the newly installed anti-intrusion devices, dimmed the lights and climbed into her bunk. For the next twenty minutes she wept violently. Then she fell asleep.

An hour or so later, she turned over on her side and said without opening her eyes, "Come, Fido!"

The plasmoid purse appeared just above the surface of the bunk between Trigger's pillow and the wall. It dropped with a small thump and stood balanced uncertainly. Trigger slept on.

Five minutes after that, the purse opened itself. A little later again, Trigger suddenly shifted her shoulder uneasily, frowned and made a little half-angry, half-whimpering cry. Then her face smoothed out. Her breathing grew quiet and slow.

Major Heslet Quillan of the Subspace Engineers came breezing into Manon Planet's spaceport very early in the morning. A Precol aircar picked him up and let him out on a platform of the Headquarters dome near Commissioner Tate's offices. Quillan was handed on toward the offices through a string of underlings and reached the door just as it opened and Trigger Argee stepped through.

He grasped her cordially by the shoulders and cried out a cheery hello. Trigger made a soft growling sound in her throat. Her left hand chopped right, her right hand chopped left. Quillan grunted and let go.

"What's the matter?" he inquired, stepping back. He rubbed one arm, then the other.

Trigger looked at him, growled again, walked past him, and disappeared through another door, her back very straight.

"Come in, Quillan," Commissioner Tate said from within the office.

Quillan went in and closed the door behind him. "What did I do?" he asked bewilderedly.

"Nothing much," said Holati. "You just share the misfortune of being a male human being. At the moment, Trigger's against 'em. She blew up the Brule Inger setup last night."

"Oh!" Quillan sat down. "I never did like that idea much," he said.

The Commissioner shrugged. "You don't know the girl yet. If I'd hauled Inger in, she would never have really forgiven me for it. I had to let her handle it herself. Actually she understands that."

"How did it go?"

"Her cover reported it was one hell of a good fight for some seconds. If you'd looked closer, you might have just spotted the traces of the shiner Inger gave her. It was a beaut last night."

Quillan went white.

"But if you're thinking of having a chat with Inger re that part of it," the Commissioner went on, "forget it." He glanced at a report from the medical department on his desk. "Dislocated shoulder . . . broken thumb . . . moderate concussion. And so on. It was the throat punch that finished the matter. He can't talk yet. We'll call it square."

Quillan grunted. "What are you going to do with him now?"

"Nothing," Holati said. "We know his contacts. Why bother? He'll resign end of the month."

Quillan cleared his throat and glanced at the door. "I suppose she'll want him put up for rehabilitation—seemed pretty fond of him."

"Relax, son," said the Commissioner. "Trigger's an individualist. If Inger goes up for rehabilitation, it will be because he wants it. And he doesn't, of course. Being a slob suits him fine.

He's just likely to be more cautious about it in future. So we'll let him go his happy way. Now—let's get down to business. How does Pluly's yacht harem stack up?"

A reminiscent smile spread slowly over Quillan's face. He shook his head. "Awesome, brother!" he said. "Plain awesome!"

"Pick up anything useful?"

"Nothing definite. But whenever Belchy comes out of the esthetic trances, he's a worried man. Count him in."

"For sure?"

"Yes."

"All right. He's in. Crack the Aurora yet?"

"No," said Quillan. "The girls are working on it. But the Ermetyne keeps a mighty taut ship and a mighty disciplined crew. We'll have a couple of those boys wrapped up in another week. No earlier."

"A week might be soon enough," said the Commissioner. "It also might not."

"I know it," said Quillan. "But the Aurora does look a little bit obvious, doesn't she?"

"Yes," Holati Tate admitted. "Just a little bit."

19

By LUNCHTIME, TRIGGER WAS acting almost cordial again. "I've got the Precol job lined up," she reported to Holati Tate. "I'll handle it like I used to, whenever I can. When I can't, the kids will shift in automatically." The kids were the five assistants among whom her duties had been divided in her absence.

"Major Quillan called me up to Mantelish's lab around ten," she went on. "They wanted to see Repulsive, so I took him up there. Then it turned out Mantelish wanted to take Repulsive along on a field trip this afternoon."

Holati looked startled. "He can't do that, and he knows it!" He reached for the desk transmitter.

"Don't bother, Commissioner. I told Mantelish I'd been put in charge of Repulsive, and that he'd lose an arm if he tried to walk out of the lab with him."

Holati cleared his throat. "I see! How did Mantelish react?"

"Oh, he huffed a bit. Like he does. Then he calmed down and agreed he could get by without Repulsive out there. So we stood by while he measured and weighed the thing, and so on. After that he got friendly and said you'd asked him to fill me in on current plasmoid theory."

"So I did," said Holati. "Did he?"

"He tried, I think. But it's like you say. I got lost in about three sentences and never caught up." She looked curiously at the Commissioner. "I didn't have a chance to talk to Major Quillan alone, so I'm wondering why Mantelish was told the I-Fleets in the Vishni area are hunting for planets with plasmoids on them. I thought you felt he was too woolly-minded to be trusted."

"We couldn't keep that from him very well," Holati said. "He was the boy who thought of it."

"You didn't have to tell him they'd found some possibles did you?"

"He did, unfortunately. He's had those plasmoid detectors of his for about a month, but he didn't happen to think of mentioning them. The reason he was to come back to Manon originally was to sort over the stuff the Fleets have been sending back here. It's as weird a collection of low-grade life-forms as I've ever seen, but not plasmoid. Mantelish went into a temper and wanted to know why the idiots weren't using detectors."

"Oh, Lord!" Trigger said.

"That's what it's like when you're working with

him," said the Commissioner. "We started making up detectors wholesale and rushing them out there, but the new results haven't come in yet."

"Well, that explains it." Trigger looked down at the desk a moment, then glanced up and met the Commissioner's eye. She colored slightly.

"Incidentally," she said, "I did take the opportunity to apologize to Major Quillan for clipping him a couple this morning. I shouldn't have done that."

"He didn't seem offended," said Holati.

"No, not really," she agreed.

"And I explained to him that you had a very good reason to feel disturbed."

"Thanks," said Trigger. "By the way, was he really a smuggler at one time? And a hijacker?"

"Yes—very successful at it. It's excellent cover for some phases of Intelligence work. As I heard it, though, Quillan happened to scramble up one of the Hub's nastier dope rings in the process, and was broken two grades in rank."

"Broken?" Trigger said. "Why?"

"Unwarranted interference with a political situation. The Scouts are rough about that. You're supposed to see those things. Sometimes you don't. Sometimes you do and go ahead anyway. They may pat you on the back privately, but they also give you the axe."

"I see," she said. She smiled.

"Just how far did we get in bringing you up to date yesterday?" the Commissioner asked.

"The remains that weren't Doctor Azol," Trigger said.

If it hadn't been for the funny business with Trigger, Holati said, he mightn't have been immediately skeptical about Doctor Azol's supposed demise by plasmoid during a thrombosis-induced spell of unconsciousness. There had been no previous indications that the U-League's screening of its scientists, in connection with the plasmoid find, might have been strategically loused up from the start.

But as things stood, he did look on the event with very considerable skepticism. Doctor Azol's death, in that particular form, seemed too much of a coincidence. For, beside himself, only Azol knew that another person already had suddenly and mysteriously lost consciousness on Harvest Moon. Only Azol therefore might expect that the Commissioner would quietly inform the official investigators of the preceding incident, thus cinching the accidental death theory in Azol's case much more neatly than the assumed heart attack had done.

The Commissioner went on from there to the reflection that if Azol had chosen to disappear, it might well have been with the intention of conveying important information secretly back to somebody waiting for it in the Hub. He saw to it that the remains were preserved, and that word of what could have happened was passed on to a high Federation official whom he knew to be trustworthy. That was all he was in a position to do, or interested in doing, himself. Security men presently came and took the supposed vestiges of Doctor Azol's body back to the Hub.

"It wasn't until some months later, when the works blew up and I was put on this job, that I heard any more about it," Holati Tate said. "It wasn't Azol. It was part of some unidentifiable cadaver which he'd presumably brought with him for just such a use. Anyway, they had Azol's gene patterns on record, and they didn't jibe."

His desk transmitter buzzed and Trigger took it on an earphone extension.

"Argee," she said. She listened a moment. "All right. Coming over." She stood up, replacing the earphone. "Office tangle," she explained. "Guess they feel I'm fluffing, now I'm back. I'll get back here as soon as it's straightened out. Oh, by the way."

"Yes?"

"The Psychology Service ship messaged in during the morning. It'll arrive some time tomorrow and wants a station assigned to it outside the system, where it won't be likely to attract attention. Are they really as huge as all that?"

"I've seen one or two that were bigger," the Commissioner said. "But not much."

"When they're stationed, they'll send someone over in a shuttle to pick me up."

The Commissioner nodded. "I'll check on the arrangements for that. The idea of the interview still bothering you?"

"Well, I'd sooner it wasn't necessary," Trigger admitted. "But I guess it is." She grinned briefly. "Anyway, I'll be able to tell my grandchildren some day that I once talked to one of the real egg heads!"

The Psychology Service woman who stood up
from a couch as Trigger came into the small
spaceport lounge next evening looked startlingly
similar to Major Quillan's Dawn City assistant,
Gaya. Standing, you could see that she was considerably more slender than Gaya. She had all of
Gaya's good looks.

"The name is Pilch," she said. She looked at
Trigger and smiled. It was a good smile, Trigger
thought; not the professional job she'd expected.
"And everyone who knows Gaya," she went on,
"thinks we must be twins."

Trigger laughed. "Aren't you?"

"Just first cousins." The voice was all right
too—clear and easy. Trigger felt herself relax
somewhat. "That's one reason they picked me to
come and get you. We're already almost ac-
quainted. Another is that I've been assigned to
take you through the preliminary work for your
interview after we get to the ship. We can chat a
bit on the way, and that should make it seem less
disagreeable. Boat's in the speedboat park over
there."

They started down a short hallway to the park
area. "Just how disagreeable is it going to be?"
Trigger asked.

"Not at all bad in your case. You're conditioned
to the processes more than you know. Your inter-
viewer will just pick up where the last job ended
and go on from there. It's when you have to work
down through barriers that you have a little trouble."

Trigger was still mulling that over as she

stepped ahead of Pilch into the smaller of two
needle-nosed craft parked side by side. Pilch followed her in and closed the lock behind them.
"The other one's a combat job," she remarked.
"Our escort. Commissioner Tate made very sure
we had one, too! She motioned Trigger to a low
soft seat that took up half the space of the tiny
room behind the lock, sat down beside her and
spoke at a wall pickup. "All set. Let's ride!"

Blue-green tinted sky moved past them in the
little room's viewer screen; then a tilted land-
scape flashed by and dropped back. Pilch winked
at Trigger. "Takes off like a scared yazong, that
boy! He'll race the combat job to the ship. About
those barriers. Supposing I told you something
like this. There's no significant privacy invasion
in this line of work. We go directly to the specific
information we're looking for and deal only with
that. Your private life, your personal thoughts,
remain secret, sacred and inviolate. What would
you say?"

"I'd say you're a liar," Trigger said promptly.

"Of course. That sort of thing is sometimes told
to nervous interviewees. We don't bother with it.
But now supposing I told you very sincerely that
no recording will be made of any little personal
glimpses we may get?"

"Lying again."

"Right again," said Pilch. "You've been
scanned about as thoroughly as anyone ever gets
to be outside of a total therapy. Your personal
secrets are already on record, and since I'm doing
most of the preparatory work with you, I've

studied all the significant-looking ones very closely. You're a pretty good person, for my money. All right?"

Trigger studied her face uncomfortably. Hardly all right, but . . .

"I guess I can stand it," she said. "As far as you're concerned, anyway." She hesitated. "What's the egghead like?"

"Old Cranadon?" said Pilch. "You won't mind her a bit, I think. Very motherly old type. Let's get through the preparations first, and then I'll introduce you to her. If you think it would make you more comfortable, I'll just stay around while she's working. I've sat in on her interviews before. How's that?"

"Sounds better," Trigger said. She did feel a good deal relieved.

They slid presently into a tunnel-like lock of the space vehicle Holati Tate had described as a flying mountain. From what Trigger could see of it in the guide lights on the approach, it did rather closely resemble a very large mountain of the craggier sort. They went through a series of lifts, portals and passages, and wound up in a small and softly lit room with a small desk, a very large couch, a huge wall-screen, and assorted gadgetry. Pilch sat down at the desk and invited Trigger to make herself comfortable on the couch.

Trigger lay down on the couch. She had a very brief sensation of falling gently through dimness.

Half an hour later she sat up on the couch. Pilch switched on a desk light and looked at her thoughtfully. Trigger blinked. Then her eyes widened, first with surprise, then in comprehension.

"Liar!" she said.

"Hm-m-m," said Pilch. "Yes."

"That *was* the interview!"

"True."

"Then you're the egghead!"

"Tcha!" said Pilch. "Well, I believe I can modestly describe myself as being like that. Yes. You're another, by the way. We're just smart about different things. Not so very different."

"You were smart about this," Trigger said. She swung her legs off the couch and regarded Pilch dubiously. Pilch grinned.

"Took most of the disagreeableness out of it, didn't it?"

"Yes," Trigger admitted, "it did. Now what do we do?"

"Now," said Pilch, "I'll explain."

The thing that had caught their attention was a quite simple process. It just happened to be a process the Psychology Service hadn't observed under those particular circumstances before.

"Here's what our investigators had the last time," Pilch said. "Lines and lines of stuff, of course. But here's a simple continuity which makes it clear. Your mother dies when you're six months old. Then there are a few nurses whom you don't like very much. Good nurses but frankly much too stupid for you, though you don't know that, and they don't either, naturally. Next, you're seven years old—a bit over—and there's a mud pond on the farm near Ceyce where you spend all your vacations. You just love that old mud pond."

Trigger laughed. "A smelly old hole, actually! Full of froggy sorts of things. I went out to that farm six years ago, just to look around it again. But you're right. I did love that mud pond, once."

"Right up to that seventh summer," Pilch said. "Which was the summer your father's cousin spent her vacation on the farm with you."

Trigger nodded. "Perhaps. I don't remember the time too well."

"Well," Pilch said, "she was a brilliant woman. In some ways. She was about the age your mother had been when she died. She was very good-looking. And she was nice! She played games with a little girl, sang to her. Told her stories. Cuddled her."

Trigger blinked. "Did she? I don't—"

"However," said Pilch, "she did not play games with, tell stories to, cuddle, etcetera, little girls who"—her voice went suddenly thin and edged—"come in all filthy and smelling from that dirty, slimy old mud pond!"

Trigger looked startled. "You know," she said, "I do believe I remember her saying that—just that way!"

"You remember it," said Pilch, "now. You never saw her again after that summer. Your father had good sense. He didn't marry her, as he apparently intended to do before he saw how she was going to be with you. You went back to your old mud pond just once more, on you next vacation. She wasn't there. What had you done? You waded around, feeling pretty sad. And you stepped on a sharp stick and cut your foot badly. Sort of a self-punishment."

She flipped over a few pages of some record on her desk. "Now before you start asking what's interesting about that, I'll run over a few crossed-in items. Age twelve. There's that Maccadon animal like a dryland jellyfish—a mingo, isn't it?—that swallowed your kitten."

"The mingo!" Trigger said. "I remember that. I killed it."

"Right. You kicked it apart and pulled out the kitten, but the kitten was dead and partly digested. You bawled all day and half the night about that."

"I might have, I suppose."

"You did. Now those are two centering points. There's other stuff connected with them. No need to go into details. As classes—you've stepped now and then on things that squirmed or squashed. Bad smells. Etcetera. How do you feel about plasmoids?"

Trigger wrinkled her nose. "I just think they're unpleasant things. All except—"

Oops! She checked herself.

"—Repulsive," said Pilch. "It's quite all right about Repulsive. We've been informed of that supersecret little item you're guarding. If we hadn't been told, we'd know now, of course. Go ahead."

"Well, it's odd!" Trigger remarked thoughtfully. "I just said I thought plasmoids were rather unpleasant. But that's the way I used to feel about them. I don't feel that way now."

"Except again," said Pilch, "for that little monstrosity on the ship. If it was a plasmoid. You rather suspect it was, don't you?"

Trigger nodded. "That would be pretty bad!"

"Very bad," said Pilch. "Plasmoids generally, you feel about them now as you feel about potatoes . . . rocks . . . neutral things like that?"

"That's about it," Trigger said. She still looked puzzled.

"We'll go over what seems to have changed your attitude there in a minute or so. Here's another thing—" Pilch paused a moment, then said, "Night before last, about an hour after you'd gone to bed, you had a very light touch of the same pattern of mental blankness you experienced on that plasmoid station."

"While I was asleep?" Trigger said, startled.

"That's right. Comparatively very light, very brief. Five or six minutes. Dream activity, etcetera, smooths out. Some blocking on various sense lines. Then, normal sleep until about five minutes before you woke up. At that point there may have been another minute touch of the same pattern. Too brief to be actually definable. A few seconds at most. The point is that this is a continuing process."

She looked at Trigger a moment. "Not particularly alarmed, are you?"

"No," said Trigger. "It just seems very odd." She added, "I got rather frightened when Commissioner Tate was first telling me what had been going on."

"Yes, I know."

20

Pɪʟᴄʜ ᴡᴀs sɪʟᴇɴᴛ ғᴏʀ sᴏᴍᴇ moments again, considering the wall-screen as if thinking about something connected with it. "Well, we'll drop that for now," she said finally. "Let me tell you what's been happening these months, starting with that first amensia-covered blankout on Harvest Moon. The Maccadon Colonial School has sound basic psychology courses, so there won't be much explaining to do. The connection between those incidents I mentioned and your earlier feeling of disliking plasmoids is obvious, isn't it?"

Trigger nodded.

"Good. When you got the first Service checkup at Commissioner Tate's demand, there was very little to go on. The amensia didn't lift immediately—not very unusual. The blankout might be interesting because of the circumstances. Otherwise the check showed you

were in a good deal better than normal condition.
Outside of total therapy processes—and I believe
you know that's a long haul—there wasn't much
to be done for you, and no particular reason to do
it. So an amensia-resolving process was initiated
and you were left alone for a while.

"Actually something already was going on at
the time, but it wasn't spotted until your next
check. What it's amounted to has been a relatively
minor but extremely precise and apparently purposeful therapy process. Your unconscious
memories of those groupings of incidents I was
talking about, along with various linked groupings, have gradually been cleared up. Emotion
has been drained away, fixed evaluations have
faded. Associative lines have shifted.

"Now that's nothing remarkable in itself. Any
good therapist could have done the same for you,
and much more rapidly. Say in a few hours' hard
work, spread over several weeks to permit pro-
gressive assimilation without conscious distur-
bances. The very interesting thing is that this or-
derly little process appears to have been going on
all by itself. And that just doesn't happen. You
disturbed now?"

Trigger nodded. "A little. Mainly I'm wondering why somebody wants me to not-dislike plasmoids."

"So am I wondering," said Pilch. "Somebody
does, obviously. And a very slick somebody it is.
We'll find out by and by. Incidentally, this particular part of the business has been concluded.
Apparently, somebody doesn't intend to make

you wild for plasmoids. It's enough that you don't dislike them."

Trigger smiled. "I can't see anyone making me wild for the things, whatever they tried!"

Pilch nodded. "Could be done," she said. "Rather easily. You'd be bats, of course. But that's very different from a simple neutralizing process like the one we've been discussing . . . Now here's something else. You were pretty unhappy about this business for a while. That wasn't somebody's fault. That was us. I'll explain.

"Your investigators could have interfered with the little therapy process in a number of ways. That wouldn't have taught them a thing, so they didn't. But on your third check they found something else. Again it wasn't in the least obtrusive; in someone else they mightn't have given it a second look. But it didn't fit at all with your major personality patterns. You wanted to stay where you were."

"Stay where I was?"

"In the Manon System."

"Oh!" Trigger flushed a little. "Well—"

"I know. Let's go on a moment. We had this inharmonious inclination. So we told Commissioner Tate to bring you to the Hub and keep you there, to see what would happen. And on Maccadon, in just a few weeks, you'd begun working that moderate inclination to be back in the Manon System up to a dandy first-rate compulsion."

Trigger licked her lips. "I—"

"Sure," said Pilch. "You had to have a good sensible reason. You gave yourself one."

"Well!"

"Oh, you were fond of that young man, all right. Who wouldn't be? Wonderful-looking lug. I'd go for him myself—till I got him on that couch, that is. But that was the first time you hadn't been able to stand a couple of months away from him. It was also the first time you'd started worrying about competition. You now had your justification. And we," Pilch said darkly, "had a fine, solid compulsion with no doubt very revealing ramifications to it to work on. Just one thing went wrong with that, Trigger. You don't have the compulsion any more."

"Oh?"

"You don't even," said Pilch, "have the original moderate inclination. Now one might have some suspicions there! But we'll let them ride for the moment."

She did something on the desk. The huge wallscreen suddenly lit up. A soft, amber-glowing plane of blankness, with a suggestion of receding depths within it.

"Last night, shortly before you woke up," Pilch said, "you had a dream. Actually you had a series of eight dreams during the night which seem pertinent here. But the earlier ones were rather vague preliminary structures. In one way and another, their content is included in this final symbol grouping. Let's see what we can make of them."

A shape appeared on the screen.

Trigger started, then laughed.

"What do you think of it?" Pilch asked.

"A little green man!" she said. "Well, it could

be a sort of counterpart to the little yellow thing on the ship, couldn't it? The good little dwarf and the very bad little dwarf."

"Could be," said Pilch. "How do you feel about the notion?"

"Good plasmoids and bad plasmoids?" Trigger shook her head. "No. It doesn't feel right."

"What else feels right?" Pilch asked.

"The farmer. The little old man who owned the farm where the mud pond was."

"Liked him, didn't you?"

"Very much! He knew a lot of fascinating things." She laughed again. "You know, I'd hate to have him find out—but that little green man also reminds me quite a bit of Commissioner Tate."

"I don't think he'd mind hearing it," Pilch said. She paused a moment. "All right—what's this?

A second shape appeared.

"A sort of caricature of a wild, mean horse," Trigger said. She added thoughtfully, "there was a horse like that on that farm, too. I suppose you know that?"

"Yes. Any thoughts about it?"

"No-o-o. Well, one. The little farmer was the only one who could handle that horse. It was mutated horse, actually—one of the Life Bank deals that didn't work out so well. Enormously strong. It could work forty-eight hours at a stretch without even noticing it. But it was just a plain mean animal."

" 'Crazy-mean,' " observed Pilch, "was the dream feeling about it."

Trigger nodded. "I remember I used to think it was crazy for that horse to want to go around kicking and biting things to pieces. Which was about all it really wanted to do. I imagine it was crazy, at that."

"You weren't ever in any danger from it yourself, were you?"

Trigger laughed. "I couldn't have got anywhere near it! You should have seen the kind of place the old farmer kept it when it wasn't working."

"I did," said Pilch. "Long, wide, straight-walled pit in the ground. Cover for shade, plenty of food, running water. He was a good farmer. Very high locked fence around it to keep little girls and anyone else from getting too close to his useful monster."

"Right," said Trigger. She shook her head. "When you people look into somebody's mind, you *look*!"

"We work at it," Pilch said. "Let's see what you can do with this one."

Trigger was silent for almost a minute before she said in a subdued voice, "I just get what it shows. It doesn't seem to mean anything?"

"What does it show?"

"Laughing giants stamping on a farm. A tiny sort of farm. It looks like it might be the little green man's farm. No, wait. It's not his! But it belongs to other little green people."

"How do you feel about that?"

"Well—I hate those giants!" Trigger said. "They're cruel. And they laugh about being cruel."

"Are you afraid of them?"

Trigger blinked at the screen for a few seconds. "No," she said in a low, sleepy voice. "Not yet."

Pilch was silent a moment. She said then, "One more."

Trigger looked and frowned. Presently she said, "I have a feeling that does mean something. But all I get is that it's the faces of two clocks. On one of them the hands are going around very fast. And on the other they go around slowly."

"Yes," Pilch said. She waited a little. "No other thought about those clocks? Just that they should mean something?"

Trigger shook her head. "That's all."

Pilch's hand moved on the desk again. The wall-screen went blank, and the light in the little room brightened slowly. Pilch's face was reflective.

"That will have to do for now," she said. "Trigger, this ship is working on an urgent job somewhere else. We'll have to go back and finish that job. But I'll be able to return to Manon in about ten days, and then we'll have another session. And I think that will get this little mystery cleared up."

"All of it?"

"All of it, I'd say. The whole pattern seems to be moving into view. More details will show up in the ten-day interval; and one more cautious boost then should bring it out in full."

Trigger nodded. "That's good news. I've been getting a little fed up with being a kind of walking enigma."

"Don't blame you at all," Pilch said, sounding almost exactly like Commissioner Tate. "Incidentally, you're a busy lady at present, but if you do have half an hour to spare from time to time, you might just sit down comfortably somewhere and listen to yourself thinking. The way things are going, that should bring quite a bit of information to view."

Trigger looked doubtful. "Listen to myself thinking?"

"You'll find yourself getting the knack of it rather quickly," Pilch said. She smiled. "Just head off in that general direction whenever you find the time, and don't work too hard at it. Are there any questions now before we start back to Manon?"

Trigger studied her a moment. "There's one thing I'd like to be sure about," she said. "But I suppose you people have your problems with Security too."

"Who doesn't?" said Pilch. "You're secure enough for me. Fire away."

"All right," Trigger said. "Commissioner Tate told me people like you don't work much with individuals."

"Not as much as we'd like to. That's true."

"So you wouldn't have been working with me if whatever has been going on weren't somehow connected with the plasmoids."

"Oh, yes, I would," said Pilch. "Or old Cranadon. Someone like that. We do give service as required when somebody has the good sense to ask for it. But obviously, we couldn't have dropped that other job just now and come to Manon to clear up some individual difficulty."

"So I am involved with the plasmoid mess?"

"You're right in the middle of it, Trigger. That's definite. In just what way is something we should be able to determine next session."

Pilch turned off the desk light and stood up. "I always hate to run off and leave something half finished like this," she admitted, "but I'll have to run anyway. The plasmoids are nowhere near the head of the Federation's problem list at present. They're just coming up mighty fast."

When Trigger reached her office next morning, she learned that the Psychology Service ship had moved out of the Manon area within an hour after she'd been returned to the Headquarters dome the night before.

None of the members of the plasmoid team were around. The Commissioner, who had a poor opinion of sleep, had been up for the past three hours; he'd left word Trigger could reach him, if necessary, in the larger of his two ships, parked next to the dome in Precol Port. Presumably he had the ship sealed up and was sitting in the transmitter cabinet, swapping messages with the I-Fleets in the Vishni area. He was likely to be at that for hours more. Professor Mantelish hadn't yet got back from his latest field trip, and Major Heslet Quillan just wasn't there.

It looked, Trigger decided, not at all reluctantly, like a good day to lean into her Precol job a bit. She told the staff to pitch everything not utterly routine her way, and leaned.

A set of vitally important reports from Precol's Giant Planet Survey Squad had been mislaid somewhere around Headquarters during yesterday's conferences. She soothed down the G P Squad and instituted a check search. A team of Hub ecologists, who had decided for themselves that outworld booster shots weren't required on Manon, called in nervously from a polar station to report that their hair was falling out. Trigger tapped the "Manon Fever" button on her desk, and suggested toupees.

The ecologists were displeased. A medical emergency skip-boat zoomed out of the dome to go to their rescue; and Trigger gave it its directions while dialing for the medical checker who'd allowed the visitors to avoid their shots. She had a brief chat with the young man, and left him twitching as the G P Squad came back on to inquire whether the reports had been found yet. Trigger began to get a comfortable feeling of being back in the good old groove.

Then a message from the Medical Department popped out on her desk. It was addressed to Commissioner Tate and stated that Brule Inger was now able to speak again.

Trigger frowned, sighed, bit her lip and thought a moment. She dialed for Doctor Leehaven. "Got your message," she said. "How's he doing?"

"All right," the old medic said.

"Has he said anything?"

"No. He's scared. If he could get up the courage, he'd ask for a personnel lawyer."

"Yes, I imagine. Tell him this then—from the Commissioner; not from me—there'll be no charges, but Precol expects his resignation, end of the month."

"That on the level?" Doctor Leehaven demanded incredulously.

"Of course."

The doctor snorted. "You people are getting soft-headed! But I'll tell him."

The morning went on. Trigger was suspiciously studying a traffic control note stating that a Devagas missionary shop had checked in and berthed at the spaceport when the G C Center's management called in to report, with some nervousness, that the Center's much advertised meteor-repellent roof had just flipped several dozen tons of falling Moon Belt material into the spaceport area. Most of it, unfortunately, had dropped around and upon a Devagas missionary ship.

"Not damaged, is it?" she asked.

The Center said no, but the Missionary Captain insisted on speaking to the person in charge here. To whom should they refer him?

"Refer him to me," Trigger said expectantly. She switched on the vision screen.

The Missionary Captain was a tall, gray-haired, gray-eyed, square-jawed man in uniform. After confirming to his satisfaction that Trigger was indeed in charge, he informed her in chilled tones

that the Devagas Union would hold her personally responsible for the unprovoked outrage unless an apology was promptly forthcoming.

Trigger apologized promptly. He acknowledged with a curt nod.

"The ship will now require new spacepaint,"
he pointed out, unmollifed.

Trigger nodded. "We'll send a work squad out
immediately."

"We," the Missionary Captain said, "shall
supervise the work. Only the best grade of paint
will be acceptable!"

"The very best only," Trigger agreed.

He gave her another curt nod, and switched off.

"Ass," she said. She cut in the don't-disturb
barrier and dialed Holati's ship.

It took a while to get through; he was probably
busy somewhere in the crate. Like Belchik Pluly,
the Commissioner, while still a very wealthy man,
would have been a very much wealthier one if it
weren't for his hobby. In his case, the hobby was
ships, of which he now owned two. What made
them expensive was that they had been tailor-
made to the Commissioner's specifications, and
his specifications had provided him with two
rather exact duplicates of the two types of Scout
fighting ships in which Squadron Commander
Tate had made space hideous for evildoers in the
good old days. Nobody as yet had got up the
nerve to point out to him that private battlecraft
definitely were not allowable in the Manon System.

He came on finally. Trigger told him about the Devagas. "Did you know those characters were in the area?" she asked.

The Commissioner knew. They'd stopped in at the system check station three days before. The ship was clean. "Their missionaries all go armed, of course; but that's their privilege by treaty. They've been browsing around and going hither and yon in skiffs. The ship's been in orbit till this morning."

"Think they're here in connection with whatever Balmordan is up to?" Trigger inquired.

"We'll take that for granted. Balmordan, by the way, attended a big shindig on the Pluly yacht yesterday. Unless his tail goofed, he's still up there, apparently staying on as a guest."

"Are you having these other Devagas watched?"

"Not individually. Too many of them, and they're scattered all over the place. Mantelish got back. He checked in an hour ago."

"You mean he's upstairs in his quarters now?" she asked.

"Right. He had a few more crates hauled into the lab, and he's locked himself in with them and spy-blocked the place. May have got something important, and may just be going through one of his secrecy periods again. We'll find out by and by. Oh, and here's a social note. The First Lady of Tranest is shopping in the Grand Commerce Center this morning."

"Well, that should boost business," said Trigger. "Are you going to be back in the dome by lunchtime?"

"I think so. Might have some interesting news, too, incidentally."

"Fine," she said. "See you then."

Twenty minutes later the desk transmitter gave her the "to be shielded" signal. Up went the barrier again.

Major Quillan's face looked out at her from the screen. He was, Trigger saw, in Mantelish's lab. Mantelish stood at a work bench behind him.

"Hi!" he said.

"Hi, yourself. When did you get in?"

"Just now. Could you pick up the whoosis-and-whichis and bring it up here?"

"Right now?"

"If you can," Quillan said. "The professor's got something new, he thinks."

"I'm on my way," said Trigger. "Take about five minutes."

She hurried down to her quarters, summoned Repulsive's container into the room and slung the strap over her shoulder.

Then she stood still a moment, frowning slightly. Something—something like a wisp of memory, something she *should* be remembering—was stirring in the back of her mind. Then it was gone.

Trigger shook her head. It would keep. She opened the door and stepped out into the hall.

She fell down.

As she fell, she tried to give the bag the send-off

squeeze, but she couldn't move her fingers. She couldn't move anything.

There were people around her. They were doing things swiftly. She was turned over on her back and, for a few moments then, she saw her own face smiling down at her from just a few feet away.

21

SHE WAS, SUDDENLY, IN A large room, well lit, with elaborate furnishings—sitting leaned back in a soft chair before a highly polished little table. On the opposite side of the table two people sat looking at her with expressions of mild surprise. One of them was Lyad Ermetyne. The other was a man she didn't know.

The man glanced aside at Lyad. "Very fast snap-back!" he said. He looked again at Trigger. He was a small man with salt-and-pepper hair, a deeply lined face, beautiful liquid-black eyes.

"Very!" Lyad said. "We must remember that. Hello, Trigger!"

"Hello," Trigger said. Her glance went once around the room and came back to Lyad's amiably observant face. Repulsive's container was nowhere around. There seemed to be nobody else in the room. An ornamental ComWeb stood

against one wall. Two of the walls were covered
with heavy hangings, and a great gold-brocaded
canopy bellied from the ceiling. No doors or portals in sight; they might be camouflaged, or behind those hangings. Any number of people
could be in call range—and a few certainly must
be watching her right now, because that small
man was no rough-and-tumble type.

The small man was regarding her with something like restrained amusement.

"A cool one," he murmured. "Very cool!"

Trigger looked at him a moment, then turned
her eyes back to Lyad. She didn't feel cool. She felt
tense and scared cold. This was probably very
bad!

"What did you want to see me about?" she
asked.

Lyad smiled. "A business matter. Do you know
where you are?"

"Not on your ship, First Lady."

The light-amber eyes barely narrowed. But
Lyad had become, at that moment, very alert.

"Why do you think so?" she asked pleasantly.

"This room," said Trigger. "You don't gush, I
think. What was the business matter?"

"In a moment," Lyad said. She smiled again.
"Where else might you be?"

Trigger thought she could guess. But she didn't
intend to. Not out loud. She shrugged. "It's no
place I want to be." She settled back a little in her
chair. Her right hand brushed the porgee pouch.

The porgee pouch.

It would have been like the Ermetyne to investigate the pouch carefully, take out the gun and put the pouch back. But they might not have.

Somebody was bound to be watching. She couldn't find out—not until the instant after she decided to try the Denton.

"I can believe that," Lyad said. "Forgive me the discourtesy of so urgent an invitation, Trigger. A quite recent event made it seem necessary. As to the business—as a start, this gentleman is Doctor Veetonia. He is an investigator of extraordinary talents along his line. At the moment, he is a trifle tired because of the very long hours he worked last night."

Doctor Veetonia turned his head to look at her. "I did, First Lady? Well, that does explain this odd weariness. Did I work well?"

"Splendidly," Lyad assured him. "You were never better, Doctor."

He nodded, smiled vaguely and looked back at Trigger. "This must go, too, I suppose?"

"I'm afraid it must," Lyad said.

"A great pity!" Doctor Veetonia said. "A great pity. It would have been a pleasant memory. This very cool one!" The vague smile shifted in the lined face again. "You are so beautiful, child," he told Trigger, "in your anger and terror and despair. And above it still the gauging purpose, the strong, quick thinking. You will not give in easily. Oh, no! Not easily at all. First Lady," Doctor Veetonia said plaintively, "I should like to remember this one! It should be possible, I think."

Small, icy fingers were working up and down Trigger's spine. The Ermetyne gave her a light wink.

"I'm afraid it isn't, Doctor," she said. "There are such very important matters to be discussed. Besides, Trigger Argee and I will come to an amicable agreement very quickly."

"No." Doctor Veetonia's face had turned very sullen.

"No?" said Lyad.

"She will agree to nothing. Any fool can see that. I recommend, then, a simple chemical approach. Your creatures can handle it. Drain her. Throw her away. I will have nothing to do with the matter."

"Oh, but Doctor!" the Ermetyne protested. "That would be so crude. And so very uncertain. Why, we might be here for hours still!"

He shook his head.

Lyad smiled. She stroked the lined cheek with light finger tips. "Have you forgotten the palace at Hamal Lake?" she asked. "The great library? The laboratories? Haven't I been very generous?"

Doctor Veetonia turned his face toward her. He smiled thoughtfully.

"Now that is true!" he admitted. "For the moment I did forget." He looked back at Trigger. "The First Lady gives," he told her, "and the First Lady takes away. She has given me wealth and much leisure. She takes from me now and then a memory. Very skillfully, since she was my pupil. But still the mind must be dim by a little each time it is done."

His face suddenly grew concerned. He looked at Lyad again. "Two more years only!" he said. "In two years I shall be free to retire, Lyad?"

Lyad nodded. "That was our bargain, Doctor. You know I keep bargains."

Doctor Veetonia said, "Yes. You do. It is strange in an Ermetyne. Very well! I shall do it." He looked at Trigger's face. The black-liquid eyes blinked once or twice. "She is almost certain she is being watched," he said, "but she has been thinking of using the ComWeb. The child, I believe, is prepared to attack us at any opportune moment." He smiled. "Show her first why her position is hopeless. Then we shall see."

"Why, it's not in the least hopeless," Lyad said. "And please feel no concern about the Doctor, Trigger. His methods are quite painless and involve none of the indignities of a chemical investigation. If you are at all reasonable, we'll just sit here and talk for twenty minutes or so. Then you will tell me what sum you wish to have deposited for you in what bank, and you will be free to go."

"What will we talk about?" Trigger said.

"Well, for one," said the Ermetyne, "there is that rather handsome little purse you've been carrying about lately. My technicians inform me there may be some risk of damaging its contents if they attempt to force it open. We don't want that. So we'll talk a bit about the proper way of opening it." She gave Trigger her little smile. "And Doctor Veetonia will verify the accuracy of any statements made on the matter."

She considered. "Oh, and then I shall ask a few

questions. Not many. And you will answer them.
It really will be quite simple. But now let me tell
you why I so very much wanted to see you today.
We had a guest here last night. A gentleman
whom you've met—Balmordan. He was mind-
blocked on some quite important subjects, and
so—though the doctor and I were very patient and
careful—he died in the end. But before he died, he
had told me as much as I really needed to know
from him.

"Now with that information," she went on,
"and with the contents of your purse and with
another little piece of information, which you
possess, I shall presently go away. On Orado, a
few hours later, Tranest's ambassador will have a
quiet talk with some members of the Federation
Council. And that will be all, really." She smiled.
"No dramatic pursuit! No hue and cry! A few
treaties will be considerably revised. And the
whole hubbub about the plasmoids will be over."
She nodded. "Because they can be made to work,
you know. And very well!"

Doctor Veetonia hadn't looked away from Trigger while Lyad was speaking. He said now, "My
congratulations, First Lady! But the girl has not
been convinced in the least that she should cooperate. She may hope to be rescued before the
information you want can be forced from
her."

The Ermetyne sighed. "Oh, really now, Trigger!" she very nearly pouted. "Well, if I must
explain about that to you, too, I shall."

She considered a moment.

"Did you see your facsimile?"

Trigger nodded. "Very briefly."

Lyad smiled. "How she and my other people passed in and out of that dome, and how it happened that your room guards were found unconscious and were very hurriedly taken to the medical department's contagious ward, makes an amusing little story. But it would be too long in the telling just now. Your facsimile is one of Tranest's finest actresses. She's been studying and practicing being you for months. She knows where to go and what to do in that dome to avoid contact with people who know you too intimately. If it seems that discovery is imminent, she needs only a minute by herself to turn into an entirely different personality. So hours might pass without anyone even suspecting you were gone.

"But on the other hand," Lyad admitted fairly, "your double might be caught immediately or within minutes. She would not be conscious then, and I doubt your fierce little Commissioner would go to the unethical limits of dead-braining a live woman. If he did, of course, he would learn nothing from her.

"Let's assume, nevertheless, that for one reason and another your friends suspect me immediately, and only me. At the time you were being taken from the dome, I was observed leaving the Grand Commerce Center. I'd shopped rather freely; a number of fairly large crates and so forth were loaded into my speedboat. And we were observed returning to the Aurora."

"Not bad," Trigger admitted. "Another facsimile, I suppose?"

"Of course." The Ermetyne glanced at a small jeweled wrist watch. "Now the Aurora, if my orders were being followed, and they were, dived approximately five minutes ago—unless somebody who might be your wrathful rescuers approached her before that time, in which case she dived then. In either case, the dive was seen by the Commissioner's watchers; and the proper conclusions sooner or later will be drawn from that."

"Supposing they dive after her and run her down?" Trigger said.

"They might! The Aurora is not an easy ship to run down in subspace; but they might. After some hours. It would be of no consequence at all, would it?" The amber eyes regarded Trigger with very little expression for a moment. "How many hours or minutes do you think you could hold out here, Trigger Argee, if it became necessary to put on real pressure?"

"I don't know," Trigger admitted. She moistened her lips.

"I could give you a rather close estimate, I think," the Ermetyne said. "But forgive me for bringing up that matter. It was an unnecessary discourtesy. Let's assume instead that the rather clever people with whom you've been working are quite clever enough to see through all these little maneuverings. Let's assume further that they are even able to conclude immediately where you and I must be at the moment.

"We are, as it happens, on the Griffin, which is

Belchik Pluly's outsize yacht, and which is orbiting Manon at present. This room is on a sealed level of the yacht, where Belchik's private life normally goes on undisturbed. I persuaded him two days ago to clear out this section of it for my own use. There is only one portal entry to the level, and that entry is locked and heavily guarded at the moment. There are two portal exits. One of them opens into a special lock in which there is a small speedboat of mine, prepared to leave. It's a very fast boat. If there have been faster ones built in the Hub, I haven't heard of them yet. And it can dive directly from the lock."

She smiled at Trigger. "You have the picture now, haven't you? If your friends decide to board the Griffin, they'll be able to do it without too much argument. After all, we don't want to be blown up accidentally. But they'll have quite a time working their way into this level. If a boarding party is reported, we'll just all quietly go away together with no fuss or hurry. I guarantee that no one is going to trace or overtake that boat. You see?"

"Yes," Trigger said disconsolately, slumping back a little. Her right hand dropped to her lap. Well, she thought, last chance!

Doctor Veetonia frowned. "First—" he began.

Trigger slapped the porgee pouch. And the Denton's soundless blast slammed the talented investigator back and over in his chair.

"Gun," Trigger explained unnecessarily.

The Ermetyne's face had turned white with

shock. She flicked a glance down at the man, then
looked back at Trigger.

"There're guns on me too, I imagine," Trigger
said. "But this one goes off very easily, First Lady!
It would take hardly any jolt at all."

Lyad nodded slightly. "They're no fools! They
won't risk shooting. Don't worry." Her voice was
careful but quite even. A tough cookie, as the
Commissioner had remarked.

"We won't bother about them at the moment,"
Trigger said. "Let's stand up together."

They stood up.

"We'll stay about five feet apart," Trigger went
on. "I don't know if you're the gun-grabbing
type."

The Ermetyne almost smiled. "I'm not!" she
said.

"No point in taking chances," Trigger said.
"Five feet." She gave Doctor Veetonia a quick
glance. He did look very unpleasantly dead.

"We'll go over to that ComWeb in a moment,"
she told Lyad. "I imagine you wouldn't have left it
on open circuit?"

Lyad shook her head. "Calls go through the
ship's communication office."

"Your own people on duty there?"

"No. Pluly's"

"Will they take your orders?"

"Certainly!"

"Can they listen in?" Trigger asked.

"Not if we seal the set here."

Trigger nodded. "You'll do the talking," she
said. "I'll give you Commissioner Tate's personal

number. Tell them to dial it. The Precol transmitters pick up ComWeb circuits. Switch on the screen after the call is in; he'll want to see me. When he comes on, just tell him what's happened, where we are, what the layout is. He's to come over with a squad to get us. I won't say much, if anything. I'll just keep the gun on you. If there's any fumble, we both get it."

"There won't be any fumble, Trigger," Lyad said.

"All right. Let's set up the rest of it before we move. After the Commissioner signs off, he'll be up here in three minutes flat. Or less. How about this ship's officers—do they take your orders too?"

"With the obvious exception of yourself," Lyad said, "everyone on the Griffin takes my orders at the moment."

"Then just tell whoever's in charge of the yacht to let the squad in before there's any shooting. The Commissioner can get awfully short-tempered. Then get the guards away from that entry portal. That's for their own good."

The Ermetyne nodded. "Will do."

"All right. That covers it, I think."

They looked at each other for a moment.

"With the information you got from Balmordan," Trigger remarked, "you should still be able to make a very good dicker with the Council, First Lady. I understand they're very eager to get the plasmoid mess straightened out quietly."

Lyad lifted one shoulder in a brief shrug. "Perhaps," she said.

"Let's move!" said Trigger.

They walked toward the ComWeb rather edgily, not very fast, not very slow, Trigger four or five steps behind. There had been no sound from the walls and no other sign of what must be very considerable excitement nearby. Trigger's spine kept tingling. A needlebeam and a good marksman could pluck away the Denton and her hand along with it, without much real risk to Ermetyne. But probably even the smallest of risks was more than the Tranest people would be willing to take when the First Lady's person was involved.

Lyad reached the ComWeb and stopped. Trigger stopped too, five feet away. "Go ahead," she said quietly.

Lyad turned to face her. "Let me make one last—well, call it an appeal," she said. "Don't be an overethical fool, Trigger Argee! The arrangement I've planned will do no harm to anybody. Come in with me, and you can write your own ticket for the rest of your life."

"No ticket," Trigger said. She waggled the Denton slightly. "Go ahead! You can talk to the Council later."

Lyad shrugged resignedly, turned again and reached toward the ComWeb.

Trigger might have relaxed just a trifle at that moment. Or perhaps there was some other cue that Pilli could pick up. There came no sound from the ceiling canopy. What she caught was a sense of something moving above her. Then the great golden bulk landed with a terrifying lightness on the thick carpet between Lyad and herself.

The eyeless nightmare head wasn't three feet from her own.

The lights in the room went out.

Trigger flung herself backwards, rolled six feet to one side, stood up, backed away and stopped again.

22

THE BLACKNESS IN THE ROOM was complete. She spun
the Denton to kill. There was silence around her
and then a soft rustling at some distance. It might
have been the cautious shuffle of a heavy foot over
thick carpeting. It stopped again. Where was
Lyad?

Her eyes shifted about, trying to pierce the
darkness. Black-light, she thought. She said,
"Lyad?"

"Yes?" Lyad's voice came easily in the dark.
She might be standing about thirty feet away, at
the far end of the room.

"Call your animal off," Trigger said quietly. "I
don't want to kill it." She began moving in the
direction from which Lyad had spoken.

"Pilli won't hurt you, Trigger," the Ermetyne
said. "He's been sent in to disarm you, that's all.
Throw your gun away and he won't even touch

you." She laughed. "Don't bother shooting in my
direction either! I'm not in the room any more."

Trigger stopped. Not because of what that hate-
ful, laughing voice had said. But because in the
dark about her a fresh, pungent smell was growing. The smell of ripe apples.

She moistened her lips. She whispered,
"Pilli—keep away!" Eyeless, the dark would
mean nothing to it. Seconds later, she heard the
thing breathing.

She faced the sound. It stopped for a moment,
then it came again. A slow animal breathing. It
seemed to circle slowly to her left. After a little it
stopped. Then it was coming toward her.

She said softly, almost pleadingly, "Pilli, stop!
Go back, Pilli!"

Silence. Pilli's odor lay heavily all around.
Trigger heard her blood drumming in her ears;
and, for a second then, she imagined she could
feel, like a tangible fog, the body warmth of the
monster standing in the dark before her.

It wasn't imagination. Something like a
smooth, heavy pad of rubber closed around her
right wrist and tightened terribly.

The Denton went off, two, three, four times
before she was jerked violently sideways, flung
away, sent stumbling backward against some low
piece of furniture and, sprawling, over it. The gun
was lost.

As she scrambled dizzily to her feet, Pilli
screamed. It was a thin, high, breathless sound
like the screaming of a terrified human child. It

stopped abruptly. And, as if that had been a signal, the room came full of light again.

Trigger blinked dazedly against the light. Virod stood before her, looking at her, a pair of opaque yellow goggles shoved up on his forehead. Black-light glasses. The golden-haired thing lay in a great shapeless huddle on the floor twenty feet to one side. She couldn't see her gun. But Virod held one, pointing at her.

Virod's other hand moved suddenly. Its palm caught the side of her face in a hefty slap. Trigger staggered dumbly sideways, got her balance and stood facing him again. She didn't even feel anger. Her cheek began to burn.

"Stop amusing yourself, Virod!" It was Lyad's voice. Trigger saw her then, standing in a small half-opened door across the room, where a wall hanging had been folded away.

"She appeared to be in shock, First Lady," Virod explained blandly.

"Is Pilli dead?"

"Yes. I have her gun. He got it from her." Virod slapped a pocket of his jacket, and some part of Trigger's mind noted the gesture and suddenly came awake.

"So I saw. Well—too bad about Pilli. But it was necessary. Bring her here then. And be reasonably gentle." Lyad still sounded unruffled. "And put that gun in a different pocket, fool, or she'll take it away from you."

She looked at Trigger impersonally as Virod brought her to the little door, his left hand clamped on her arm just above the elbow.

She said, "Too bad you killed my expert, Trigger! We'll have to use a chemical approach now. Flam and Virod are quite good at that, but there will be some pain. Not too much, because I'll be watching them. But it will be rather undignified, I'm afraid. And it will take a great deal longer."

Tanned, tall, sinuous Flam stood in the small room beyond the door. Trigger saw a long, low, plastic-covered table, clamps and glittering gadgetry. That would have been where cold-fish Balmordan hadn't been able to make it against his mind-blocks finally. There was still one thing she could do. The yacht was orbiting.

"That sort of thing won't be at all necessary!" she said shakily. Her voice shook with great ease, as if it had been practicing it all along.

"No?" Lyad said.

"You've won," Trigger said resignedly. "I'll play along now. I'll show you how to open that handbag, to start with."

Lyad nodded. "How do you open it?"

"You have to press it in the right places. Have them bring it here. I'll show you."

Lyad laughed. "You're a little too eager. And much too docile, Trigger! Considering what's in that handbag, it's not at all likely it will detonate if we brightly hand it to you and let you start pressing. But something or other of a very undesirable nature would certainly happen! Flam—"

The tall redhead nodded and smiled. She went over to a wall cabinet, unlocked it and took out Repulsive's container.

Lyad said. "Put it on that shelf for the moment. Then bring me Virod's gun, and hers."

"I'm afraid you'll have to go up on that table now, Trigger," she said. "If you've really decided to cooperate, it won't be too bad. And, by and by, you'll start telling us very exactly what should be done with that handbag. And a few other things."

She might have caught Trigger's expression then. She added drily, "I was informed a few nights ago that you're quite an artist in rough-and-tumble tactics. So are Virod and Flam. So if you want to give Virod an opportunity to amuse himself a little, go right ahead!"

At that point, the graceful thing undoubtedly would have been to just smile and get up on the table. Trigger discovered she couldn't do it. She gave them a fast, silent, vicious tussle, mouth clenched, breathing hard through her nose. It was quite insanely useless. They weren't letting her get anywhere near Lyad. After Virod had amused himself a little, he picked her up and plunked her down on the table. A minute later, she was stretched out on it, face down, wrists and ankles secured with padded clamps to its surface.

Flam took a small knife and neatly slit the back of the Precol uniform open along the line of her spine. She folded the cloth away. Then Trigger felt the thin icy touches of some vanilla-smelling spray walk up her, ending at the base of her skull.

It wasn't so very painful; Lyad had told the truth about that. But presently it became extremely undignified. Then her thoughts were speeding up

and slowing down and swirling around in an odd,
confusing fashion. And at last her voice began to
say things she didn't want it to say.

After this, there might have been a pause. She
seemed to be floating up out of a small pool of
sleep when Lyad's voice said somewhere, with
cold fury in it: "There's nothing inside?"

A whole little series of memory-pictures
popped up suddenly then, like a chain of fire-
crackers somebody had set off. They formed
themselves into a pattern; and there the pattern
was in Trigger's mind. She looked at it. Her eyes
flew open in surprise. She began to laugh weakly.

Light footsteps came quickly over to her.
"Where is that plasmoid, Trigger?"

The Ermetyne was in a fine, towering rage.
She'd better say something.

"Ask the Commissioner," she said, mumbling a
little.

"It's wearing off, First Lady," said Flam. "Shall
I?"

Trigger's thoughts went eddying away for a
moment, and she didn't hear Lyad's reply. But
then the vanilla smell was there agin, and the thin
icy touches. This time, they stopped abruptly,
halfway.

And then there was a very odd stillness all
around Trigger. As if everybody and everything
had stopped moving together.

A deep, savage voice said, "I hope there'll be no
trouble, folks. I just want her a lot worse than you
do."

Trigger frowned in puzzlement. Next came an angry roar, some thumping sounds, a sudden crack.

"Oops!" the deep voice said happily. "A little too hard, I'm afraid!"

Why, of course, Trigger thought. She opened her eyes and twisted her head around.

"Still awake, Trigger?" Quillan asked from the door of the room. He looked pleasantly surprised. There was a very large bellmouthed gun in his hand.

That was an odd-looking little group in the doorway, Trigger felt. On his knees before Quillan was a fat, elderly man, blinking dazedly at her. He wore a brilliantly purple bath towel knotted about his loins and nothing else. It was a moment before she recognized Belchik Pluly. Old Belchy! And on the floor before Belchy, motionless as if in devout prostration, Virod lay on his face. Dead, no doubt. He shouldn't have got gay with Quillan.

"Yes," Trigger said then, remembering Quillan's question. "I've got a very fast snap-back—but they fed me a fresh load of dope just a moment ago."

"So I saw," said Quillan. His glance shifted beyond Trigger.

"Lyad," he said, almost gently.

"Yes, Quillan?" Lyad's voice came from the other side of Trigger. Trigger turned her head toward it. Lyad and Flam both stood at the far side of the room. Their expressions were unhappy.

"I don't like at all," Quillan said, "what's been going on here. Not one bit! Which is why Big

Boy got the neck broken finally. Can the rest of us take a hint?"

"Certainly," the Ermetyne said.

"So the Flam girl quits ogling those guns on the shelf and stays put, or they'll amputate a leg. First Lady, you come up to the table and get Trigger unclamped."

Trigger realized her eyes had fallen shut again. She left them that way for a moment. There was motion near her, and the wrist clamps came off in turn. Lyad moved down to her feet.

"The fancy-looking gun is Trigger's?" Quillan inquired.

"Yes," said Lyad

"Is that what happened to Pilli and the other gent out there?"

"Yes."

"Imagine!" said Quillan thoughtfully. "Uh—got something to seal up the clothes?"

"Yes," Lyad said. "Bring it here, Flam."

"Toss it, Flam!" cautioned Quillan. "Remember the leg."

Lyad's hands did things to the clothes at her back. Then they went away.

"You can sit up now, Trigger!" Quillan's voice informed her loudly. "Sort of slide down easy off the table and see if you can stand."

Trigger opened her eyes, twisted about, slid her legs over the edge of the table, came down on her feet, stood.

"I want my gun and the handbag," she announced. She saw them again then, on the shelf, walked over and picked up the plasmoid container. She looked inside, snapped it shut and slung the strap over her shoulder. She picked up the Denton, looked at its setting, spun it and turned.

"First Lady—" she said.

Lyad went white around the lips. Quillan made some kind of startled sound. Trigger shot.

Flam ran at her then, screaming, arms waving, eyes wild and green like an animal's. Trigger half turned and shot again.

She looked at Quillan. "Just stunned," she explained. She waited.

Quillan let his breath out slowly. "Glad to hear it!" He glanced down at Pluly. "Purse was open," he remarked significantly.

"Uh-huh," Trigger agreed.

"How's the doohinkus?"

She laughed. "Safe and sound! Believe me."

"Good," he said. He still looked somewhat puzzled. "Put the eye on Belchy for a few seconds then. We're taking Lyad along. I'll have to carry her now."

"Right," Trigger said. She felt rather jaunty at the moment. She put the eye on Belchik. Belchik moaned.

They started out of the little room, Pluly in the van, clutching his towel. The Ermetyne, dangling loosely over Quillan's left shoulder, looked fairly gruesomely dead. "You walk this side of me, Trigger," Quillan said. "Still all right?"

She nodded. "Yes." Actually she wasn't quite. It was mainly a problem with her thoughts, which showed a tendency to move along in odd little leaps and bounds, with short stops in between, as if something were trying to freeze them up. But if it was going to be like the first time, she should last till they got to wherever they were going.

Halfway across the room, she saw the golden thing like a huge furry sack on the carpet and shivered. "Poor Pilli!" she said.

"Alas!" Quillan said politely. "I gather you didn't just stun Pilli?"

She shook her head. "Couldn't," she said. "Too big. Too fast."

"How about the other one?"

"Oh, him. Stunned. He's an investigator. They thought he was dead, though. That's what scared Lyad and Flam."

"Yeah," Quillan said thoughtfully. "It would."

Another section of wall hanging had folded aside, and a wide door stood open behind it. They went through the door and turned into a mirrored passageway, Pluly still tottering rapidly ahead. "Might keep that gun ready, Trigger," Quillan warned. "We just could get jumped here. Don't think so, though. They'd have to get past the Commissioner."

"Oh, he's here, too?"

She didn't hear what Quillan answered, because things faded out around then. When they faded in again, the passageway with the mirrors had disappeared, and they were coming to the top of a short flight of low, wide stairs and into a very beautiful room. This room was high and long, not very wide. In the center was a small square swimming pool, and against the walls on either side was a long row of tall square crystal pillars through which strange lights undulated slowly. Trigger glanced curiously at the nearest pillar. She stopped short.

"Galaxy!" she said, startled.

Quillan reached back and grabbed her arm with his gun hand. "Keep moving, girl! That's just how Belchik keeps his harem grouped around him when he's working. Not too bad an idea—it does cut down the chatter. This is his office."

"Office!" Then she saw the large business desk with prosaic standard equipment which stood on the carpet on the other side of the pool. They moved rapidly past the pool, Quillan still hauling at her arm. Trigger kept staring at the pillars they passed. Long-limbed, supple and languid, they floated in their crystal cages, in tinted, shifting lights, eyes closed, hair drifting about their faces.

"Awesome, isn't it?" Quillan's voice said.

"Yes," said Trigger. "Awesome. One in each— he is a pig! They look drowned."

"He is and they aren't," said Quillan. "Very lively girls when he lets them out. Now around this turn and . . . oops!"

Pluly had reached the turn at the end of the row of pillars, moaned again and fallen forwards.

"Fainted!" Quillan said. "Well, we don't need him any more. Watch your step, Trigger—dead one just behind Pluly."

Trigger stretched her stride and cleared the dead one behind Pluly neatly. There were three more dead ones lying inside the entrance to the next big room. She went past them, feeling rather dreamy. The sight of a squat, black subtub parked squarely on the thick purple carpeting ahead of her, with its canopy up, didn't strike her as unusual. Then she saw that the man leaning against the canopy, a gun in one hand, was Commissioner Tate. She smiled.

She waved her hand at him as they came up. "Hi, Holati!"

"Hi, yourself," said the Commissioner. He asked Quillan, "How's she doing?"

"Not bad," Quillan said. "A bit ta-ta at the moment. Double dose of ceridim, by the smell of it. Had a little trouble here, I see."

"A little," the Commissioner acknowledged. "They went for their guns."

"Very uninformed gentlemen," said Quillan. He let Lyad's limp form slide off his shoulder, and bent forward to lower her into the subtub's back seat. Trigger had been waiting for a chance to get into the conversation.

"Just who," she demanded now, frowning, "is a bit ta-ta at the moment?"

"You," said Quillan. "You're doped, remember? You'll ride up front with the Commissioner. Here." He picked her up, plasmoid purse and all, and set her down on the front seat. Holati Tate, she discovered then, was already inside. Quillan swung down into the seat behind her. The canopy snapped shut above.

The Commissioner shifted the tub's controls. In the screens, the room outside vanished. A darkness went rushing downwards past them.

A thought suddenly popped to mind again, and Trigger burst into tears. The Commissioner glanced over at her.

"What's the matter, Trigger girl?"

"I'm so s-sorry I killed Pilli. He s-screamed."

Then her mind froze up with a jolt, and thinking stopped completely. Quillan reached over the back of the seat and eased her over on her side.

"Got to her finally!" he said. He sat down again. He brooded a moment. "She shouldn't get so disturbed about that Pilli thing," he remarked then. "It couldn't have lived anyway."

"Eh?" the Commissioner said absently, watching the screens. "Why not?"

"Its brains," Quillan explained, "were too far apart."

The Commissioner blinked. "It's getting to you too, son!" he said.

23

TRIGGER CAME OUT OF THE ceridim trance hours before Lyad awoke from the stunner blast she'd absorbed. The Commissioner was sitting in a chair beside her bunk, napping.

She looked around a moment, feeling very comfortable and secure. This was her personal cabin on Commissioner Tate's ship, the one he referred to as the Big Job, modeled after the long-range patrol ships of the Space Scouts. It wasn't actually very big, but six or seven people could go traveling around in it very comfortably. At the moment it appeared to be howling through subspace at its hellish rate again, going somewhere.

Well, that could keep.

Trigger reached out and poked the Commissioner's knee. "Hey, Holati!" she whispered. "Wake up."

His eyes opened. He looked at her and smiled. "Back again, eh?" he said.

Trigger motioned at the door. "Close it," she whispered. "Got something to tell you."

"Talk away," he said. "Quillan's piloting, the First Lady's out cold, and Mantelish got dive-sick and I doped him. Nobody else on board."

Trigger lay back and looked at him. "This is going to sound pretty odd!" she warned him. Then she told him what Repulsive had done and what he was trying to do.

The Commissioner looked badly shaken.

"You sure of that, Trigger?"

"Sure, I'm sure."

"Trying to talk to you?"

"That's it."

He blinked at her. "I looked in the bag, and the thing was gone."

"Lyad knows it was gone," Trigger said. "So in case she gets a chance to blab to someone, we'll say you had it."

He nodded and stood up. "You stay here," he said. "Prescription for the kind of treatment you've had is a day of bed rest."

"Where are you going?"

"I'm going to go talk to that Psychology ship," he said. "And just let 'em try to stall me this time!"

He went off up the passage toward the transmitter cabinet in the forward part of the ship. Some minutes passed. Then Trigger suddenly heard Commissioner Tate's voice raised in great wrath. She listened. It appeared the Psychology Service had got off on the wrong foot by advising him once more to stay calm.

He came back presently and sat down beside the bunk, still a little red in the face. "They're going to follow us," he said. "If they hadn't, I would have turned back and gunned our way on board that lopsided disgrace of theirs."

"Follow us? Where?"

He grunted. "A place called Luscious. We'll be there in under a week. It'll take them about three. But they're starting immediately."

Trigger blinked. "Looks like the plasmoids have made it to the head of the problem list!"

"I wouldn't be surprised," said the Commissioner. "I was put through to that Pilch after a while. She said to remind you to listen to your thinking whenever you can get around to it. Know what she meant?"

"I'm not sure I do," Trigger said hesitantly. "But she's mentioned it. I'll give it a whirl. Why are we going to Luscious?"

"Selan's Fleet found plasmoids on it. It's in the Vishni area."

"What kind of plasmoids?"

He shrugged. "They don't amount to much, from what I heard. Small stuff. But definitely plasmoid. It looks like somebody might have done some experimenting there for a while. And not long ago."

"Did they find the big one?"

"Not yet. No trace of any people on Luscious either." He chewed his lip thoughtfully for a moment. "About an hour after we picked you and Lyad up," he said, "we had a Council Order transmitted to the ship. Told us to swing off course a bit and rendezvous with a fast courier boat of theirs."

"What for?"

"The order said the courier was to take Lyad on board and head for the Hub with her. Some diplomatic business." He scratched his chin. "It also instructed us to treat the First Lady of Tranest with the courtesy due to her station meanwhile."

"Brother!" Trigger said, outraged.

"Just too bad I couldn't read that message," said Holati Tate. "Some gravitic disturbance! Rendezvous point's hours behind us. They'll never catch up."

"Ho-ho!" said Trigger. "But that's being pretty insubordinate, Holati!"

"It was till just now," he said. "I mentioned that we had Lyad on board to that Pilch person. She said she'd speak to the Council. We're to hang on to Lyad and when Pilch gets to Luscious she'll interview her."

Trigger grinned. "Now that," she remarked, "gives me a feeling of great satisfaction, somehow. When Pilch gets her little mitts on someone, there isn't much left out."

"I had that impression. Meanwhile, we'll put the Ermetyne through a routine questioning ourselves when she gets over being groggy. Courtesy will be on the moderate side. She'll probably spill part of what she knows, especially if you sit there and hand her the beady stare from time to time."

"That," Trigger assured him, "will be hardly an effort at all!"

"I can imagine. You're pretty sure that thing will show up again?"

Trigger nodded. "Just leave the handbag with me."

"All right." He stood up. "I've got a hot lunch prepared for you. I'll bring the bag along. Then you can tell me what happened after they grabbed you."

"How did you find out I was gone?" Trigger asked.

"Your fac," he said. "The girl was darn good actually. I talked to you—her—on office transmitter once and didn't spot a sour note. Mostly she just kept out of everybody's way. Very slick at it! We would have got her fairly fast because we were preparing for take-off to Luscious by then. But she spilled it herself."

"How?"

"I located her finally again, on transmitter screen. There was no one on her side to impress. She took a sniff of porgee."

Trigger laughed delightedly. "Good old porgee pouch! It beat them twice. But how did you know where I was?"

"No problem there. We knew Lyad had strings on Pluly. Quillan knew about that sealed level on Pluly's yacht and got Pluly to invite him over to admire the harem right after the Dawn City arrived. While he was admiring, he was also recording floor patterns for a subtub jump. That gimmick's pretty much of a spilled secret now, but on a swap for you and Lyad it was worth it. We came aboard five minutes after we'd nabbed your fac."

"The Ermetyne figured you'd go chasing after the Aurora," Trigger said.

"Well," the Commissioner said tolerantly, "the Ermetyne's pretty young. The Aurora was a bit obvious."

"How come Quillan didn't start wondering when I didn't show up in Mantelish's lab with Repulsive?"

"So that's what he was for!" Holati said. He rubbed the side of his jaw. "I was curious about that angle! That wasn't Quillan. That was Quillan's fac."

"In Mantelish's lab?" Trigger said, startled.

"Sure. That's how they all got in. In those specimen crates Mantelish has been lugging into the dome the past couple of days. It looks like the prof's been hypnotized up to his ears for months."

The last five hours of her day of recuperative rest Trigger spent asleep, her cabin door locked and the plasmoid purse open on the bunk beside her. Holati had come by just before to report that the Ermetyne was now awake but very groggy, apparently more than a little shocked, and not yet quite able to believe she was still alive. He'd dose her with this and that, and interrogations would be postponed until everybody was on their feet.

When Trigger woke up from her five hour nap, the purse was shut. She opened it and looked inside. Repulsive was down there, quietly curled up.

"Smart little bugger, aren't you?" she said, not

entirely with approval. Then she reached in and
gave him a pat. She locked the purse, got dressed
and went up to the front of the ship, carrying
Repulsive along.

All four of the others were up in the lounge area
which included the partitioned control section.
The partition had been slid into the wall and the
Commissioner, who was at the controls at the
moment, had swung his seat half around toward
the lounge.

He glanced at the plasmoid purse as Trigger
came in, grinned and gave her a small wink.

"Come in and sit down," he said. "We've been
waiting for you."

Trigger sat down and looked at them. Something apparently had been going on. Quillan's
tanned face was thoughtful, perhaps a trifle
amused. Mantelish looked very red and angry.
His shock of white hair was wildly rumpled. The
Ermetyne appeared a bit wilted.

"What's been going on?" Trigger asked.

It was the wrong question. Mantelish took a
deep breath and began bellowing like a wounded
thunder-ork. Trigger listened, with some admira-
tion. It was one of the best jobs of well-verbalized
huffing she'd heard, even from the professor. He
ran down in less than five minutes, though—
apparently he'd already let off considerable
steam.

Lyad had dehypnotized him, at the Commissioner's suggestion. It had been a lengthy job,
requiring a couple of hours, but it was a complete
one. Which was understandable, since it was the

First Lady herself, Trigger gathered gradually from the noise, who had put Mantelish under the influence, back in his own garden on Maccadon, and within two weeks after his first return from Harvest Moon.

It was again Lyad who had given Mantelish his call to bemused duty via a transmitted verbal cue on her arrival in Manon, and instructed him to get lost from his League guards for a few hours in Manon's swamps. There she had met and conferred with him and pumped him of all he could tell her. As the final outrage, she had instructed him to lug her crated cohorts, preserved like Pluly's harem ladies, into the Precol dome—to care for them tenderly there and at the proper cued moment to release them for action—all under the illusion that they were priceless biological specimens!

Mantelish wasn't in the least appeased by the fact that—again at the Commissioner's suggestion—Lyad had installed one minor new hypno-command which, she said, would clear up permanently his tendency toward attacks of dive sickness. But he just ran down finally and sat there, glowering at the Ermetyne now and then.

"Well," the Commissioner remarked, "this might be as good a time as any to ask a few questions. Got your little quizzer with you, Quillan?"

Quillan nodded. Lyad looked at both of them in turn and then, briefly and for the first time, glanced in Trigger's direction.

It wasn't exactly an appealing glance. It might have been a questioning one. And Trigger discovered suddenly that she felt just a little sympathy

for Lyad. Lyad had lost out on a very big gamble.
And, each in his own way, there were three very
formidable males among whom she was sitting.
None of them was friendly; two were oversized,
and the undersized one had a fairly bloodchilling
record for anyone on the wrong side of law and
order. Trigger decided to forget about beady
stares for the moment.

"Cheer up, Lyad!" she said. "Nobody's going to
hurt you. Just give 'em the answers!"

She got another glance. Not a grateful one,
exactly. Not an ungrateful one either. Temporary
support had been acknowledged.

"Commissioner Tate has informed me," the
Ermetyne said, "that this group does not recog-
nize the principle of diplomatic immunity in my
case. Under the circumstances I must accept that.
And so I shall answer any questions I can." She
looked at the pocket quizzer Quillan was checking over unhurriedly. "But such verification instruments are of no use in questioning me."

"Why not?" Quillan asked idly.

"I've been conditioned against them, of
course," Lyad said. "I'm an Ermetyne of Tranest.
By the time I was twelve years old, that toy of
yours couldn't have registered a reaction from me
that I didn't want it to show."

Quillan slipped the toy back in his pocket.

"True enough, First Lady," he said. "And that's
one small strike in your favor. We thought you
might try to gimmick the gadget. Now we'll just
pitch you some questions. A recorder's on. Don't
stall on the answers."

And he and the Commissioner started flipping

out questions. The Ermetyne flipped back the answers. So far as Trigger could tell, there wasn't any stalling. Or any time for it.

Azol: Doctor Azol had been her boy from the start. He was now on Tranest. The main item in his report to her had been the significance of the 112-113 plasmoid unit. He'd also reported that Trigger Argee had become unconscious on Harvest Moon. They'd considered the possibility that somebody was controlling Trigger Argee, or attempting to control her, because of her connections with the plasmoid operations.

Gess Fayle: Lyad had been looking for Doctor Fayle as earnestly as everyone else after his disappearance. She had not been able to buy him. So far as she knew, nobody had been able to buy him. Doctor Fayle had appeared to intend to work for himself. He was at present well outside the Hub's area of space. He still had 112-113 with him. Yes, she could become more specific about the location—with the help of star maps.

"Let's get them out," said Commissioner Tate.

They got them out. The Ermetyne presently circled a largish section of the Vishni Fleet's area. The questions began again.

113-A: Professor Mantelish had told her of his experiments with this plasmoid—

There was an interruption here while Mantelish huffed reflexively. But it was very brief. The professor wanted to learn more about the First Lady's depravities himself.

—and its various possible associations with the main unit. But by the time this information became available to her, 113-A had been placed under heavy guard. Professor Mantelish had made one attempt to smuggle it out to her.

Huff-huff!

—but had been unable to walk past the guards with it. Tranest agents had made several unsuccessful attempts to pick up the plasmoid. She knew that another group had made similarly unsuccessful attempts. The Devagas. She did not yet know the specific nature of 113-A's importance. But it was important.

Trigger: Trigger Argee might be able to tell them why Trigger was important. Doctor Fayle certainly could. So could the top ranks of the Devagas hierarchy. Lyad, at the moment, could not. She did know that Trigger Argee's importance was associated directly with that of plasmoid 113-A. This information had been obtained from a Devagas operator, now dead. Not Balmordan. The operator had been in charge of the attempted pickup on Evalee. The much more elaborate affair at the Colonial School had been a Tranest job. A Devagas group had made attempts to interfere with it, but had been disposed of.

Pluly: Lyad had strings on Belchik. He was afraid of the Devagas but somewhat more terrified of her. His fear of the Devagas was due to the fact that he and an associate had provided the hierarchy with a very large quantity of contraband materials. The nature of the materials indicated the Devagas were constructing a major fortified outpost on a world either airless or with poisonous atmosphere. Pluly's associate had since been murdered. Pluly believed he was next in line to be silenced.

Balmordan: Balmordan had been a rather high-ranking Devagas Intelligence agent. Lyad had heard of him only recently. He had been in charge of the attempts to obtain 113-A. Lyad had convinced him that she would make a very dangerous competitor in the Manon area. She also had made information regarding her activities there available to him. So Balmordan and a select group of his gunmen had attended Pluly's party on Pluly's yacht. They had been allowed to force their way into the sealed level and were there caught in a black-light trap. The gunmen had been killed. Balmordan had been questioned.

The questioning revealed that the Devagas had found Doctor Fayle and the 112-113 unit, almost immediately after Fayle's disappearance. They had succeeded in creating some working plasmoids. To go into satisfactory operation, they still needed 113-A. Balmordan had not known why. But they no longer needed Trigger Argee. Trigger Argee was now to be destroyed at the earliest opportunity. Again Balmordan had not known why. Fayle and his unit were in the fortress dome the Devagas had been building. It was in the area Lyad had indicated. It was supposed to be very thoroughly concealed. Balmordan might or might not have known its exact coordinates. His investigators made the inevitable slip finally and triggered a violent mind-block reaction. Balmordan had died. Dead-braining him had produced no further relevant information.

The little drumfire of questions ended abruptly. Trigger glanced at her watch. It had been going on for only fifteen minutes, but she felt somewhat dizzy by now. The Ermetyne just looked a little more wilted.

After a minute, Commissioner Tate inquired politely whether there was any further information the First Lady could think of to give them at this time.

She shook her head. No.

Only Professor Mantelish believed her.

But the interrogation was over, apparently.

24

QUILLAN TOOK OVER THE SHIP controls, and the Commissioner and Trigger went with the recorder into the little office back of the transmitter cabinet, to slam out some fast reports to the Hub and other points. Lyad was appologizing profoundly to Mantelish as they left the lounge. The professor was huffing back at her, rather mildly.

A little while later, Lyad, showing indications of restrained surprise, was helping Trigger prepare dinner. They took it into the lounge. Quillan remained at the controls while the others started eating. Trigger fixed up a tray and brought it to him.

"Thanks for the rescue, Major!" she said.

He grinned up at her. "It was a pleasure."

Trigger glanced back at the little group in the lounge. "Think she was fibbing a bit?"

"Sure. Mainly she'd decided in advance how

much to tell and how much not. She thinks fast in action though! No slips. What she told of what she knows makes a solid story, and with angles we can check on fast. So it's bound to have plenty of information in it. It'll do for the moment."

"She's already started buttering up Mantelish," said Trigger.

"She'll do that," Quillan said. "By the time we reach Luscious, the prof probably might as well be back in the trances. The Commissioner intends to give her a little rope, I think."

"How close is Luscious to that area she showed?"

Quillan flicked on their course screen and superimposed the map Lyad had marked. "Red dot's well inside," he pointed out. "That bit was probably quite solid info." He looked up at her. "Did it bother you much to hear the Devagas have dropped the grab idea and are out to do you in?"

Trigger shook her head. "Not really," she said. "Wouldn't make much difference one way or the other, would it?"

"Very little." He patted her hand. "Well, they're not going to get you, doll—one way or the other!"

Trigger smiled. "I believe you," she said. "Thanks." She looked back into the lounge again. Just at present she did have a feeling of relaxed, unconcerned security. It probably wasn't going to last, though. She glanced at Quillan.

"Those computers of yours," she said. "What did they have to say about that not-catassin you squashed?"

"The crazy things claim now it was a plasmoid," Quillan said, "Revolting notion! But it makes some sense for once. Checks with some of the things Lyad just told us, too. Do you remember that Vethi sponge Blamordan was carrying?"

"Yes."

"It didn't come off the ship with him. He checked it out as having died en route."

"That is a revolting notion!" Trigger said after a moment. "Well, at least we've got detectors now."

But the feeling of security had faded somewhat again.

Before dinner was half over, the long-range transmitters abruptly came to life. For the next thirty minutes or so, messages rattled in incessantly, as assorted Headquarters here and there reacted to the Ermetyne's report. The Commissioner sat in the little office and sorted over the incoming information. Trigger stayed at the transmitters, feeding it to him as it arrived. None of it affected them directly—they were already headed for the point in space a great many other people would now start heading for very soon.

Then business dropped off again almost as suddenly as it had picked up. A half dozen low priority items straggled in, in as many minutes. The transmitters purred idly. Then the person-to-person buzzer sounded.

Trigger punched the screen button. A voice pronounced the ship's dial number.

"Acknowledging," Trigger said. "Who is it?"

"Orado ComWeb Center," said the voice. "Stand by for contact with Federation Councilman Roadgear."

Trigger whacked the panic button. Roadgear was a NAME! "Standing by," she said.

Commissioner Tate came in through the door and slipped into the chair she'd already vacated. Trigger took another seat a few feet away. She felt a little nervous, but she'd always wanted to see a high-powered diplomat in action.

The screen lit up. She recognized Roadgear from his pics. Tall, fine-looking man of the silvered sideburns type. He was in an armchair in a very plush office.

"Congratulations, Commissioner!" he said, smiling. "I believe you're aware by now that your latest report has set many wheels spinning rapidly!"

"I rather expected it would," the Commissioner admitted. He also smiled.

They pitched it back and forth a few times, very chummy. Roadgear didn't appear to be involved in any specific way with the operations which soon would center about Luscious. Trigger began to wonder what he was after.

"A few of us are rather curious to know," Roadgear said, "why you didn't acknowledge the last Council Order sent you."

Trigger didn't quite start nervously.

"When was this?" asked the Commissioner.

Roadgear smiled softly and told him.

"Got a record here of some scrambled item that arrived about then," the Commissioner said. "Very good of you to call me about it, Councilman. What was the order content?"

"It's dated now, as it happens," Roadgear said.

"Actually I'm calling about another matter. The First Lady of Tranest appears to have been very obliging about informing you of some of her recent activities."

The Commissioner nodded. "Yes, very obliging."

"And in so short a time after her, ah, detainment. You must have been very persuasive?"

"Well," Holati Tate said, "no more than usually."

"Yes," said Councilman Roadgear. "Now there's been some slight concern expressed by some members of the Council—well, let's say they'd just like to be reassured that the amenities one observes in dealing with a head of state actually are being observed in this case. I'm sure they are, of course."

The Commissioner was silent a moment. "I was informed a while ago," he said, "that full responsibility for this Head of State has been assigned to my group. Is that correct?"

The Councilman reddened very slightly. "Quite," he said. "The official Council Order should reach you in a day or so."

"Well, then," said the Commissioner, "I'll assure you and you can assure the Councilmen who were feeling concerned that the amenities are being observed. Then everybody can relax again. Is that all right?"

"No, not quite," Roadgear said annoyedly. "In fact, the Councilmen would very much prefer it, Commissioner, if I were given an opportunity to speak to the First Lady directly to reassure myself on the point."

"Well," Commissioner Tate said, "she can't come to the transmitters right now. She's washing the dishes."

The Councilman reddened very considerably this time. He stared at the Commissioner a moment longer. Then he said in a very soft voice, "Oh, the hell with it!" He added, "Good luck, Commissioner—you're going to need it some time."

The screen went blank.

The scouts of Selan's Independent Fleet, who had first looked this planet over and decided to call it Luscious, had selected a name, Trigger thought, which probably would stick. Because that was what it was, at least in the area where they were camping.

She rolled over from her side to her face and gave herself a push away from the rock she'd been regarding contemplatively for the past few minutes. Feet first, she went drifting out into a somewhat deeper section of Plasmoid Creek.

None of it was very deep. There were pools here and there, in the stretch of the creek she usually came to, where she could stand on her toes in the warm clear water and, arms stretched straight up, barely tickle the surface with her finger tips. But along most of the stretch the bigger rocks weren't even submerged.

She came sliding over the sand to another rock, turned on her back and leaned up against the rock, blinking at sun reflections along the water. Camp was a couple of hundred yards down the valley, its sounds cut off by a rise of the ground. The Commissioner's ship was there, plus a half dozen tents, plus a sizable I-Fleet unit with lab facilities which Selan's outfit had loaned Mantelish for the duration. There were some fifteen, twenty people in all about the camp at the moment. They knew she was loafing around in the water up here and wouldn't disturb her.

Strictly speaking, of course, she wasn't loafing. She was learning how to listen to herself think. She didn't feel she was getting the knack of it too quickly; but it was coming. The best way seemed to be to let go mentally as much as possible; to wait without impatience, really to more-or-less listen quietly within yourself, as if you were looking around in some strange forest, letting whatever wanted to come to view come, and fade again, as something else rose to view instead. The main difficulty was with the business of relaxing mentally, which wasn't at all her natural method of approaching a problem.

But when she could do it, information of a kind that was beginning to look very interesting was likely to come filtering into her awareness. Whatever was at work deep in her mind—and she could give a pretty fair guess at what it was now—seemed as weak and slow as the Psychology Service people had indicated. The traces of its work were usually faint and vague. But gradually the traces were forming into some very definite pictures.

Lazing around in the waters of Plasmoid Creek for an hour or so every morning had turned out to be a helpful part of the process. On the flashing, all-out run to Luscious, subspace all the way, with the Commissioner and Quillan spelling each other around the clock at the controls, the transmitters clattering for attention every half hour, the ship's housekeeping had to be handled, and somebody besides Mantelish needed to keep a moderately beady eye on the Ermetyne, she hadn't even thought of acting on Pilch's suggestion.

But once they'd landed, there suddenly wasn't much to keep her busy, and she could shift priority to listening to herself think. It was one of those interim periods where everything was being prepared and nothing had got started. As a plasmoid planet, Luscious was pretty much of a bust. It was true that plasmoids were here. It was also true that until fairly recently plasmoids were being produced here.

By the simple method of looking where they were thickest, Selan's people even had located the plasmoid which had been producing the others, several days before Mantelish arrived to confirm their find. This one, by the plasmoid standards of Luscious, was a regular monster, some twenty-five inches high; a gray, mummylike thing, dead and half rotted inside. It was the first plasmoid—with the possible exception of whatever had flattened itself out on Quillan's gravity mine—known to have died. There had been very considerable excitement when it was first discovered, because the description made it sound very much as if they'd finally located 112-113.

They hadn't. This one—if Trigger had followed Mantelish correctly—could be regarded as a cheap imitation of 112. And its productions, compared with the working plastic life of Harvest Moon, appeared to be strictly on a kindergarten level: nuts and bolts and less than that. To Trigger, most of the ones that had been collected looked like assorted bugs and worms, though one at least was the size of a small pig.

"No form, no pattern," Mantelish rumbled. "Was the thing practicing? Did it attempt to construct an assistant and set it down here to test it? Well, now!" He went off again to incomprehensibilities, apparently no longer entirely dissatisfied. "Get me 112!" he bellowed. "Then this business will be solved! Meanwhile we now at least have plasmoid material to waste. We can experiment boldly! Come, Lyad, my dear."

And Lyad followed him into the lab unit, where they went to work again, dissecting, burning, stimulating, inoculating and so forth great numbers of more or less pancake-sized subplasmoids.

This morning Trigger wasn't getting down to the best semidrowsy level at all readily. And it might very well be that Lyad-my-dear business. "You know," she had told the Commissioner thoughtfully the day before, "by the time we're done, Lyad will know more about plasmoids than anyone in the Hub except Mantelish!"

He didn't look concerned. "Won't matter much.

By the time we're done, she and the rest of the
Ermetynes will have had to cough up control of
Tranest. They've broken treaty with this busi-
ness."

"Oh," Trigger said. "Does Lyad know that?"

"Sure. She also knows she's getting off easy. If
she were a Federation citizen, she'd be up for
compulsory rehabilitation right now."

"She'll try something if she gets half a chance!"
Trigger warned.

"She sure will!" the Commissioner said absently. He went on with his work.

It didn't seem to be Lyad that was bothering.
Trigger lay flat on her back in the shallow sand
bar, arms behind her head, feeling the sun's
warmth on her closed eyelids. She watched her
thoughts drifting by slowly.

It just might be Quillan.

Ole Major Quillan. The rescuer in time of need.
The not-catassin smasher. Quite a guy. The water
murmured past her.

On the ride out here they'd run by one another
now and then, going from job to job. After they'd
arrived, Quillan was gone three quarters of the
time, helping out in the hunt for the concealed
Devagas fortress. It was still concealed; they
hadn't yet picked up a trace.

But every so often he made it back to camp. And
every so often when he was back in camp and
didn't think she was looking, he'd be sitting there
looking at her.

Trigger grinned happily. Ole Major Quillan—
being bashful! Well now!

And that did it. She could feel herself relaxing, slipping down and away, drifting down through her mind . . . farther . . . deeper . . . toward the tiny voice that spoke in such a strange language and still was becoming daily more comprehensible.

"Uh, say, Trigger!"

25

TRIGGER GASPED. Her eyes flew open. She made a convulsive effort to vanish beneath the surface of the creek. Being flat on the sand as it was, that didn't work. So she stopped splashing about and made rapid covering-up motions here and there instead.

"You've got a nerve!" she snapped as her breath came back. "Beat it! Fast!"

Ole bashful Quillan, standing on the bank fifteen feet above her, looked hurt. He also looked.

"Look!" he said plaintively. "I just came over to make sure you were all right—wild animals around! I wasn't studying the color scheme."

"*Beat it! At once!*"

Quillan inhaled with apparent difficulty.

"Though now it's been mentioned," he went on, speaking rapidly and unevenly, "there is all that brown and that sort of pink and that lovely white." He was getting more enthusiastic by the moment; Trigger became afraid he would fall off the bank and land in the creek beside her. "And the—ooh-ummh!—wet red hair and the freckles!" he rattled along, his eyes starting out of his head. "And the lovely—"

"Quillan!" she yelled. "Please!"

Quillan checked himself. "Uh!" he said. He drew a deep breath. The wild look faded. Sanity appeared to return. "Well, it's the truth about those wild animals! Some sort of large, uncouth critter was observed just now ducking into the forest at the upper end of the valley!"

Trigger darted a glance along the bank. Her clothes were forty feet away, just beside the water.

"I'm observing some sort of large, uncouth critter right here!" she said coldly. "What's worse, it's observing me. Turn around!"

Quillan sighed. "You're a hard woman, Argee," he said. But he turned. He was carrying a holstered gun, as a matter of fact; but he usually did that nowadays anyway. "This thing," he went on, "is supposed to have a head like a bat, three feet across. It flies."

"Very interesting," Trigger told him. She decided he wasn't going to turn around again. "So now I'll just get into my clothes, and then—"

It came quietly out of the trees around the upper bend of the creek sixty feet away. It had a head like a bat, and was blue on top and yellow below. Its flopping wing tips barely cleared the bank on either side. The three-foot mouth was wide open, showing very long thin white teeth. It came skimming swiftly over the surface of the water toward her.

"Quiiii-LLAN!"

They walked back along the trail to camp. Trigger walked a few steps ahead, her back very straight. The worst of it had been the smug look on his face.

"Heel!" she observed. "Heel! Heel! Heel!"

"Now, Trigger," Quillan said calmly behind her. "After all, it was you who came flying up the bank and wrapped yourself around my neck. All wet, too."

"I was scared!" Trigger snarled. "Who wouldn't be? You certainly didn't hesitate an instant to take full advantage of the situation!"

"True," Quillan admitted. "I'd dropped the bat. There you were. Who'd hesitate. I'm not out of my mind."

She did two dance steps of pure rage and spun to face him. She put her hands on her hips. Quillan stopped warily.

"Your mind!" she said. "I'd hate to have one like it. What do you think I am? One of Belchik's houris?"

For a man his size, he was really extremely quick. Before she could move, he was there, one big arm wrapped about her shoulders, pinning her arms to her sides. "Easy, Trigger!" he said softly.

Well, others had tried to hold her like that when she didn't want to be held. A twist, a jerk a heave—and over and down they went. Trigger

braced herself quietly. If she was quick enough
now— She twisted, jerked, heaved. She stopped,
discouraged. The situation hadn't altered appre-
ciably.

She *had* been afraid it wasn't going to work
with Quillan.

"Let go!" she said furiously, aiming a fast heel
at his instep. But the instep flicked aside. Her shoe
dug into the turf of the path. The ape might even
have an extra pair of eyes on his feet!

Then his free palm was cupped under her chin,
tilting it carefully. His other eyes appeared above
hers. Very close. Very dark.

"I'll bite!" Trigger whispered fiercely. "I'll
bi—mmph!

"Mmmph—grrmm!

"Grr-mm-mhm . . . Hm-m-m . . . mhm!"

They walked on along the trail, hand in hand.
They came up over the last little rise. Trigger
looked down on the camp. She frowned.

"Pretty dull!" she observed.

"Eh?" Quillan asked, startled.

"Not that, ape!" she said. She squeezed his
hand. "Your morals aren't good, but dull it
wasn't. I meant generally. We're just sitting here
now waiting. Nothing seems to be happening."

It was true, at least on the surface. There were a
great number of ships and men around and near
Luscious, but they weren't in view. They were
ready to jump in any direction, at any moment,
but they had nothing to jump at yet. The Commissioner's transmitters hadn't signaled more than

two or three times in the last two days. Even the short communicators remained mostly silent.

"Cheer up, Doll!" Quillan said. "Something's bound to break pretty soon."

That evening, a Devagas ship came zooming in on Luscious.

They were prepared for it, of course. That somebody came round from time to time to look over the local plasmoid crop was only to be expected. As the ship surfaced in atmosphere on the other side of the planet, four one-man Scout fighters flashed in on it from four points of the horizon, radiation screens up. They tacked holding beams on it and braced themselves. A Federation destroyer appeared in the air above it.

The Devagas ship couldn't escape. So it blew itself up.

They were prepared for that, too. The Devagas pilot was being dead-brained three minutes later. He didn't know a significant thing except the exact coordinates of an armed, subterranean Devagas dome, three days' run away.

The Scout ships that had been hunting for the dome went howling in toward it from every direction. The more massive naval vessels of the Federation followed behind. There was no hurry for the heavies. The captured Devagas ship's attempt to beam a warning to its base had been smothered without effort. The Scouts were getting in fast enough to block escape attempts.

"And now we split forces," the Commissioner said. He was the only one, Trigger thought, who didn't seem too enormously excited by it all.

"Quillan, you and your group get going! They can use you there a whole lot better than we can here."

For just a second, Quillan looked like a man being dragged violently in two directions. He didn't look at Trigger. He asked, "Think it's wise to leave you people unguarded?"

"Quillan," said Commissioner Tate, "that's the first time in my life anybody has suggested I need guarding."

"Sorry sir," said Quillan.

"You mean," Trigger said, "we're not going? We're just staying here?"

"You've got an appointment, remember?" the Commissioner said.

Quillan and company were gone within the hour. Mantelish, Holati Tate, Lyad and Trigger stayed at camp.

Luscious looked very lonely.

"It isn't just the king plasmoid they're hoping to catch there," the Commissioner told Trigger. "And I wouldn't care, frankly, if the thing stayed lost the next few thousand years. But we had a very odd report last week. The Federation's undercover boys have been scanning the Devagas worlds and Tranest very closely of late, naturally. The report is that there isn't the slightest evidence that a single one of the top members of the Devagas hierarchy has been on any of their worlds in the past two months."

"Oh," she said. "They think they're out here? In that dome?"

"That's what's suspected."

"But why?"

He scratched his chin. "If anyone knows, they haven't told me. It's probably nothing nice."

Trigger pondered. "You'd think they'd use facsimiles," she said. "Like Lyad."

"Oh, they did," he said. "They did. That's one of the reasons for being pretty sure they're gone. They're nowhere near as expert at that facsimile business as the Tranest characters. A little study of the recordings showed the facs were just that."

Trigger pondered again. "Did they find anything on Tranest?"

"Yes. One combat-strength squadron of those souped-up frigates of the Aurora class they're allowed by treaty can't be accounted for."

Trigger cupped her chin in her hands and looked at him. "Is that why we've stayed on Luscious, Holati—the four of us?"

"It's one reason. That Repulsive thing of yours is another."

"What about him?"

"I have a pretty strong feeling," he said, "that while they'll probably find the hierarchy in that Devagas dome, they won't find the 112-113 item there."

"So Lyad still is gambling," Trigger said. "And we're gambling we'll get more out of her next play than she does." She hesitated. "Holati—"

"Yes?"

"When did you decide it would be better if nobody ever got to see that king plasmoid again?"

Holati Tate said, "About the time I saw the

reconstruct of that yellow monster of Balmordan's. Frankly, Trigger, there was a good deal of discussion of possibilities along that line before we decided to announce the discovery of Harvest Moon. If we could have just kept it hidden away for a couple of centuries—until there was considerably more good sense around the Hub—we probably would have done it. But somebody was bound to run across it sometime. And the stuff did look as if it might be extremely valuable. So we took the chance."

"And now you'd like to untake it?"

"If it's still possible. Half the Fed Council probably would like to see it happen. But they don't even dare think along those lines. There could be a blowup that would throw Hub politics back into the kind of snarl they haven't been in for a hundred years. If anything is done, it will have to look as if it had been something nobody could have helped. And that still might be bad enough."

"I suppose so. Holati—"

"Yes?"

She shook her head. "Nothing. Or if it is, I'll ask you later." She stood up. "I think I'll go have my swim."

She still went loafing in Plasmoid Creek in the mornings. The bat had been identified as an innocent victim of appearances, a very mild-mannered beast dedicated to the pursuit and engulfment of huge mothlike bugs which hung around watercourses. Luscious still looked like the safest of all possible worlds for any creature as vigorous as a human being. But she kept the Denton near now, just in case.

She stretched out again in the sun-warmed water, selected a smooth rock to rest her head on, wriggled into the sand a little so the current wouldn't shift her, and closed her eyes. She lay still, breathing slowly. Contact was coming more easily and quickly every morning. But the information which had begun to filter through in the last few days wasn't at all calculated to make one happy.

She was afraid now she was going to die in this thing. She had almost let it slip out to Holati, which wouldn't have helped in the least. She'd have to watch that in future.

Repulsive hadn't exactly said she would die. He'd said, "Maybe." Repulsive was scared too. Scared badly.

Trigger lay quiet, her thoughts, her attention drifting softly inward and down. Creek water rippled against her cheek.

It was all because that one clock moved so slowly. That was the thing that couldn't be changed. Ever.

26

THREE MORNINGS LATER, the emergency signal called her back to camp on the double.

Trigger ran over the developments of the past days in her mind as she trotted along the path, getting dressed more or less on the way. The Devagas dome was solidly invested by now, its transmitters blanked out. It hadn't tried to communicate with its attackers. On their part, the Fed ships weren't pushing the attack. They were holding the point, waiting for the big, slow wrecking boats to arrive, which would very gently and delicately start uncovering and opening the dome, taking it apart, piece by piece. The hierarchy could surrender themselves and whatever they were hiding in there at any point in the process. They didn't have a chance. Nobody and nothing had escaped. The Scouts had swatted down a few Devagas vessels on the way in; but those had been headed toward the dome, not away from it.

Perhaps the Psychology Service ship had arrived, several days ahead of time.

The other three weren't in camp, but the lock to the Commissioner's ship stood open. Trigger went in and found them gathered up front. The Commissioner had swung the transmitter cabinet aside and was back there, prowling among the power leads.

"What's wrong?" Trigger asked.

"Transmitters went out," he said. "Don't know why yet. Grab some tools and help me check."

She slipped on her work gloves, grabbed some tools and joined him. Lyad and Mantelish watched them silently.

They found the first spots of the fungus a few minutes later.

"Fungus!" Mantelish said, startled. He began to fumble in his pockets. "My microscope—"

"I have it." Lyad handed it to him. She looked at him with concern. "You don't think—"

"It seems possible. We did come in here last night, remember? And we came straight from the lab."

"But we had been decontaminated," Lyad said puzzledly.

"Don't try to walk in here, Professor!" Trigger warned as he lumbered forward. "We might have to de-electrocute you. The Commissioner will scrape off a sample and hand it out. This stuff—if it's what you think it might be—is poisonous?"

"Quite harmless to life, my dear," said the professor, bending over the patch of greenish-gray scum the Commissioner had reached out to him.

"But ruinous in delicate instruments! That's why we're so careful."

Holati Tate glanced at Trigger. "Better look in the black box, Trig," he said.

She nodded and wormed herself farther into the innards of the transmitters. A minute later she announced, "Full of it! And that's the one part we can't repair or replace, of course. Is it your beast, Professor?"

"It seems to be," Mantelish said unhappily. "But we have, at least, a solvent which will remove it from the equipment."

Trigger came sliding out from under the transmitters, the detached black box under one arm. "Better use it then before the stuff gets to the rest of the ship. It won't help the black box." She shook it. It tinkled. "Shot!" she said. "There went another quarter million of your credits, Commissioner."

Mantelish and Lyad headed for the lock to get the solvent. Trigger slipped off her work gloves and turned to follow them. "Might be a while before I'm back," she said.

The Commissioner started to say something, then nodded and climbed back into the transmitters. After a few minutes, Mantelish came puffing in with sprayers and cans of solvent. "It's at least fortunate you tried to put out a call just now," he said. "It might have done incalculable damage."

"Doubt it," said Holati. "A few more instruments might have gone. Like the communicators. The main equipment is fungus-proof. How do you attach this thing?"

Mantelish showed him.

The Commissioner thanked him. He directed a fine spray of the solvent into the black box and watched the fungus melt. "Happen to notice where Trigger and Lyad went?" he asked.

"Eh?" said Mantelish. He reflected. "I saw them walking down toward camp talking together as I came in," he called. "Should I go get them?"

"Don't bother," Holati said. "They'll be back."

They came walking back into the ship around half an hour later. Both faces looked rather white and strained.

"Lyad has something she wants to tell you, Holati," Trigger said. "Where's Mantelish?"

"In his lab. Taking a nap, I believe."

"That's good. We don't want him here for this. Go ahead, Lyad. Just the important stuff. You can give us the details after we've left."

Three hours later, the ship was well away from Luscious, traveling subspace, traveling fast. Trigger walked up into the control section.

"Mantelish is still asleep," she said. They'd fed the professor a doped drink to get him aboard without detailed explanation and argument about how much of the lab should be loaded on the ship first. "Shall I get Lyad out of her cabin for the rest of the story or wait till he wakes up?"

"Better wait," said the Commissioner. "He'll come out of it in about an hour, and he might as well hear it with us. Looks like navigating's going to be a little rough for a spell anyway."

Trigger nodded and sat down in the control next to his. After a while he glanced over at her.

"How did you get her to talk?" he asked.

"We went back into the woods a bit. I tied her over a stump and broke two sticks across the first seat of Tranest. Got the idea from Mihul sort of," Trigger added vaguely. "When I picked up a third stick, Lyad got awfully anxious to keep things at just a fast conversational level. We kept it there."

"Hm," said the Commissioner. "You don't feel she did any lying this time?"

"I doubt it. I tapped her one now and then, just to make sure she didn't slow down enough to do much thinking. Besides I'd got the whole business down on a pocket recorder, and Lyad knew it. If she makes one more goof till this deal is over, the recording gets released to the Hub's news viewer outfits, yowls and all. She'd sooner lose Tranest than risk having that happen. She'll be good."

"Yeah, probably," he said thoughtfully. "About that substation—would you feel more comfortable if we went after the bunch round the Devagas dome first and got us an escort for the trip?"

"Sure," Trigger said. "But that would just about kill any chances of doing anything personally, wouldn't it?"

"I'm afraid so. Scout Intelligence will go along pretty far with me. But they couldn't go that far. We might be able to contact Quillan individually though. He's a topnotch man in a fighter."

"It doesn't seem to me," Trigger said, "that we ought to run any risk of being spotted till we know exactly what this thing is like."

"Well," said the Commissioner, "I'm with you there. We shouldn't."

"What about Mantelish and Lyad? You can't let them know either."

The Commissioner motioned with his head. "The rest cubicle back of the cabins. If we see a chance to do anything, we'll pop them both into Rest. I can dream up something to make that look plausible afterwards, I think."

Trigger was silent a moment. Lyad had told them she'd dispatched the Aurora to stand guard over a subspace station where the missing king plasmoid presently was housed, until both she and the combat squadron from Tranest could arrive there. The exact location of that station had been the most valuable of the bits of information she had extracted so painstakingly from Balmordan. The coordinates were centered on the Commissioner's course screen at the moment.

"How about that Tranest squadron?" Trigger asked. "Think Lyad might have risked a lie, and they could get out here in time to interfere?"

"No," said the Commissioner. "She had to have some idea of where to send them before starting them out of the Hub. They'll be doing fine if they make it to the substation in another two weeks. Now the Aurora—if they started for Luscious right after Lyad called them last night, at best they can't get there any sooner than we can get to the substation. I figure that at four days. If they turn right around then, and start back—"

Trigger laughed. "You can bet on that!" she said. The Commissioner had used his ship's guns to brand the substation's coordinates in twenty-mile figures into a mountain plateau above Plasmoid Creek. They'd left much more detailed information in camp, but there was a chance it would be overlooked in too hurried a search.

"Then they'll show up at the substation again four or five days behind us," the Commissioner said. "So they're no problem. But our own outfit's fastest ships can cut across from the Devagas dome in less than three days after their search party messages from Luscious to tell them why we've stopped transmitting and where we've gone. Or the Psychology ship might get to Lusscious before the search party does and start transmitting about the coordinates."

"In any case," said Trigger, "it's our own boys who are likely to be the problem."

"Yes. I'd say we should have two days, give or take a few hours, after we get to the station to see if we can do anything useful and get it done. Of course, somebody might come wandering into Luscious right now and start wondering about those coordinate figures, or drop in at our camp and discover we're gone. But that's not very likely, after all."

"Couldn't be helped anyway," Trigger said.

"No. If we knock ourselves out on this job, somebody besides Lyad's Tranest squadron and the Devagas has to know just where the station is." He shook his head. "That Lyad! I figured she'd know how to run the transmitters, so I gave her the chance. But I never imagined she'd be a good enough engineer to get inside them and mess them up without killing herself."

"Lyad has her points," Trigger said. "Too bad

she grew up a rat. You had a playback attachment stuck in there then?"

"Naturally."

"Full of the fungus, I suppose?"

"Full of it," said the Commissioner. "Well, Lyad still lost on that maneuver. Much less comfortably then she might have, too."

"I think she'd agree with you there," Trigger said.

Lyad's first assignment after Professor Mantelish came out of the dope was to snap him back into trance and explain to him how he had once more been put under hypno control and used for her felonious ends by the First Lady of Tranest. They let him work off his rage while he was still under partial control. Then the Ermetyne woke him up.

He stared at her coldly.

"You are a deceitful woman, Lyad Ermetyne!" he declared. "I don't wish to see you about my labs again! At any time. Under any pretext. Is that understood?"

"Yes, Professor," Lyad said. "And I'm sorry that I believed it necessary to—"

Mantelish snorted. "Sorry! Necessary! Just to be certain it doesn't happen again, I shall make up a batch of antihypno pills. If I can remember the prescription."

"I happen," the Ermetyne ventured, "to know a very good prescription for the purpose, Professor. If you will permit me!"

Mantelish stood up. "I'll accept no prescriptions from you!" he said icily. He looked at Trigger as he turned to walk out of the cabin. "Or drinks from you either, Trigger Argee!" he growled. "Who in the great spiraling galaxy is there left to trust!"

"Sorry, Professor," Trigger said meekly.

In half an hour or so, he calmed down enough to join the others in the lounge, to get the final story on Gess Fayle and the missing king plasmoid from the Ermetyne.

Doctor Gess Fayle, Lyad reported, had died very shortly after leaving the Manon System. And with him had died every man on board the U-League's transport ship. It might be simplest, she went on, to relate the first series of events from the plasmoid's point of view.

"Point of view?" Professor Mantelish interrupted. "The plasmoid has awareness then?"

"Oh, yes. That one does."

"Self-awareness?"

"Definitely."

"Oho! But then—"

"Professor," Trigger interrupted politely in turn, "may I get you a drink?"

He glared at her, growled, then grinned. "I'll shut up," he said. Lyad went on.

Doctor Fayle had resumed experimentation with the 112-113 unit almost as soon as he was alone with it; and one of the first things he did was to detach the small 113 section from the main one. The point Doctor Fayle hadn't adequately considered when he took this step was that 113's function appeared to be that of a restraining, limiting or counteracting device on its vastly larger partner. The Old Galactics obviously had been aware of dangerous potentialities in their more advanced creations, and had used this means of regulating them. That the method was reliable was indicated by the fact that, in the thirty thousand years since the Old Galactics had vanished, plasmoid 112 had remained restricted to the operations required for the maintenance of Harvest Moon.

But it hadn't like being restricted.

And it had been very much aware of the possibilities offered by the new life-forms which lately had intruded on Harvest Moon.

The instant it found itself free, it attempted to take control of the human minds in its environment.

"Mind-level control?" Mantelish exclaimed, looking startled. "Not unheard-of, of course. And wo'd been considering . . . But of human minds?"

Lyad nodded. "It can contact human minds," she said, "though, perhaps rather fortunately, it can project that particular field effect only within a quite limited radius. A little less, the Devagas found later, than five miles."

Mantelish shook his head, frowning. He turned toward the Commissioner. "Holati," he said emphatically, "I believe that thing could be dangerous!"

For a moment, they all looked at him. Then the

Commissioner cleared his throat. "It's a possibility, Mantelish," he admitted. "We will give it thought later."

"What," Trigger asked Lyad, "killed the people on the ship?"

"The attempt to control them," Lyad said. Doctor Fayle apparently had died as he was leaving the laboratory with the 113 unit. The other men died wherever they were. The ship, running subspace and pilotless, plowed headlong into the next gravitic twister and broke up.

A Devagas ship's detectors picked up the wreckage three days later. Balmordan was on board the Devagas ship and in charge.

The Devagas, at that time, were at least as plasmoid-hungry as anybody else, and knew they were not likely to see their hunger gratified for several decades. The wreck of a U-League ship in the Manon area decidedly was worth investigating.

If the big plasmoid hadn't been capable of learning from its mistakes, the Devagas investigating party also would have died. Since it could and did learn, they lived. The searchers discovered human remains and the crushed remnants of the 113 unit in a collapsed section of the ship. Then they discovered the big plasmoid—alive in subspace, undamaged and very conscious of the difficulties it now faced.

It had already initiated its first attempt to solve the difficulties. It was incapable of outward motion and could not change its own structure, but it was no longer alone. It had constructed a small work-plasmoid with visual and manipulating organs, as indifferent to exposure to subspace as its designer. When the boarding party encountered the twain, the working plasmoid apparently was attempting to perform some operation on the frozen and shriveled brain of one of the human cadavers.

Balmordan was a scientist of no mean stature among the Devagas. He did not understand immediately what he saw, but he realized the probable importance of understanding it. He had the plasmoids and their lifeless human research object transferred to the Devagas ship and settled down to observe what they did.

Released, the working plasmoid went back immediately to its task. It completed it. Then Balmordan and, presumably, the plasmoids waited. Nothing happened.

Finally, Balmordan investigated the dead brain. Installed in it he found what appeared to be near-microscopic energy receivers of plasmoid material. There was nothing to indicate what type of energy they were to—or could—receive.

Devagas scientists, when they happened to be of the hierarchy, always had enjoyed one great advantage over most of their colleagues in the Federation. They had no difficulty in obtaining human volunteers to act as subjects for experimental work. Balmordan appointed three of his least valuable crew members as volunteers for the plasmoids's experiments.

The first of the three died almost immediately. The plasmoid, it turned out, lacked understand-

ing of, among other things, the use and need
of anesthetics. Balmordan accordingly assisted
obligingly in the second operation. He was delighted when it became apparent that his assistance was being willingly and comprehendingly
accepted. This subject did not die immediately.
But he did not regain consciousness after the
plasmoid devices had been installed; and some
hours later he did die, in convulsions.

Number Three was more fortunate. He regained
consciousness. He complained of headaches and,
after he had slept, of nightmares. The next day he
went into shock for a period of several hours.
When he came out of it, he reported tremblingly
that the big plasmoid was talking to him, though
he could not understand what it said.

There were two more test operations, both successful. In all three cases, the headaches and
nightmares stopped in about a week. The first
subject in the series was beginning to understand
the plasmoid. Balmordan listened to his reports.
He had his three surviving volunteers given very
extensive physical and psychological tests. They
seemed to be in fine condition.

Balmordan now had the operation performed
on himself. When he woke up, he disposed of his
three predecessors. Then he devoted his full attention to learning what the plasmoid was trying
to say. In about three weeks it became clear . . .

The plasmoid had established contact with
human beings because it needed their help. It
needed a base like Harvest Moon from which to
operate and on which to provide for its require-

ments. It did not have the understanding to permit it to construct such a base.

So it made the Devagas a proposition. It would work for them, somewhat as it had worked for the Old Galactics, if—unlike the Old Galactics—they would work for it.

Balmordan, newly become a person of foremost importance, transmitted the offer to the hierarchy in the Hub. With no hesitation it was accepted, but Balmordan was warned not to bring his monster into the Hub area. If it was discovered on a Devagas world, the hierarchy would be faced with the choice between another war with the Federation and submission to more severely restrictive Federation controls. It didn't care for either alternative; it had lost three wars with the Federated worlds in the past and each time had been reduced in strength.

They contacted Vishni's Independent Fleet, Vishni's area was not too far from Balmordan's ship position, and the Devagas had had previous dealings with him and his men. This time they hired the I-Fleet to become the plasmoid's temporary caretaker. Within a few weeks it was parked on Luscious, where it devoted itself to the minor creative experimentation which presently was to puzzle Professor Mantelish.

The Devagas meanwhile toiled prodigiously to complete the constructions which were to be a central feature in the new alliance. On a base very far removed from the Hub, on a base securely anchored and concealed among the gravitic swirlings and shiftings of a subspace turbulance area, virtually indetectable, the monster could make a very valuable partner. If it was discovered, the partnership could be disowned. So could the fact that they had constructed the substation for it—in itself a grave breach of Federation treaties.

They built the substation. They built the armed subterranean observer's dome three days' travel away from it. The plasmoid was installed in its new quarters. It then requested the use of the Vishni Fleet people for further experimentation.

The hierarchy was glad to grant the request. It would have had to get rid of those too well informed hirelings in any case.

Having received its experimental material, the plasmoid requested the Devagas to stay away from the substation for a while.

27

THE DEVAGAS, SAID LYAD, while not too happy with their ally's increasingly independent attitude, were more anxious than ever to see the alliance progress to the working stage. As an indication of its potential usefulness, the monster had provided them with a variety of working plasmoid robots, built to their own specifications.

"What kind of specifications?" Trigger inquired.

Lyad hadn't learned in detail, but some of the robots appeared to have demonstrated rather alarming possibilities. Those possibilities, however, were precisely what intrigued the hierarchy most.

Mantelish smacked his lips thoughtfully and shook his head. "Not good!" he said. "Not at all good! I'm beginning to think—" He paused a moment. "Go on, Lyad."

The hierarchy was now giving renewed consideration to a curious request the plasmoid had made almost as soon as Balmordan became capable of understanding it. The request had been to find and destroy plasmoid 113-A.

The Ermetyne's amber eyes switched to Trigger. "Shall I?" she asked.

Trigger nodded.

And a specific human being. The Devagas already had established that this human being must be Trigger Argee.

"*What?*" Mantelish's thick white eyebrows shot up. "113-A we can understand—it is afraid of being in some way brought back under control. But why Trigger?"

"Because," Lyad said carefully, "112 was aware that 113-A intended to condition Trigger into being *its* interpreter."

Professor Mantelish's jaw dropped. He swung his head toward Trigger. "Is that true?"

She nodded. "It's true, all right. We've been working on it, but we haven't got too far along. Tell you later. Go ahead, Lyad."

The Devagas, naturally, hadn't acted on the king plasmoid's naïve suggestion. Whatever it feared was more than likely to be very useful to them. Instead they made preparations to bring both 113-A and Trigger Argee into their possession. They would then have a new, strong bargaining point in their dealings with their dubious partner. But they discovered promptly that neither Trigger nor 113-A were at all easy to come by.

Balmordan now suggested a modification of

tactics. The hierarchy had seen to it that a number
of interpreters were available for 112; Balmordan
in consequence had lost much of his early importance and was anxious to regain it. His proposal
was that all efforts should be directed at obtaining
113-A. Once it was obtained, he himself would
volunteer to become its first interpreter. Trigger
Argee, because of the information she might re-
veal to others, should be destroyed—a far simpler
operation than attempting to take her alive.

This was agreed to; and Balmordan was au-
thorized to carry out both operations.

Mantelish had begun shaking his head again.
"No!" he said suddenly and loudly. He looked at
Lyad, then at Trigger. "Trigger!" he said.

"Yes?" said Trigger.

"Take that deceitful woman to her cabin," Mantelish ordered. "Lock her up. I have something to
say to the Commissioner."

Trigger arose. "All right," she said. "Come on,
Lyad."

The two of them left the lounge. Mantelish
stood up and went over to the Commissioner. He
grasped the Commissioner's jacket lapels.

"Holati, old friend!" he began emotionally.

"What is it, old friend?" the Commissioner inquired.

"What I have to say," Mantelish rumbled, "will
shock you. Profoundly."

"No!" exclaimed the Commissioner.

"Yes," said Mantelish. "That plasmoid 112—it
has, of course, an almost inestimable potential
value to civilization."

"Of course," the Commissioner agreed.

"But it also," said Mantelish, "represents a quite intolerable threat to civilization."

"Mantelish!" cried the Commissioner.

"It does. You don't comprehend these matters as I do. Holati, that plasmoid must be destroyed! Secretly, if possible. And by us!"

"Mantelish!" gasped the Commissioner. "You can't be serious!"

"I am."

"Well," said Commissioner Tate, "sit down. I'm open to suggestions." Space-armor drill hadn't been featured much in the Colonial School's crowded curriculum. But the Commissioner broke out one of the ship's two heavy-duty suits; and when Trigger wasn't at the controls, eating, sleeping, or taking care of the ship's housekeeping with Lyad and Mantelish, she drilled.

She wasn't at the controls too often. When she was, they had to surface and proceed in normal space. But Lyad, not too suprisingly, turned out to be a qualified subspace pilot. Even less surprisingly, she already had made a careful study of the ship's controls. After a few hours of instruction, she went on shift with the Commissioner along the less rugged stretches. In this area, none of the stretches were smooth.

When not on duty, Lyad lay on her bunk and brooded.

Mantelish tried to be useful.

Repulsive might have been brooding too. He didn't make himself noticeable.

Time passed. The stretches got rougher. The last ten hours, the Commissioner didn't stir out of the control seat. Lyad had been locked in her cabin again as the critical period approached. In normal space, the substation should have been in clear detector range by now. Here, the detectors gave occasional blurry, uncertain indications that somewhere in the swirling energies about them might be something more solidly material. It was like creeping through jungle thickets towards the point where a dangerous quarry lurked.

They eased down on the coordinate points. They came sliding out between two monstrous twisters. The detectors leaped to life.

"Ship!" said the Commissioner. He swore. "Frigate class," he said an instant later. He turned his head toward Trigger. "Get Lyad! They're in communication range. We'll let her communicate."

Trigger, heart hammering, ran to get Lyad. The Commissioner had the short-range communicator on when they came hurrying back to the control room together.

"That the Aurora?" he asked.

Lyad glanced at the outline in the detectors. "It is!" Her face went white.

"Talk to 'em," he ordered. "Know their call number?"

"Of course," Lyad sat down at the communicator. Her hands shook for a moment, then steadied. "What am I to say?"

"Just find out what's happened, to start with. Why they're still here. Then we'll improvise. Get them to come to the screen if you can."

Lyad's fingers flew over the tabs. The communicator signaled contact.

Lyad said evenly, "Come in, Aurora! This is the Ermetyne."

There was a pause, a rather unaccountably long pause, Trigger thought. Then a voice said, "Yes, First Lady?"

Lyad's eyes widened for an instant. "Come in on visual, Captain!" There was the snap of command in the words.

Again a pause. Then suddenly the communicator was looking into the Aurora's control room. A brown-bearded, rather lumpy-faced man in uniform sat before the other screen. There were other uniformed men behind him. Trigger heard the Ermetyne's breath suck in and turned to watch Lyad's face.

"Why haven't you carried out your instructions, Captain?" The voice was still even.

"There was a difficulty with the engines, First Lady."

Lyad nodded. "Very well. Stand by for new instructions."

She switched off the communicator. She twisted around toward the Commissioner. "Get us out of here!" she said, chalk-faced. "*Fast!* Those aren't my men."

Flame bellowed about them in subspace. The Commissioner's hand slapped a button. The flame vanished and stars shone all around. The engines hurled them forward. Twelve seconds later, they angled and dived again. Subspace reappeared.

"Guess you were right!" the Commissioner said. He idled the engines and scratched his chin. "But what were they?"

"Everything about it was wrong!" Lyad was saying presently, her face still white. "Their faces, in particular, were deformed!" She looked at Trigger. "You saw it?"

Trigger nodded. She suspected she was on the white-faced side herself. "The captain," she said. "I didn't look at the others. It looked as if his cheeks and forehead were pushed out of shape!"

There was a short silence. "Well," said the Commissioner, "seems like that plasmoid has been doing some more experimenting. Question is, how did it get to them?"

They didn't find any answers to that. Lyad insisted the Aurora had been given specific orders to avoid the immediate vicinity of the substation. Its only purpose there was to observe and report on anything that seemed to be going on in the area. She couldn't imagine her crew disobeying the orders.

"That mind-level control business," Trigger said finally. "Maybe it found a way of going out to them."

She could see by their faces that the idea had occurred, and that they didn't like it. Well, neither did she.

They pitched a few more ideas around. None of them seemed helpful.

"Unless we just want to hightail it," the Commissioner said finally, "about the only thing we can do is go back and slug it out with the frigate first. We can't risk snooping around the station while she's there and likely to start pounding on our backs any second."

Mantelish looked startled. "Holati," he cautioned, "That's a warship!"

"Mantelish," the Commissioner said, a trifle coldly, "what you've been riding in isn't a canoe." He glanced at Lyad. "I suppose you'd feel happier if you weren't locked up in your cabin during the ruckus?"

Lyad gave him a strained smile. "Commissioner," she said, "You're so right!"

"Then keep your seat," he said. "We'll start prowling."

They prowled. It took an hour to recontact the Aurora, presumably because the Aurora was also prowling for them. Suddenly the detectors came alive.

The ship's guns went off at once. Then subspace went careening crazily past in the screens. Trigger looked at the screens for a few seconds, gulped and started studying the floor.

Whatever the plasmoid had done to the frigate's crew, they appeared to have lost none of their ability to give battle. It was a very brisk affair. But neither had the onetime Squadron Commander Tate lost much of his talent along those lines. The frigate had many more guns but no better range. And he had the faster ship. Four minutes after the first shots were exchanged, the Aurora blew up.

The ripped hunk of the Aurora's hull which the Commissioner presently brought into the lock appeared to have had three approximately quarter-inch holes driven at a slant through it, which subsequently had been plugged again. The plugging material was plasmoid in character.

"There were two holes in another piece," the Commissioner said, very thoughtfully. "If that's the average, she was punched in a few thousand spots. Let's go have a better look."

He and Mantelish maneuvered the gravity crane carrying the holed slab of steel-alloy into the ship's workshop. Lyad was locked back into her cabin, and Trigger went on guard in the control room and looked out wistfully at the stars of normal space.

Half an hour later, the two men came up the passage and joined her. They appeared preoccupied.

"It's an unpleasant picture, Trigger girl," the Commissioner said. "Those holes look sort of chewed through. Whatever did the chewing was also apparently capable of sealing up the portion behind it as it went along. What it did to the men when it got inside we don't know. Mantelish feels we might compare it roughly to the effects of ordinary germ invasion. It doesn't really matter. It fixed them."

"Mighty large germs!" Trigger said. "Why didn't their meteor reflectors stop them?"

"If the ship was hove to and these things just drifted in gradually—"

. "Oh, I see. That wouldn't activate the reflectors. Then, if we keep moving ourselves—"

"That," said the Commisioner, "was what I had in mind."

28

TRIGGER COULDN'T KEEP FROM staring at the subspace
station. It was unbelievable.

One could still tell that the human construction
gangs had put up a standard type of armored
station down there. A very big, very massive one,
but normally shaped, nearly spherical. One could
tell it only by the fact that at the gun pits
the original material still showed through.
Everywhere else it had vanished under great
black masses of material which the plasmoids had
added to the station's structure.

All over that black, lumpy, lavalike surface the
plasmoids crawled, walked, soared and wriggled.
There were thousands of them, perhaps hundreds
of different types. It looked like a wet, black, rot-
ten stump swarming with life inside and out.

Neither she nor the two men had made much

mention of its appearance. All you could say was
that it was horrible.

The plasmoids they could see ignored the ship.
They also gave no noticeable attention to the eight
space flares the Commissioner had set in a rough
cube about the station. But for the first two hours
after their arrival, the ship's meteor reflectors remained active. An occasional tap at first, then an
almost continuous pecking, finally a twenty
minute drumfire that filled the reflector screens
with madly dancing clouds of tiny sparks. Suddenly it ended. Either the king plasmoid had
exhausted its supply of that particular weapon or
it preferred to conserve what it had left.

"Might test their guns," the Commissioner
muttered. He looked very unhappy, Trigger
thought.

He circled off, put on speed, came back and
flicked the ship past the station's flank. He drew
bursts from two pits with a promptness which
confirmed what already had been almost a
certainty—that the gun installations operated automatically. They seemed remarkably feeble
weapons for a station of that size. The Devagas
apparently had had sense enough not to give the
plasmoid every advantage.

The Commissioner plunked a test shot next into
one of the black protuberances. A small fiery crater appeared. It darkened quickly again. Out of the
biggest opening, down near what would have
been the foot of the stump if it had been a stump,
something, long, red and wormlike wriggled
rapidly. It flowed up over the structure's surface

to the damaged point and thrust the tip of its front end into the crater. Black material began to flow from the tip. The plasmoid moved its front end back and forth across the damaged area. Others of the same kind came out and joined it. The crater began to fill out.

They hauled away a little and surfaced. Normal space looked clean, beautiful, homelike, calmly shining. None of them except Lyad had slept for over twenty hours. "What do you think?" the Commissioner asked.

They discussed what they had seen in subdued voices. Nobody had a plan. They agreed that one thing they could be sure of was that the Vishni Fleet people and any other human beings who might have been on the station when it was turned over to the king plasmoid were no longer alive. Unless, of course, something had been done to them much more drastic than had happened to the Aurora's crew. The ship had passed by the biggest opening, like a low wide black mouth, close enough to make out that it extended far back into the original station's interior. The station was open and airless as Harvest Moon had been before the humans got there.

"Some of those things down there," the Commissioner said, "had attachments that would crack any suit wide open. A lot of them are big, and a lot of them are fast. Once we were inside, we'd have no maneuverability to speak of. If the termites didn't get to us before we got inside. Suits won't do it here." He was a gambler, and a gambler doesn't buck impossible odds.

"What could you do with the guns?" Trigger asked.

"Not too much. They're not meant to take down a fortress. Scratching around on the surface with them would just mark the thing up. We can widen that opening by quite a bit, and once it's widened, I can flip in the bomb. But it would be just blind luck if we nailed the one we're after that way. With a dozen bombs we could break up the station. But we don't have them."

They nodded thoughtfully.

"The worst part of that," he went on, "is that it would be completely obvious. The Council's right when it worries about fumbles here. Tranest and the Devagas know the thing is in there. If the Federation can't produce it, both those outfits have the Council over a barrel. Or we could be setting the Hub up for fifty years of fighting among the member worlds, sometime in the next few hours."

Mantelish and Trigger nodded again. More thoughtfully.

"Nevertheless—" Mantelish began suddenly. He checked himself.

"Well, you're right," the Commissioner said. "That stuff down there just can't be turned loose, that's all! The thing's still only experimenting. We don't know what it's going to wind up with. So I guess we'll be trying the guns and the bomb finally, and then see what else we can do . . . Now look, we've got—what is it?—nine or ten hours left. The first of the boys are pretty sure to come helling in around then. Or maybe something's happened we don't know about, and they'll be here in thirty minutes. We can't tell. But I'm in favor of knocking off now and just grabbing a couple of hours' sleep. Then we'll get our brains together again. Maybe by then somebody has come up with something like an idea. What do you say?"

"Where," Mantelish said, "is the ship going to be while we're sleeping?"

"Subspace," said the Commissioner. He saw their expressions. "Don't worry! I'll put her on a wide orbit and I'll stick out every alarm on board. I'll also sleep in the control chair. But in case someboy gets here early, we've got to be around to tell them about that space termite trick."

Trigger hadn't expected she would be able to sleep, not where they were. But afterwards she couldn't even remember getting stretched out all the way on the bunk.

She woke up less than an hour later, feeling very uncomfortable. Repulsive had been talking to her.

She sat up and looked around the dark cabin with frightened eyes. After a moment, she got out of the bunk and went up the passage toward the lounge and the control section.

Holati Tate was lying slumped back in his chair, eyes closed, breathing slowly and evenly. Trigger put out a hand to touch his shoulder and then drew it back. She glanced up for a moment at the plasmoid station in the screen, seeming to turn slowly as they went orbiting by it. She noticed that one of the space flares they'd planted there had gone out, or else it had been plucked away by a passing twister's touch. She looked away quickly again, turned and went restlessly back through the lounge, and up the passage, toward the cabins. She went by the two suits of space armor at the lock without looking at them. She opened the door to Mantelish's cabin and looked inside. The professor lay sprawled across the bunk in his clothes, breathing slowly and regularly.

Trigger closed his door again. Lyad might be wakeful, she thought. She crossed the passage and unlocked the door to the Ermetyne's cabin. The lights in the cabin were on, but Lyad also lay there placidly asleep, her face relaxed and young looking.

Trigger put her fist to her mouth and bit down hard on her knuckles for a moment. She frowned intensely at nothing. Then she closed and locked the cabin door, went back up the passage and into the control room. She sat down before the communicator, glanced up once more at the plasmoid station in the screen, got up restlessly and went over to the Commissioner's chair. She stood there, looking down at him. The Commissioner slept on.

Then Repulsive said it again.

"No!" Trigger whispered fiercely. "I won't! I can't! You can't make me do it!"

There was a stillness then. In the stillness, it was made very clear that nobody intended to make her do anything.

And then the stillness just waited.

She cried a little.
So this was it.
"All right," she said.

The armor suit's triple light-beam blazed into
the wide, low, black, wet-looking mouth rushing
toward her. It was much bigger than she had
thought when looking at it from the ship. Far
behind her, the fire needles of the single gun pit
which her passage to the station had aroused still
slashed mindlessly about. They weren't geared to
stop suits, and they hadn't come anywhere near
her. But the plasmoids looked geared to stop suits.

They were swarming in clusters in the black
mouth like maggots in a rotting skull. Part of the
swarms had spilled out over the lips of the mouth,
clingling, crawling, rippling swiftly about. Trigger shifted the flight controls with the fingers of
one hand, dropping a little, then straightening
again. She might be coming in too fast. But she
had to get past that mass at the opening.

Then the black mouth suddenly yawned wide
before her. Her left hand pressed the gun handle.
Twin blasts stabbed ahead, blinding white, struck
the churning masses, blazed over them. They
burned, scattered, exploded, and rolled back,
burning and exploding, in a double wave to meet
her.

"Too fast!" Repulsive said anxiously. "Much
too fast!"

She knew it. But she couldn't have forced herself to do it slowly. The armor suit slammed at a

slant into a piled, writhing, burning hardness of
plasmoid bodies, bounced upward. She went over
and over, yanking down all the way on the flight
controls. She closed her eyes for a moment.

When she opened them again, the suit hung
poised a little above black uneven flooring, turned
back half toward the entrance mouth. A black
ceiling was less than twenty feet above her head.

The plasmoids were there. The suit's light
beams played over the massed, moving ranks:
squat bodies and sinuous ones, immensities that
scraped the ceiling, stalked limbs and gaping
nutcracker jaws, blurs of motion her eyes couldn't
step down to define into shapes. Some still blazed
with her guns' white fire. The closest were thirty
feet away.

They stayed there. They didn't come any closer.

She swung the suit slowly away from the entrance. The ring was closed all about her. But it
wasn't tightening.

Repulsive had thought he could do it.

She asked in her mind, "Which way?"

She got a feeling of direction, turned the suit a
little more and started it gliding forward. The
ranks ahead didn't give way, but they went down.
Those that could go down. Some weren't built for
it. The suit bumped up gently against one huge
bulk, and a six-inch pale blue eye looked at her for
a moment as she went circling around it. "Eyes for
what?" somebody in the back of her mind wondered briefly. She glanced into the suit's rear view
screen and saw that the ones who had gone down

were getting up again, mixed with the ones who
came crowding after her. Thirty feet away!

Repulsive was doing it.

So far there weren't any guns. If they hit guns,
that would be her job and the suit's. The king
plasmoid should be regretting by now that it had
wasted its experimental human material. Though
it mightn't have been really wasted; it might be
incorporated in the stuff that came crowding after
her, and kept going down ahead.

Black ceiling, black floor seemed to stretch on
endlessly. She kept the suit moving slowly along.
At last the beams picked up low walls ahead, con-
verging at the point toward which the suit was
gliding. At the point of convergence there seemed
to be a narrow passage.

Plasmoid bodies were wedged into it.

The suit pulled them out one by one, its steel
grippers clamping down upon things no softer
than itself. But it had power to work with and they
didn't, at the moment. Behind the ones it pulled
out there were presently glimpses of the swiftly
weaving motion of giant red worm-shapes sealing
up the passage. After a while, they stopped weaving each time the suit returned and started again
as it withdrew, dragging out another plasmoid
body.

Then the suit went gliding over a stilled tangle
of red worm bodies. And there was the sealed end
of the passage.

The stuff was still soft. The guns blazed, bit into

it, ate it away, their brilliance washing back over the suit. The sealing gave way before the suit did. They went through and came out into . . .

She didn't know what they had come out into. It was like a fog of darkness, growing thicker as they went sliding forward. The light beams seemed to be dimming. Then they quietly went out as if they'd switched themselves off.

In blackness, she fingered the light controls and knew they weren't switched off.

"Repulsive!" she cried in her mind.

Repulsive couldn't help with the blackness. She got the feeling of direction. The blackness seemed to be soaking behind her eyes. She held the speed throttle steady in fingers slippery with sweat, and that was the only way she could tell they were still moving forward.

After a while, they bumped gently against something that had to be a wall, it was so big, though at first she wasn't sure it was a wall. They moved along it for a time, then came to the end of it and were moving in the right direction again.

They seemed to be in a passage now, a rather narrow one. They touched walls and ceiling from time to time. She thought they were moving downward.

There was a picture in front of her. She realized suddenly that she had been watching it for some time. But it wasn't until this moment that she became really aware of it.

The beast was big, strong and angry. It bellowed and screamed, shaking and covered with foam.

She couldn't see it too clearly, but she had the impression of mad, staring eyes and a terrible lust to crush and destroy.

But something was holding it. Something held it quietly and firmly, for all its plunging. It reared once more now, a gross, lumbering hugeness, and came crashing down to its knees. Then it went over on its side.

The suit's beams flashed on. Trigger squeezed her eyes tight shut, blinded by the light that flashed back from black walls all around. Then her fingers remembered the right drill and dimmed the lights. She opened her eyes again and stared for a long moment at the great gray mummy-shape before one of the black walls.

"Repulsive?" she asked in her mind.

Repulsive didn't answer. The suit hung quietly in the huge black chamber. She didn't remember having stopped it. She turned it now slowly. There were eight or nine passages leading out of here, through walls, ceiling, floor.

"Repulsive!" she cried plaintively.

Silence.

She glanced once more at the king plasmoid against the wall. It stayed silent too. And it was as if the two silences cancelled each other out.

She remembered the last feeling of moving downward and lifted the suit toward a passage that came in through the ceiling. She hung before it, considering. Far up and back in its darkness, a bright light suddenly blazed, vanished, and blazed again. Something was coming down the passage, fast . . .

Her hand started for the gun handle. Then it remembered another drill and flashed to the suit's communicator. A voice crashed in around her.

"Trigger, Trigger, Trigger!" it sobbed.

"Ape!" she screamed. "You aren't hurt?"

29

Mantelish's garden in the highland south of Ceyce had a certain renown all over the Hub. It had been donated to the professor twenty-five years ago by the populace of another Federation world. That populace had negligently permitted a hideous pestilence of some kind to be imported, and had been saved in the nick of time by the appropriate pestilence-killer, hastily developed and forwarded to it by Mantelish. In return, a lifetime ambition had been fulfilled for him—his own private botanical garden plus an unlimited fund for stocking and upkeep.

To one side of the big garden house, where Mantelish stayed whenever he found the time to go puttering around among his specimens, stood a giant sequoia, generally reputed to be the oldest living thing in the Hub outside of the Life Banks. It was certainly extremely old, even for a sequoia.

For the last decade there had been considerable talk about the advisability of removing it before it collapsed and crushed the house and everyone in it. But it was one of the professor's great favorites, and so far he had vetoed the suggestion.

Elbows propped on the broad white balustrade of the porch before her third-story bedroom, Trigger was studying the sequoia's crown with a pair of field glasses when Pilch arrived. She laid the glasses down and invited her guest to pull up a chair and help her admire the view.

They admired the view for a little in silence. "It certainly is a beautiful place!" Pilch said then. She glanced down at Professor Mantelish, a couple of hundred yards from the house, dressed in a pair of tanned shorts and busily grubbing away with a spade around some new sort of shrub he'd just planted, and smiled. "I took the first opportunity I've had to come see you," she said.

Trigger looked at her and laughed. "I thought you might. You weren't satisfied with the reports then?"

Pilch said, "Of course not! But it was obvious the emergency was over, so I was whisked away to something else." She frowned slightly. "Sometimes," she admitted, "the Service keeps me the least bit busier than I'd prefer to be. So now it's been six months!"

"I would have come in for another interview if you'd called me," Trigger said.

"I know," said Pilch. "But that would have made it official. I can keep this visit off the record." Her eyes met Trigger's for a moment. "And

I have a feeling I will. Also, of course, I'm not pushing for any answers you mightn't care to give."

"Just push away," Trigger said agreeably.

"Well, we got the Commissioner's call from his ship. A worried man he was. So it seems now that we've had one of the Old Galactics around for a while. When did you first find out about it?"

"On the morning after our interview. Right after I got up."

"How?"

Trigger laughed. "I watch my weight. When I noticed I'd turned three and a half pounds heavier overnight than I'd averaged the past four years, I knew all right!"

Pilch smiled faintly. "You weren't alarmed at all?"

"No. I guess I'd been prepared just enough by that time. But then, you know, I forgot all about it again until Lyad and Flam opened that purse—and he wasn't inside. Then I remembered, and after that I didn't forget again."

"No. Of course." Pilch's slim fingers tapped the surface of the table between them. She said then, paying Repulsive the highest compliment Pilch could give, "It—he—was a good therapist!" After a moment, she added. "I had a talk with Commissioner Tate an hour or so ago. He's preparing to leave Maccadon again, I understand."

"That's right. He's been organizing that big exploration trip of Mantelish's the past couple of months. He'll be in charge of it when they take off."

"You're not going along?" Pilch asked.

Trigger shook her head. "Not this time. Ape and I—Captain Quillan and I, that is—"

"I heard," Pilch said. She smiled. "You picked a good one on the second try!"

"Quillan's all right," Trigger agreed. "If you watch him a little."

"Anyway," said Pilch, "Commissioner Tate seems to be just the least bit worried about you still."

Trigger put a finger to her temple and made a small circling motion. "A bit ta-ta?"

"Not exactly that, perhaps. But it seems," said Pilch, "that you've told him a good deal about the history of the Old Galactics, including what ended them as a race thirty-two thousand years ago."

Trigger's face clouded a little. "Yes," she said. She sat silent for a moment. "Well, I got that from Repulsive somewhere along the line," she said then. "It didn't really come clear until some time after we'd got back. But it was there in those pictures in the interview."

"The giants stamping on the farm?"

Trigger nodded. "And the fast clock and the slow one. He was trying to tell it then. The Jesters—that's the giants—they're fast and tough like us. Apparently," Trigger said thoughtfully, "they're a good deal like us in a lot of ways. But worse. Much worse! And the Old Galactics were just slow. They thought slow; they moved slow— they did almost everything slow. At full gallop, old Repulsive couldn't have kept up with a healthy snail. Besides, they just liked to grow things and tinker with things and so on. They didn't go in for fighting, and they never got to be at all good at it. So they just got wiped out, practically."

"The Jesters were good at fighting, eh?"

Trigger nodded. "Very good. Like us, again."

"Where did they come from?"

"Repulsive thought they were outsiders. He wasn't sure. He and that other O.G. were on the sidelines, running their protein collecting station, when the Jesters arrived; and it was all over and they were gone before he had learned much about it."

"From outside the galaxy!" Pilch said thoughtfully. She cleared her throat. "What's this business about they might be back again?"

"Well," Trigger said, "he thought they might be. Just might. Actually he believed the Jesters got wiped out too."

"Eh?" Pilch said. "How's that?"

"Quite a lot of the Old Galactics went along with them like Repulsive went along with me. And one of the things they did know," Trigger said, "was how to spread diseases like nobody's business. About like we use weed-killers. Wholesale. They could clean out the average planet of any particular thing they didn't want there in about a week. So it's not really too likely the Jesters will be back."

"Oh!" said Pilch.

"But if they are coming, Repulsive thought they'd be due in this area in about another eight centuries. That looked like a very short time to him, of course. He thought it would be best to pass on a warning."

"You know," Pilch said after a brief pause, "I find myself agreeing with him there, Trigger! I might turn in a short report on this, after all."

"I think you should, really," Trigger said. She smiled suddenly. "Of course, it might wind up with people thinking both of us are ta-ta!"

"I'll risk that," said Pilch. "It's been thought of me before."

"If they did come," Trigger said, "I guess we'd take them anyway. We've taken everything else like that that came long. And besides—"

Her voice trailed off thoughtfully. She studied the table top for a moment. Then she looked up at Pilch.

"Well," she said, smiling, "any other questions?"

"A few," said Pilch, passing up the "and besides—" She considered. "Did you ever actually see him make contact with you?"

"No," Trigger said. "I was always asleep, and I suppose he made sure I'd stay asleep. They're built sort of like a leech, you know. I guess he knew I wouldn't feel comfortable about having something like that go oozing into the side of my neck or start oozing out again. Anyway, he never did let me see it."

"Considerate little fellow!" said Pilch. She sighed. "Well, everything came out very satisfactorily—much more so than anyone could have dared hope at one time. All that's left is a very intriguing mystery which the Hub will be chatting about for years . . . What happened aboard Doctor Fayle's vanished ship that caused the king plasmoid to awaken to awful life?" she cried. "What equally mysterious event brought about its death on that strangely hideous structure it had built in subspace? *What was it planning to do there?* Etcetera." She smiled at Trigger. "Yes, very good!"

"I saw they camouflaged out what was still visible of the original substation before they let in the news viewers," Trigger remarked. "Bright idea somebody had there!"

"Yes. It was I. And the Devagas hierarchy is broken, and the Ermetynes run out of Tranest. Two very bad spots, those were! I don't recall having heard what they did to your friend, Pluly."

"I heard," Trigger said. "He just got black-listed by Grand Commerce finally and lost all his shipping concessions. However, his daughter is married to an up and coming young businessman who happened to be on hand and have the money and other qualifications to pick up those concessions." She laughed. "It's the Inger Lines now. They're smart characters, in a way!"

"Yes," said Pilch. "In a way. Did you know Lyad Ermetyne put in for voluntary rehabilitation with us, and then changed her mind and joined the Service?"

"I'd heard of it." Trigger hesitated. "Did you know Lyad paid me a short visit about an hour before you got here this morning?"

"I thought she would," Pilch said. "We came in to Maccadon together."

Trigger had been a little startled when she answered the doorchime and saw Lyad standing there. She invited the Ermetyne in.

"I thought I'd thank you personally," Lyad said casually, "for a recording which was delivered to me some months ago."

"That's quite all right," Trigger said, also casually. "I was sure I wasn't going to have any use for it."

Lyad studied her face for a moment. "To be honest about it, Trigger Argee," she said, "I still don't feel entirely cordial toward you! However, I did appreciate the gesture of letting me have the recording. So I decided to drop by to tell you there isn't really too much left in the way of hard feelings, on my part."

They shook hands restrainedly, and the Ermetyne sauntered out again.

"The other reason she came here," Pilch said, "is to take care of the financing of Mantelish's expedition."

"I didn't know that!" Trigger said, surprised.

"It's her way of making amends. Her legitimate Hub holdings are still enormous, of course. She can afford it."

"Well," Trigger said, "that's one thing about Lyad—she's wholehearted!"

"She's that," said Pilch. "Rarely have I seen anyone rip into total therapy with the verve displayed by the Ermetyne. She mentioned on one occasion that there simply had to be some way of getting ahead of you again."

"Oh," said Trigger.

"Yes," said Pilch. "By the way, what are your own plans nowadays? Aside from getting married."

Trigger stretched slim tanned arms over her head and grinned. "No immediate plans!" she said. "I've resigned from Precol. Got a couple of checks from the Federation. One to cover my expenses on that plasmoid business—that was the Dawn City fare mainly—and the other for the five weeks special duty they figured I was on for them. So I'm up to five thousand crowns again, and I thought I'd just loaf around and sort of think things over till Quillan gets back from his current assignment."

"I see. When is Major Quillan returning?"

"In about a month. It's Captain Quillan at present, by the way."

"Oh?" said Pilch. "What happened?"

"That unwarranted interference with a political situation business. They'd broadcast a warning against taking individual action of any kind against the plasmoid station. But when he got there and heard the Commissioner was in a kind of coma, and I wasn't even on board, he lost his head and came charging into the station after me, flinging grenades and so on around. The plasmoids would have finished him off pretty quick, except most of them had started slowing down as soon as Repulsive turned off the main one. The lunatic was lucky the termites didn't get to him before he even reached the station!"

Pilch said, "Termites?"

Trigger told her about the termites.

"Ugh!" said Pilch. "I hadn't heard about those. So they broke him for that. It hardly seems right."

"Well, you have to have discipline," Trigger said tolerantly. "Ape's a bit short on that end anyway. They'll be upgrading him again fairly soon, I imagine. I might just be going into Space Scout Intelligence myself, by the way. They said they'd be glad to have me."

"Not at all incidentally," remarked Pilch, "my Service also would be glad to have you."

"Would they?" Trigger looked at her thoughtfully. "That includes that total therapy process, doesn't it?"

"Usually," said Pilch.

"Well, I might some day. But not just yet." She smiled. "Let's let Lyad get a head start! Actually, it's just I've found out there are so many interesting things going on all around that I'd like to look them over a bit before I go charging seriously into a career again." She reached across the table and tapped Pilch's wrist. "And I'll show you one interesting thing that's going on right here! Take Mantelish's big tree out there!"

"The sequoia?"

"Yes. Now just last year it was looking so bad they almost talked the professor into having it taken away. Hardly a green branch left on it."

Pilch shaded her eyes and looked at the sequoia's crown far above them. "It looks," she observed reflectively, "in fairly good shape at the moment, I'd say!"

"Yes, and it's getting greener every week. Mantelish brags about a new solvent he's been dosing its roots with. You see that great big branch like an L turned upward, just a little above the center?"

Pilch looked again. "Yes," she said after a moment, "I think so."

"Just before the L turns upward, there's a little cluster of green branches," Trigger said.

"I see those, yes."

Trigger picked up the field glasses and handed them to her. "Get those little branches in the glasses," she said.

Pilch said presently, "Got them."

Trigger stood up and faced up to the sequoia. She cupped her hands to her mouth, took a deep breath, and yelled. "Yoo-hoo! Reee-pul-sive!"

Down in the garden, Mantelish straightened and looked about angrily. Then he saw Trigger and smiled.

"Yoo-hoo yourself, Trigger!" he shouted, and turned back to his spading.

Trigger watched Pilch's face from the side. She saw her give a sudden start.

"Great Galaxies!" Pilch breathed. She kept on looking. "That's one for the book, isn't it?" Finally she put the glasses down. She appeared somewhat stunned. "He really *is* a little green man!"

"Only when he's trying to be. It's a sort of sign of friendliness."

"What's he doing up there?"

"He moved over into the sequoia right after we got back," Trigger said. "And that's where he'll probably stay indefinitely now. It's just the right kind of place for Repulsive."

"Have you been doing any more—well, talking?"

"No. Too strenuous both ways. Until a few days before we got back here, there wasn't even a sign from him. He just about knocked himself out on that big plasmoid."

"Who else knows about this?" asked Pilch.

"Nobody. I would have told Holati, except he's still mad enough about having been put into a coma, he might go out and chop the sequoia down."

"Well, it won't go into the report then," Pilch said. "They'd just want to bother Repulsive!"

"I knew it would be all right to tell you. And here's something else very interesting that's going on at present."

"What's that?"

"The real hush-hush reason for Mantelish's expedition," Trigger explained, "is, of course, to scout around this whole area of space with planetary plasmoid detectors. They don't want anybody stumbling on another setup like Harvest Moon and accidentally activating another king plasmoid."

"Yes," Pilch said. "I'd heard that."

"It was Mantelish's idea," said Trigger. "Now Mantelish is very fond of that sequoia tree. He's got a big, comfortable bench right among its roots, where he likes to sit down around noon and have a little nap when he's out here."

"Oh!" said Pilch. "Repulsive's been up to his old tricks, eh?"

"Sure. He's given Mantelish very exact instructions. So they're going to find one of those setups, all right. And they won't come back with any plasmoids. But they will come back with something they don't know about."

Pilch looked at her for a moment. "You say it!"

Trigger's grin widened. "A little green woman," she said.